THE
OUTSIDERS

'Devi Yesodharan's *The Outsiders* expertly builds its two worlds—separated by almost two millennia and an ocean—to create a narrative braid that is as lashing as it is enthralling. Hopes of sustenance compel human migration, and to accept being an outsider is harsh business, but Yesodharan's novel illustrates that even in atmospheres of injunction, prohibition and looming violence, desire and choice do get to have their say'—**Tanuj Solanki, author of *Manjhi's Mayhem* and *The Machine Is Learning***

THE
OUTSIDERS

Devi Yesodharan

VINTAGE

An imprint of Penguin Random House

VINTAGE

Vintage is an imprint of the Penguin Random House group of companies
whose addresses can be found at global.penguinrandomhouse.com

Published by Penguin Random House India Pvt. Ltd
4th Floor, Capital Tower 1, MG Road,
Gurugram 122 002, Haryana, India

First published in Vintage by Penguin Random House India 2024

ISBN 9780143466253

Typeset in Goudy Old Style by Manipal Technologies Limited, Manipal
Printed at Gopsons Papers Pvt. Ltd., Noida

www.penguin.co.in

All sorts of things in this world behave like mirrors.

—Jacques Lacan

1

1995

She has no gravitas. Nita already knows this about herself. Some weaknesses are as obvious as they are unfixable, and don't need to be pointed out. She is five foot nothing and slight—a small-earrings, anonymous-bag kind of person. She chews her lip too much. As a kid, adults would often tell her to stop doing that: 'It makes you look nervous.'

It is probably why she is struggling with these unforgiving (*venomous*) teenagers who make up her tenth-grade class. These forty adolescents, with their antennae for coolness and self-assurance, sense that she has neither. Every day, she must stand and teach in the unwanted spotlight of their collective gaze, enduring an hour of them mentally taking her apart, docking her points for her voice with its high pitch, her flyaway hair and unfashionable saris, her market-stall slippers—really, for her overall vibe, which is a combination of excessive friendliness and a general manner of apology, as if she's just been caught picking her nose.

They pass notes to each other during her class, not trying very hard to hide it. She didn't call this out the first few times, and now, eight months later, it feels like it's too late.

Today, she thought she'd done a good job for a change, in rousing them from their hormonal fugue. She had set aside the textbook and told them about a woman warrior from a thousand years ago—a pirate queen from a Montenegro island who preyed on the Greek and Roman sea trade. She commanded a fleet of small pirate cruisers, boats with pointed beaks shaped like birds and dragons, that chased down much bigger ships and wrecked them by ramming their sharp points into them.

As the queen grew more assured, she began pillaging large cities and towns. Her crew was small and ragged but wily. They would arrive outside the city gates, holding empty water jugs and asking for help to quench their thirst—young men and pretty women, pleading with liquid eyes. Once inside, they would pull out the long blades they'd hidden in the jugs. They looted and stole as if it were child's play, cutting a bloody route down the coast.

She made her people very rich, but the Romans eventually captured her pirate crew and she fled to an isolated castle.

Centuries later, Nita tells them, excavators reached one of her castles. Buried under several floors damaged by fires, they found a giant ceramic pot that held nearly 5000 coins, the largest treasure ever from that century.

'She barely spent any of her loot,' Nita observes. 'She did it for the thrill of the chase.'

Her students listen closely, and one of the boys raises his hand. 'What happened to her in the end?'

'We don't really know because there are no records of her death. Of course, now she would have kept a journal: "Dear

Diary, today I tied up two men on a trading ship and took their ivory."'

She gets a few half-hearted laughs. She's turned to the blackboard when someone murmurs, 'Why tell a story if you don't know the ending?'

'It's probably not even real.'

Her insides shrivel at the whispers. This is not teasing but its meaner cousin, mockery. Her mind stutters, but she manages to finish writing what she'd started on the board, her neat cursive degenerating into illegibility at the end: 'Today's homework: medieval piracy'. The brittle chalk dust, as usual, tickles her nose. Don't sneeze, she tells herself, and lose whatever dignity you have left.

By now, the back of her blouse is soaked and semi-transparent with sweat. The heat feels especially unbearable at this moment. When she first came to this Catholic school, she was struck by its prettiness—the white buildings with blue-trimmed windows, the clock tower at the centre of the courtyard, the spiral staircase that connected the two wings of the school.

But this architecture, imported by missionary priests, is impractical for Kochi's tropical weather. The concrete rooms on the top floor, used for the senior grades, are great at trapping heat, and the fans above their heads have grown lazy with voltage swings and power cuts. The noon heat prickles their scalps, wilts the ribbons in braids and the starch out of the school uniforms. Perhaps it also intensifies the meanness, sapping everyone's will to be polite. Perhaps that's what Nita should blame for her shrinking authority.

Itchy-nosed and with her zippy enthusiasm gone, she barely makes it through the rest of her lesson. By the time the hour is up, the students can't wait to get out of the sweltering room.

Kochi lies in the heart of the fertile, verdant Western Ghats. At night, the breeze brings home the scents of jackfruit and rose apple, the sounds of frogmouths, wild dogs, and the whistling calls of the Malabar thrush. The city has sidled right up to the edge of the forest and then some, so snakes live under floorboards, and mongooses go mouse-hunting at night in the city's alleyways. On the right spring day, you might spot a weaver bird busily building a nest in a coconut tree, or a white-headed periyar kite against blue skies, headed to the sea. A cousin with a paper and printing store told her that nightjar birds gather outside his shop window in the mornings, drawn by the sound of his inkjet printer, which sounds like their mating call.

But noon today is quiet—the crackling heat saps even the most enthusiastic birds of their song, and people shut themselves in. You can almost mistake this sullen passivity for calm.

Underneath, it's anything but. All they can talk about in the teachers' room are the copycat *aruval* attacks. The year before, a prolific burglar had broken into houses around town for money, gold and electronics. He cut down anyone in his way with an aruval—a working man's machete used for penetrating the thick skin of coconuts and hacking dry grass.

He was caught only after eight murders and three dozen burglaries that included the Kerala Beverages Corporation, where he killed the sole night guard and robbed the place of cash, a video cassette player and several crates of dark rum. The newspapers documented the arrest on their front pages, calling him the 'Ripper Jayanandan'. The photos showed a slight, dark man with the bloodshot eyes of someone who liked his tipple, flanked by two cops and holding hands with them like lovers.

After that, everyone forgot about the whole thing, more or less, until the present summer with its series of copycat burglaries.

A rumour starts that the real Aruval killer has not been caught, even though Jayanandan had been cornered in his house with several empty bottles of rum and the missing VCR (his wife was wearing some of the stolen jewellery, but he had sold the rest).

The copycat is also using an aruval to injure, maim or murder anyone unlucky enough to be in his vicinity. Nita registers all the latest details as she eats her sambar rice and fish fry. Kripa, the maths teacher for the middle grades, narrates a gruesome detail to protesting-but-not-really shrieks from the others—a hand missing from one of the bodies was found later at *another* burglary, left behind like a totem, a taunt to those looking for him.

The students like to linger under the courtyard trees during lunch hour. The higher grades get the dibs of the shade, glaring and elbowing their way in as the younger kids scuttle out. Passing by, Nita slows down when she sees one of her students, Shruti, at the centre of a knot of her classmates. This is not unusual. Shruti is someone people jockey to be around. But it's a delicate dance— they want to be her audience, her friend, but not her target. Her minor talent is in summarizing someone in a precise, unflattering phrase, after which it's impossible for people to see them any other way. Her pet names for you can be death to your reputation and sense of self. One girl became Panty Sheela, because of the way she sat without crossing her legs. Another boy has been Mickey Mouse since the eighth grade because he'd once wept in class, no one remembers why, and the wail he'd let out sounded a bit like the high-pitched cartoon character. Then there is Cindy Crawford, a boy with a mole in the same spot as the supermodel. Only the teachers use their real names any more.

Having so much social influence at this age can be intoxicating, and Shruti is busy testing how much they let her get away with.

'I am walking up to my front door, when I hear a strange sound,' Shruti says. 'A big thud from deep inside the house.' Something heavy has fallen. To her surprise, the door is unlocked. She walks in to find upturned tables and furniture in the living room.

Instead of leaving to get help, Shruti ventures further in. 'I know that it's dangerous,' she whispers, as the others lean in. 'But this is how I am. I step on the tiger's tail, I am treacherously curious. It is my true misfortune.'

Lines ripped from a pulpy horror novel, no doubt. But to Nita's surprise, no one rolls their eyes.

Shruti swallows. 'You know the TV character who opens the door of the haunted house while we all scream, *don't do it!?* That's me.'

She goes towards the bedrooms. 'As I pass by the living room window, I see my favourite tree,' she says, 'A mango that we got as a sapling ten years ago. Its leaves tremble in the wind as if it's warning me.'

Shruti is one of those girls always trying to skirt past the rules a little. She keeps her regulation braids too loose so that stray hairs are always escaping and fringing her pretty, oval face; she applies transparent varnish on her fingernails even though nail polish is not permitted. Her father is in the Indian Foreign Service and travels a lot, and so she has music albums and cute electronics that nobody else does. She also has the kind of chutzpah that money can't buy—last term, she and another friend set up a 'tallest boy contest' for the twelfth graders, where the two of them marked the boys' heights off with a pen and ruler against a wall near the labs, writing their names against the marks. A good number of boys, including the ones without any chance of winning, turned up for the opportunity to chat her up.

The victor won by a quarter of an inch. Shruti and her friend got pulled to the principal's office for 'defacing school property' but were let off with a warning. All of this somehow makes her the kind of person whose melodrama others want to be around.

By now, Shruti has progressed to her parents' bedroom. A strange man is standing inside with his back to her. Her mother's trunk has been forced open—the one with her silk saris and wedding jewels. The man hasn't seen her yet. In one hand, he is holding a bloody aruval.

Somewhere on the way to the bedroom, Shruti has picked up the heaviest thing she could find—a small hammer. The man turns as she swings it. He leaps out of her way, rushing out of the back door as she chases him. By the time she reaches outside, he is gone.

'I run back in, and I see my mother on the floor,' she says. 'Her sari has turned from yellow to bright red from the wound in her stomach. But the frown line between her eyebrows is still there, as if she is trying to figure something out. That's how I know she is alive.'

'This is how I find her,' Shruti says, her voice breaking a little, 'with her blood inching towards my school shoes.'

'These school shoes,' she adds.

A couple of the students gasp, look down at Shruti's neat Batas.

One lone girl appears sceptical. Her hair is pulled into such a tight braid her eyebrows look raised. 'Your mother?' she asks, 'You are saying the aruval killer attacked your mother?'

They all watch Shruti's face intently.

'Yes,' Shruti says. She looks distraught. 'Papa said that I couldn't tell anyone. But you guys—you are my friends. I couldn't not.'

Nita walks up, timing her entry to disrupt any chance of a weepy group hug. 'Hello,' she says, 'What did I miss?'

Shruti frowns at the interruption. The appearance of an adult is guaranteed buzzkill; there is low-grade mumbling and a lack of eye contact as the group rapidly breaks up.

'Next time,' she tells Shruti, 'At least pick someone they won't see on Parents Day two weeks later.' The girl is silent but purses her lips as if she's barely holding back something she wants to say. Nita wonders what it is. She supposes, as Shruti looks her up and down with unconcealed disdain, that it has something to do with the fact that Nita is wearing polyester.

It occurs to Nita only then, as Shruti smirks and turns away, that her problems here may have nothing to do with her personality or the quality of her jokes, as she'd assumed, but with the plain fact that she is poor in an upper-middle-class school. The realization is unexpected, delivered via this unserious, teenaged messenger, Shruti, with her feathery fringe and the waistband she folds to make her skirt shorter. It mortifies her: that to them, she's indelibly working class and has been carrying too many signs to hide. It's a fact less obvious only from her side of the aisle. It's a gateless gate between them and her that she cannot cross.

I used to be on the other side, she wants to protest. *You would be surprised how easy it is to get from there to here.* But there wouldn't be much point. This crowd doesn't want to be seduced—at least not by her.

2

The day that is a fork in the road for Nita, the one with a switch to a far-out bomb, dawns light and cool. The heat of the last few weeks has broken and the smell of chembakam flowers is in the air. Ani spots a cloud in the sky that looks like a rabbit, points it out to her. The resemblance is uncanny, down to the two symmetrical ears and puffy tail.

Nita used to believe that these moments of shared joy would be a frequent, easy thing between mother and son. But Ani's and her moods are opposite poles. Nita is often too busy, distracted and irritable when he pulls at her clothes, wanting attention. People might think her son's name is *Ani Stopit*, she says it so often.

But this morning they hold hands as they walk to school, searching the sky for a cloud carrot that the cloud rabbit can have for breakfast.

So when she arrives at the employment agency, she is upbeat and more hopeful than usual. But nothing has changed; there are no new openings in town. Most jobs are in construction and at the cashew factories—well-paying unionized work that has been cornered by men. Occasionally there is a request for a female typist at one of the seedy second-floor businesses on the main street, in buildings with tinted windows and no ladies' bathrooms, that are run by men who reek of Hercules rum in the mornings.

'Are you willing to branch out?' the agent asks her. A chain made of manjaadi seeds, meant for good luck, peeks out of the collar of his shirt. Irreligious but superstitious is a common bent in her communist town. God is easy to let go of, but people here still believe in luck and buy lottery tickets in specific numbers, wear citrine stone rings and check the weekly astrology column in the local paper.

Nita waits as he rummages through the pile on his desk. His is the main employment agency in town, but his office is small—a single room with a storage closet. He is a pack rat, every surface is piled with files bursting with job applications, some dated from several years ago. His assistant sits in a corner, typing, his hair in a sweep across one side of his face, a damaged eye peeking through. It's unwise, Nita thinks, to hide an obvious deformity. It only makes people curious and has them imagining something far worse.

The agent pulls out a piece of paper. 'I do have a new opening, if you are willing to go outside.'

The job sounds good—great, even. An Arab family in Dubai wants a live-in English tutor for their seven-year-old daughter.

Nita has a dual MA in English and History, and taught the language to second and fourth-graders at the job before this one. The shoe fits. Maybe if she was still doing that—teaching primary school instead of these arch adolescents—she wouldn't be looking for work. Her young students had been sweet and malleable.

But even if her job had been going great, her pay is barely enough to live on for a widow with a young son. Last week, she found herself adding water to Ani's milk while trying to save money for a toy he wanted.

The Dubai salary the agent quotes makes her eyes go wide—it is five times what she's making now. That kind of money could be life-changing for her and Ani, pole-vaulting them from the working class into the upper middle; it is money that makes toy brick sets, new textbooks and even a scooter possible. It seems like a loophole someone has forgotten to close.

She needs to think about it, she tells the agent. A couple of days pass, during which time their small fridge stops working, and she has to take out a good portion of her savings from her bank account to get the compressor fixed. They are stretched thin and living dangerously. The next time she goes to the employment office, the agent has a picture of the family for her to see. It's a studio photograph, deliberately posed, the family's demons disappearing in the flash.

Nita squints at the picture, studying the little girl's wide-eyed face, trying to divine something of her personality in the fuzzy lines.

'What do *you* think?' she asks the agent. As if this man, eager to get his cut of the deal, would be an impartial observer.

He pretends to consider her question, furrowing his brows and stroking his chin before giving her the expected response.

'You should take it,' he says. He smiles counter-productively, his eyeteeth curved and sharp like a carnivore's.

'Hmm.' She is desperate to say yes.

'They are good people. Look at the mother, she looks like she has a soft heart.'

Nita, who thinks that men are particularly susceptible to reading softness in women's faces when there is none, looks anyway. She does like the mother's face. She doesn't really examine the husband.

These jobs, the agent says, tend to disappear quickly, considering the dirham–rupee exchange rates. Everyone wants to go to the Middle East.

Nita has always been the kind to do her homework. She'd asked around about people's experiences in that country and heard success stories as well as bleakly cautionary tales. Some people returned with suitcases filled with Toblerone bars and M&Ms, new electronics, good whiskey and enough savings to buy a house. But there were also the other stories, more whispered than told, often about women who left to become au pairs, nannies or household workers and were abused for years at their employers' homes, or forced into prostitution, and others who didn't come back and were never heard from again despite repeated attempts by their families to track them down.

The laws in these Middle East countries were silent on worker protections, allowing widespread exploitation. The workers with the worst luck were treated like slaves.

Still, Kochi is a port city and for the people here, the need to journey outwards is an old instinct—people have set out to sea, crowded into the bellies of junks and ships, for at least a thousand years. 'You should go,' the teachers in her school told her when she mentioned the opportunity, their eyes lighting up with something like envy.

The money is persuasive. And need is a creature that is hard to argue with. The money would help her be a better mother, she thinks. A better provider. Ani could live with her sister, Divya, and two years would pass quickly. Besides, Dubai is just three and a half hours away by plane.

Also, if she really thinks about it, it's not like she has much of a choice.

'All right,' she says, 'I'll take the job.'

She faxes over her education and passport documents, and sits through a phone interview with the agent in the Middle East. Every process is focused on vetting only her, and at the end of it, she knows nothing more about the family than she did at the start.

She spends the next two months worrying about getting along with her employers, who might be closed off, overbearing, possibly racist. Two months fretting over Ani and giving him long, overwrought hugs, and crying into her pillow after he's asleep.

She enrols for Arabic classes in a language school that teaches from a mix of faded textbooks, old magazines and instruction manuals. She learns some basic sentences and a slapdash vocabulary that includes several words for engine parts from a car repair booklet.

A week before her flight, she reads that the copycat killer has been caught in a different town while trying to pawn off some of his stolen haul. She's no longer at the school, but can imagine the excitement. Perhaps Shruti will have an 'inside story' about a cousin's part in a bike chase that nabbed the killer.

Nita is trying to spend as much time as possible with Ani before she leaves. Divya is here too, to take Ani back with her. After the first hour of being polite and considerate with each other, the sisters fall back into their old patterns. They bicker—Nita makes fun of Divya's husband, who she finds insufferably pompous, with his oddly high-waisted pants and slow way of enunciating when he talks to Nita, like she's stupid. Divya complains about Nita's cooking. They relitigate old fights, where

Divya once ironed Nita's favourite blouse on high heat, burning it ('you did it on purpose') and Divya accuses Nita of stealing a cheap but beloved piece of jewellery that teenage Divya had owned, a blue stone ring, which Nita denies to this day. It's exhausting and infuriating, but they can't be with each other any other way.

The two sisters talk about everything except Nita's impending departure and how either of them feels about it. It is their style to never openly admit to sadness, illness or misfortune, and to just wait for it to go away. The elephants in the room sit with them at the dining table, they all watch late-night TV together.

Their paternal great-grandfather, according to family lore, had died of a massive tumour that grew behind his ear over several years, one that he claimed was 'just a rash' until it became the size of a cricket ball. 'Another cricket ball tumour,' is what their mother would say when their father refused to discuss a big and uncomfortable problem, whether it was fights in the family, problems with the house or his struggling business.

Then their parents died in a bus accident when Nita was twelve and Divya eighteen, and the two sisters found themselves cricket-ball-tumouring every problem they had.

But at the last moment outside the airport, Divya hugs her close. 'My baby sister,' she says, 'I wish I had been able to take better care of you so that you didn't have to go to another country all alone.'

'I will be fine,' Nita says, even though it feels like her chest might explode right here out of sadness.

Anl, who'd seemed so unconcerned right up to now, is refusing to let go of her. She bends down and gives him the last of her smothering hugs, kissing him innumerable times on his face until he struggles to be released, his tears drying up as they wrestle. She tries to memorize the image of her son and her sister standing together—the two people left in the world who love her.

'So listen,' she tells Divya, before she heads to the departure gate, her voice thick with unshed tears, 'no matter what, do not open the top drawer of the bedroom cabinet. It's the one thing I ask.'

She leaves quickly so that she can cry by herself in the airport bathroom. Of course, Divya will go straight back to Nita's house and check that drawer. Nita has left a note in there: 'I did take the ring. It was me. I flushed it down the toilet.'

ಐ ಐ ಞ

Coming off the plane in Dubai, Nita feels the change in the world at once.

There is none of the humidity of the Kochi airport, where the heat indoors was even worse than outside and everyone sweated through their clothes while standing in serpentine queues, despite the whirring fans above. The Dubai airport has its own self-contained climate. The vast space is lit by innumerable sparkling ceiling lights, the air is scentless and cool. There is also a subtle shift in her status. Her clothes feel off at once—a too-thick material in an outdated print.

At the immigration counters, the male officials have haircuts better than hers and uniforms cut in a military style, emphasizing their biceps and broad shoulders. Even from a few feet away, she is hit by the strong incense-like scent they all seem to have doused themselves in.

When Nita presents her passport and employment documents, they look at her a beat longer than she is used to, and then never make eye contact again, handing back her papers with an abrupt gesture that emphasizes her alien ordinariness.

She is now part of a million-worker wave coming here for money and jobs. It is a set-up with little loyalty on either side—she has few rights or obligations. She cannot buy land, gets no benefits, has no path to citizenship. But she pays no taxes either.

When she steps outside the white, modernist airport, her body reacts at once. The air here has teeth. Objectively, it is 46 degrees Celsius, the temperature at which a human body becomes susceptible to heatstroke in about five minutes, and cells start to die. It feels like she's walked into a wall of thorns. She breaks out instantly into a full-body sweat, swaying on the pavement like a fighter about to go down after a one-two uppercut to the face. The sun beats down on her with a heavy club.

She manages her way to the taxi stand, lugging her wheelless suitcase. The taxi is a rundown Corolla with an Indian driver—it is not Arabic but her diffident Hindi that she practises. The man, delighted to find out that she is Indian (no matter that she is from the south), gets immediately overfamiliar. 'My sister,' he exclaims. He talks about his wife and children with longing, memories painful to listen to in the rawness of her separation from Ani.

When she opens her purse to find the address, the smell of dried jasmine flowers wafts out, already foreign, too ripe for nostalgia.

The car windows are up, the AC on full blast. She looks out as she's carried through this strange, startling place. Even in this car with its busted springs, the roads are like butter, wide, dark asphalt that stretches uninterrupted into the horizon. As they cross into the city, glass and steel skyscrapers loom over them, but they are far apart and look brand new, apostrophed by building cranes and girders. A picture of modernity is flickering into place, but for now, you can see the gaps through which the vast desert peeks through. There is constructed greenery along the road, geometric strips of lawn grass and manicured date palms, dwarf trees too brief for shade. Even the plants seem made to order and placed at exact intervals. There are few pedestrians, no bicyclists or even motorcycles. It's just a steady stream of cars, dusty Toyotas and Mazdas, as well as sleek, gleaming models she's never seen before. On a massive roundabout, she finally sees something she recognizes: a champa tree blooming among sprinklers, white blossoms against waxy green leaves. It feels like a friendly face.

'This is what brings everyone here,' the driver says, gesturing expansively at the new buildings. The immigrant who arrived slightly earlier, pretending to a greater connection with the place. 'Money and beauty, everyone wants some of it, no?' He'd seemed kind enough, but when he looks at her now in the rear-view mirror it's as if a mask has come off, and she glimpses fat-lipped lechery. Nita remembers the warnings back home about the immigrant men here, lonely and horny. She looks away.

The sand is pervasive. The pale dunes everywhere are like waves of a frozen sea. Trapped behind the growing city, the desert is both sombre and beautiful, the sun causing a play of shadow and light that would delight a landscape painter. Gusts of sand cut past the highway around the cars and slap against the taxi's windows, the fine grains collecting in the space between windows and doors. It turns the sky hazy white. The air is full of sand, the city's AQI at unhealthy, blinking-red levels. The hanging dust crystals reflect the sunlight many millions of times over, so that the noon here is brighter, sharper and hurts more than anywhere else.

As they near a bridge, she sees men in wide-brimmed sun protectors and orange jackets wielding brushes and dustcloths. They are cleaning the decorative railings and the road separators. Once she notices them, she can't miss them—they are everywhere, in a Sisyphean wiping, cleaning and dusting of the city—men with skin like hers.

When she reaches the two-storey house, a woman is waiting for her out front. The house itself is unremarkable, an upper-middle-class concrete block painted in a shade of clotted cream, with vaulted, gold-trimmed windows.

Nita recognizes her from the photo—the girl's mother. She is outside on the steps in the sun, seemingly unaffected by the heat, to greet her new employee. She is bare-headed, in a full-length, full-sleeved dress. She watches Nita climb the stairs, dragging her bag behind her. She smiles and greets her in uncertain English, sounding like she's practised it: 'Hello. Welcome to Saba's home.'

The woman's face is the kind of pale people get from sitting indoors all the time. Nita notices blue veins across her neck and forehead, and grey-green eyes like the backwaters that run parallel to the sea back home. She is in her late thirties, and formerly beautiful in a way that people tend to hold against you as if you were the custodian of something you irresponsibly lost. Nita's sister had been a looker, and the relatives who met Divya after several years often reacted to her impending middle age with near-hostility, reminiscing resentfully about her once youthful face and lush hair, like she had been careless with the family jewels.

The conversation between her and the woman, who introduces herself as Rouhi, is instantly easy, even though they are speaking in English, a second language for both. Rouhi struggles with it, her hands gesticulating as if to make up for the gaps in vocabulary.

She smiles encouragingly when Nita attempts her self-taught Arabic but continues in English as they go into the house. 'Husband in merchant ship,' she says, 'he is always in the sea. It is only Saba, me and two woman cooks here.'

The house feels smaller inside, in part because it is packed with furniture, the edges of one piece inches from the next. Rugs crowd the floor and doilies sit on the arms of fat, patterned sofas.

The walls inside are painted in new-money colours, glossy white with loud yellow trimmings. They are bare except for an oversized photograph of a wounded zebra lying in the grass, its stomach distended, apparently from a pregnancy. A man—angular, his cheekbones like knives in his face— stands over the animal holding a cleaver, raised high and ready to swing. The grass around them is stamped down with blood.

Rouhi sees Nita look at it and nods as if she'd asked a question, 'Anyone who come here looks at picture. My husband likes it to be first thing people see.'

She says it in a resigned sort of way.

Nita squints at the photograph. It is a little blurry, as if it was taken quickly and without preparation. 'Did your husband kill the zebra?'

'Yes. But that zebra dead very long time, he shot it when he was young man. I am from Egypt but my husband, he is Emirati, he is from here. He loves guns. His grandparents were Bedouin desert tribesmen. You know, when British met the Bedouins and showed them all modern things—the car, helicopter, the radio— they didn't want any of it. They wanted only the guns.'

Her tone is contemptuous but Nita can't be sure, because Rouhi is flashing that brilliant smile at her again.

'Now come,' she says, 'meet the *afreet*.'

'Afreet?'

'You will soon know all Arabic words for monsters because a small one lives here. An afreet makes storms. This one gives us fever.'

Nita follows her up the stairs, which gives her a chance to observe her new employer. Rouhi's loose dark blue dress hides most of her curves. Her hair is lush with finger-thick highlights, reds and browns mixed into the jet black, and she pushes it back from her face as they walk upstairs. The movement gets Nita's attention because each time, Rouhi's arm goes up higher than needed, over her head, pushing the hair back in a seductive move that lifts her chest, momentarily revealing its shape despite the modest dress. It's the kind of come-hither move a teenage girl may have practised in front of the mirror and then deliberately adopted, forgetting over the years how—or why—she started the habit.

The upper floor of the house is less ornately furnished and lit with bare tube lights. It seems lived-in—the couch cushions pushed to one side in acknowledgement of their uselessness, the rugs on the floor clean but worn. Nita realizes that the downstairs is a showcase, furnished more with an eye towards guests than for the people living here.

The air-conditioning is on high, and she pulls the hem of her sari around her shoulders. The room Rouhi leads her into has a small girl, wary and very un-monster-like, perched on the edge of a bed as if ready to hop off at any moment. Her face is already sharper-featured and older than her photograph. The colour is high in her cheeks as if she's just been running. Nita will later discover that this happens every time Saba is excited—two round spots of colour form on each cheek, a warning of chaos to come.

Nita waits for Rouhi to take the lead in the introductions, but she stays silent.

'Hello,' Nita finally says, 'Ahlan.'

'Ahlan!' Saba hops off the bed and rattles off what sounds like several questions in Arabic.

'No Saba, you must speak only English with Nita,' Rouhi says, 'She will help you learn, yes?'

Saba sighs. 'Hello,' she says gravely.

'Hello. My name is Nita. I just got off a plane from India.'

'Yes, Mama say,' Saba's cheeks get redder, and she hops with excitement. 'I have seven holes in my face.'

'That's exciting,' Nita says. She's met a lot of kids but this is still a new introduction. 'But are eyes holes or pockets?'

'Oh!' Saba considers this.

'Ok, Saba,' Rouhi says, 'Nita will tell you about plane, and you can talk about eye pocket. But first you finish homework, ok?'

Saba looks disappointed, but when Nita glances back as she leaves, the girl is already distracted, her fingers worrying a scab on her knee.

'That was good. No screaming,' Rouhi says.

Rouhi asks for her documents and goes over the paperwork. She keeps Nita's passport aside and returns the rest. 'Haroun will want to see,' she explains, and so Nita watches, tongue-tied, as she takes it into her bedroom and returns without it.

She sits back down and gives Nita that smile again, the one that looks like she means it. It is a gift to be able to smile like that, Nita thinks, to bestow what feels like easy friendliness on just about anyone, even a lowly employee.

'My husband say, "I want English teacher for Saba," and so you are here,' Rouhi says, 'I am not good with the English.'

'Your English is not bad. It's better than my Arabic.'

'My English so bad,' Rouhi insists, 'and my Saba is lazy. She is like k in knife. Does not do any work.'

Nita realizes a beat too late that Rouhi has cracked a joke, and that the chance to laugh has passed.

'Tell me,' Rouhi asks, 'Why you come here? You are young woman.'

'I am sorry?'

'I mean, you have no family, husband, baby? Why you come alone? You were desperate?'

'I am not desperate.' Nita giggles, and her laugh sounds awful and uncomfortable, as if she's just lied. 'I was a teacher back home, but the job didn't pay well. My parents died when I was twelve. My husband died when our son Ani was a baby. Ani is now six and staying with my sister while I work here.'

'That is hard place to be,' Rouhi says, 'This happens to us women, we lose parents, lose husband. But it has happened to you very early. You are woman alone.'

Nita can't tell if Rouhi is actually blunt or whether her sympathy was lost in translation. Anyway, it is the truth. 'Yes. I am a woman alone.'

'That needs *shagaah*. I have never been alone in my life.'

Later, Nita learns that the word means courage. That first conversation is one Nita thinks about often—Rouhi offering her a confession as soon as they met like she couldn't help but reveal herself. *I have never been alone in my life.*

3

The school bus arrives every morning at 6.30 a.m. to beat the heat. Waking up at 6 is early for Nita, and unholy for Saba.

The school bus stop is where the wealth of this place really hits home for Nita. Saba's school bus is shiny pink and white with yellow trim. There are seat belts on each spotless, cushioned seat, and as the kids climb on, an automated counter near the driver tallies them up. There are handholds that the smaller kids use to get up the steps. The name of the school and the logo— an orange tulip inside a book—are stencilled on the outside. Everything is sparkling clean.

Nothing drives poverty home harder than seeing what you can't give your children. Nita had tried the school bus for a week for Ani, before deciding to save money by walking him to school. The 'bus' had been an old blue Maruti Omni van, a model banned in some states because of its non-existent bumper and lack of crash guards. In an accident, it tended to crumple like a cardboard box. The seats were worn and the bus driver was dressed in a sleeveless vest and mundu. Kids were packed by the threes into two seats.

She wonders now whether she is a bad mother for having let Ani take that death trap to school. Had she not known any better? Everyone knew that Omnis were unsafe and used them anyway because they were cheap. She'd been wilfully blind in the face of a lack of options.

Her thoughts are interrupted by the cries of a young girl being carried to the bus stop. She's struggling hard to get away, but her father has his grip around her hips and one slippery leg. Her face is beet red and clips are falling from her hair. She looks like she is having the battle of her life. But her father's arms are octopus-like, grabbing another limb each time she pulls one free. She is the only one here who doesn't know that the fight is already lost.

The bus stop is Nita's chance to observe Rouhi's neighbours, since they usually dart from house to car and back. What she sees here is a reversal of normal life—the children, wide awake and unforgiving at 6.30 a.m., are emotionally in charge, screaming about shoelaces 'tied the wrong way', about not being able to take a chocolate bar for lunch, about feeling too hot, or too cold, about ponytails tied too tight, their faces feeling big, their teeth hurting, having a newly discovered stomach ache, being thirsty, hungry. One girl is weeping inconsolably about Zizo, her cat, not being allowed to ride to school with her. The ironed uniforms already look undone, the snot is starting to run.

The half-awake adults are barely able to manage this early morning onslaught. They are all strangers to Nita and likely to stay that way since they barely glance at her. Over the past few weeks, Nita has made up private nicknames for them. There is, for instance, Mrs Stoneface, who watches her three young sons go through emotional cartwheels with zero reaction (even her eyebrows don't twitch); Mr Everything Is Ok, who responds with the same pained cheeriness to his daughter's manic energy, her tears and refusal to climb on to the bus virtually every morning; there is Ms I Did Not Ask For This, the full-time nanny of twin third-graders, a girl and boy who are well aware of her lesser power, alternately tear at her clothes (Nita has heard a rip at least once) and try to convince her to tell their parents that the bus never came. The adults all flee the scene when the bus arrives, as soon as the children become someone else's problem.

Nita sees Saba beside this crowd of miniature despots and finds her relatively manageable. She is indeed a storm-demon, but not a tyrant—while chaos follows her wherever she goes, with books missing, bath routines ignored, clocks barely adhered to and clothes shrugged off, she is not malicious. It makes it easy for Nita to like her.

Everything related to Saba is Nita's job. She is a tutor-caretaker-sometimes-cleaning-up-after person, in that hyphenated way so many jobs that women do are. She teaches Saba English, hunts for missing textbooks, checks scrawled homework, gets her dressed and fed. Nita is awake at 5.30 a.m. in her narrow bed every morning and in the kitchen by 6 to prepare a snack for school.

Most of the time getting ready is spent on coaxing Saba to follow basic hygiene and wear an acceptable outfit. Getting her into and out of the bath takes about twenty minutes. Saba will only brush her teeth with one specific toothpaste flavour, strawberry, and if that isn't available she will go to school with room-clearing breath.

Once Saba is finally persuaded that putting her underwear on outside her school pants is not the height of style or that just a towel won't work for class, they walk to the bus.

This early, the weather is almost pleasant. By eight, the heat slams into you as soon as you step outside, a heavyweight fighter with an anger problem—it's the reason that the few people hurrying past on the pavements cannot stop to make small talk or ask for directions.

Still, this unforgiving land has, for now, been forced into submission. Busy cities are emerging out of this earth. International politicos and oil executives are presenting the ruling sheikhs with bespoke Rolls Royces and homes in the toniest European neighbourhoods to push through deals for trading licenses, oil pipelines. Money has poured in, to leash the Arabian Sea with dredging and sea breakers. Across the jagged coastline, iron railings and concrete walls separate freshly laid highways from the sea, and the waves exhaust themselves over and over against these new barriers, searching for a way in.

The sandstorms are harder to tame. If you open the windows at the wrong time, you get slapped in the face by windborne sand that is sharp-edged from erosion and cuts like tiny knives. The windows of houses and apartments are edged with rubber trim and sealed with netting on the outside, the glass tinted against the sun.

Saba sometimes does well in school and sometimes doesn't— she is smack in the middle of her class. In Arabic and Math, she brings back golden stars at the top of her pages, but in English, it's a sea of blue stars across her tests, colours near the bottom in the school star hierarchy that has gold, then silver, followed by green, blue and red.

Saba's difficulty in English is partly because it's the sole class where the teachers actually speak the language. All her other classes are in Arabic. Saba chatters with her friends in Arabic with only the rare English word peppering their conversations: *dinosaur, Barbie, walkman.*

But Nita's Arabic is worse than Saba's English, which forces Saba to use the less preferred tongue. Saba will sometimes try an

Arabic word when she doesn't know the English one and Nita will shake her head in puzzlement. Saba usually responds to this by saying the word louder, as if the higher volume will pierce Nita's incomprehension: '*Maqas*, Nita, *maqas!*'

'*Scissors*,' Rouhi will eventually say from the other room. She is the explainer of last resort, helping out when Nita and Saba are at a wordless, shriek-heavy impasse.

English is full of phonetic stumbling blocks for Saba, like her difficulty with the letter *p*, which has no Arabic equivalent. *Barrot, burse, bencil*—Saba's tongue does not comply (*combly*). Still, speaking English is easier for Saba than writing it. Having to write from left to right, instead of right to left like in Arabic, is her biggest battle. She will write TAH EHT NI SI TAC EHT and it will make perfect sense to her. Asking her to do it in the reverse direction seems to hurt her brain.

Finally, Nita makes a small bracelet with yellow thread for Saba to wear on her left wrist when she does her English homework to help her remember to start on the left.

They get along and Nita is willing to play Saba's single plot games. 'Nita,' Saba will shriek, 'Come play Throw Jaffa Out with me!'

TJO involves Nita pretending to throw Saba's stuffed giraffe Jaffa out of the bedroom window, which they open just enough for the game. Saba screams and begs for mercy while Nita dangles Jaffa outside. After a few evil cackles, Nita will pretend to give in and move away from the window, but then quickly dart back holding Jaffa by his thin neck, pinched between her thumb and forefinger, so it really looks like this time, Jaffa is doomed, and Saba screams in delight/terror and covers her eyes.

'Saba likes you,' Rouhi observes within a week of Nita's arrival, and while Nita smiles at this, she doesn't find it especially flattering. She discovered early on that while you needed to be kind with small children and patient in the face of relentless questioning, you could win their affection quickly with occasional treats, like the toffees from the corner store she used to give out generously to her young students for good behaviour. Ani's weakness was bournvita powder sprinkled on toasted milk bread. The crystals melted into a crunchy topping over the slice, and he couldn't get enough of it. Homework finished faster with the promise of it at the end.

A little sugar goes a long way is Nita's take—perhaps not the healthiest approach to child-rearing and something she feels occasionally guilty about. But she is playing the long game.

When Nita took over the preparation of Saba's mid-morning school snacks from the cooks, she asked her at the start what she wanted. Saba was surprised—no one had asked before. She demanded chocolate.

'Chocolate is difficult,' Nita had said. Rouhi was unlikely to go along with that. But Nita had checked the pantry before this conversation. 'I could do a butter jam sandwich with a cookie inside the sandwich,' she offered.

'*Inside* the sandwich?' Red spots appeared on Saba's cheeks.

'Yes, but your mother may stop me if she finds out, so you can't tell anyone.' It wasn't true, since she'd already suggested this to Rouhi, who had only shrugged. But for Saba, a secret with the sweet was irresistible.

Something that Nita, a lover of words, thinks counts in her favour: *sukkar*, sugar's root, is an Arabic word; sweetness reached them before the Europeans. It is an old love, hard to dislodge.

So Nita packs decadent sandwiches—couscous with extra raisins and sugar, cheese toast with potato chips crumbled in.

They improvise as they go, the last few minutes of evening bath-time dedicated to Nita and Saba debating the snack options for the next day, the discussion a frowny serious affair like a state event, if such meetings had as its main decision maker a tiny person covered in soap.

Most days, Nita is busy until night-time, and once back in her small room, writes letters to her sister and her son until she is ready to sleep. Sometimes, in quiet moments—while ironing Saba's dresses, or looking over her schoolwork—she finds herself gripped with a terrible homesickness. She imagines Ani's small face becoming more grown up, his milk teeth falling out, his hair growing and losing its cowlick. His memory of his mother growing fuzzy.

Stranded in this city with its wide, uncrossable streets, she finds herself longing for the chaos of home—a place with trees so dense that century-old banyans used their thick roots to break up newly laid pavements, and rains came with raging-god force, night after monsoon night.

Back home, at least half the day was entirely hers. Like Saba, the people in her home town have a sweet tooth and nearly every street has an ice cream parlour or milkshake bar, which Nita would visit with her friends for the chikoo cashew or banana pineapple.

She misses everything about her street, including the Perfect movie theatre, with its sideways *P*, the small motorcycle store, Fantom, that sells decals of fire-breathing eagles and offers Jaguar and Ferrari logo stickers for anything from a bicycle and up. Everyone calls the traffic roundabout down the street from her house the 'nuts corner', because an old woman with a cart used to sell roasted nuts in newspaper cones for over thirty years until she died, and the name stuck.

Here, she is struggling for connection. The windows of the house are always shut to keep the dust out and the streets are dead silent besides the sound of cars.

Forget the hoopoe. She waits for a sparrow or magpie, or even a pedestrian lizard. She listens hard for the noises of living things—the crack of a bird taking off, the croak of a daytime toad, the skittering of neighbourhood cats, the rustling of leaves as critters wander inside bushes and trees. But she hears nothing as she walks down footpaths with crisp black and white borders. Once, she hears a hiss, but it turns out to be a water pipe breaking in the heat.

Everything here is brand new. In the 1950s, when neighbours like Egypt had outdoor cafes, movie theatres and a divorced princess who showed off her shapely legs in Chanel dresses, Dubai was a pearling village without electricity, where people kept track of time through a one-armed local who'd walk down the beach, beating his drum to let everyone know it was past 7 p.m. People fried locusts as snacks and served them alongside dates and black coffee.

Now this place is an enclave for wealthy strangers, and all kinds of people are renting a spot. It's not just the usual mix of sports stars and celebrities, but also former Nigerian kleptocrat governors and military officials, who steadily siphoned off billions of dollars of funds meant for their provinces into Dubai bank accounts; Russian FSB and Azerbaijani arms dealers, who have set up love nests for their girlfriends and visit regularly on 'business'; Pakistani and Indian gangsters, and former CEOs and CFOs of assorted defunct banks from across Asia and the Middle East—the ones who managed to leave their countries right before the institutions they looted collapsed. They are all relocating to plush apartments and villas in Dubai with 'uninterrupted panoramic views of the Arabian Sea'.

And that is just the creamy layer. Mid-sized criminals across government, business and mafia from Mexico to Iran have realized that this new iteration of Dubai has a financial sector that comes with just a light dusting of regulation, with virtually no documentation needed to open an account. The city's Port Rashid, named after its king, has become the staging ground for smuggled goods. When it comes to money, the local banks don't see colour, whether black, white or bloody. It is the perfect set-up for everyone to get rich very fast.

Most of the residents hear little of this, but they see the change in their streets—the packed luxury stores, designer bags on many arms, and a new wave of multi-racial, super-rich immigrants wandering about the malls in Jimmy Choo stilettos and custom-made, diamond-studded Force Pumps.

Nita, confined as she is inside the house like a caged bird, rereads her books, writes her letters, stares out of the windows at the traffic. From her room, she can see an apartment building on the opposite side of the street, the only one on this villa-dominated block. She sometimes spots a teenage girl hanging out on a balcony on the second floor in cycling shorts and brief tops—gym wear— although she clearly isn't going anywhere. She's often reading a magazine or looking out onto the street like Nita. After a few weeks, she notices that the girl is on the balcony more often and is also better dressed, either in pretty tops and jean shorts or in dresses. She is also taking better care of her hair, and it falls over her shoulders in smooth waves.

It takes a few days for Nita to finally see the reason for the change. The girl is there as usual with her magazine, but then sits up slowly in her chair, her eyes intent on Nita's side of the

street. Whoever she's looking at is in Nita's blind spot. She can
only guess at what's happening from the changing expressions
on the girl's face—a brightening, a shy smile, a wave. A nod.
A shake of the head and a laugh. After a few minutes of this,
she goes back inside and doesn't come out again for the rest
of the day.

Nita makes sure to be at the window the same time the
next day. And sure enough, the girl is there, her face aglow,
communicating in improvised sign language with someone
on the pavement. From the stealthiness of it all, Nita intuits a
budding romance.

The love affair, unbeknownst to its active participants, is
a triangle—the girl, her paramour and Nita, the silent witness.
She watches its snail-like progress, the few minutes of daily
communication evolving into more complicated signs and
gestures over the next few weeks. Given only one side to watch,
Nita can't really crack the code, but some of the gestures are
repeated often and easier to figure out. A finger pointed at the
unseen lover and then hugging herself—a lover's embrace. The
girl often makes a heart shape with her hands, shyly. Other
gestures have become stand-ins for words or phrases. An entire
secret language made up by two people separated by a street,
restrictions, rules. Love somehow finding a way through the
cracks.

Then all at once, the girl is no longer there. Nita figures at
first that the family might be away on a trip, but the lights still
come on in the evenings. She turns up on schedule for the next
several days, but the balcony doors, to her disappointment, stay
closed. It happened without warning—the last communication
was as usual, full of endearments and giggles from the young
woman.

Nita can only guess at what happened. Very likely, there were several witnesses to this streetside romance and someone told the girl's parents.

There isn't much to watch on daytime television—they don't get international cable and the local Channel 33 starts its transmission with the afternoon cartoons. So Nita devours the *Khaleej Times* every morning in an effort to get some understanding of the place. But Dubai's paper of repute is a PR broadsheet when it comes to local news, splashing glossy colour photos of Dubai's crown prince on the front pages alongside foggy, adoring text of his latest horse purchase or ribbon-cutting ceremony.

It's jarring for Nita, whose home town's papers are filled with disparaging editorials of the local politicos and cartoons that border on the abusive, depicting legislators with thick noses and frog-like bodies. Here, the news favours photographs where the light catches Prince Maktoum's jawline just so.

'Would you like to come to supermarket today?' Rouhi asks her one weekend afternoon.

Nita has heard about this place from Middle Eastern returnees—a legendary, shiny destination filled with your heart's desires, much like Ali Baba's magic cave. 'Yes,' she says.

'We should get almond ice cream if they have,' Rouhi muses, 'and vegetable for my morning shakes,' she adds, to compensate.

It is a ten-minute car ride to the Giant superstore. The high-ceilinged, heavily air-conditioned place, brightly lit even in early afternoon, is unlike anything Nita has seen before. It is crowded with Arabs as well as immigrant Indians, Pakistanis, Sri Lankans, Filipinos, sunburned Aussies and Brits getting their weekly shopping in. Shopping carts are loaded to their brims in a jumble of produce, tahini cans, Cheetos, plastic toys, tins of Danish butter cookies, Blue Diamond almonds, American cereal. The Northern Europeans with their absent eyebrows and outdoor trek clothing, loom over everyone else; the Russian women shop in full-face make-up, the Iranians arrive with their entire families including the grandparents and argue strenuously in the produce section, massaging the pomegranates and popping the pistachios to check their freshness. The freezer section is enormous, packed with meat cut and minced and massaged into all kinds of shapes and options. A young girl and her father stand near the ice cream freezers, the father holding the door open and examining a massive box of butterscotch ice cream cake as white waves of cold air wash over them.

'This orange is bigger than my head,' Nita marvels, picking it up.

'That is not orange, it is the grapefruit,' Rouhi says, amused, taking it from her and putting it in the shopping cart. 'We will try today.' Along with almond chocobars, they get tubs of yoghurt (again, bigger than Nita's head), dates still on the stem, a variety of green vegetables Nita has not seen before and cannot name, exotic, non-desert fruit from other people's summers (imported but still somewhat affordable thanks to zero taxes), white bread, tahini, jam, wedge cheese, butter, sesame oil, fresh olives, jarred artichokes, spiced kebabs, freshly roasted assorted nuts in a warm brown paper bag, pencils for Saba and a cotton t-shirt that Saba picks out, which says 'I <3 cats', part of Saba's ongoing campaign with her mother. Nita notices Rouhi taking pains to avoid the cereal aisle, where the shelves are a riot of sweet American brands, the cartoon characters on the boxes waiting siren-like to entice Saba.

Nita's hands are icy from the air-conditioning. She steps outside the store for a moment while Rouhi and Saba negotiate how many cardboard picture books she can buy. They are cheap but making them feel hard to get is part of Rouhi's discipline arsenal—they are effective bribes for Saba's obedience.

Nita waits in the parking lot, where the blinking, epileptic-unfriendly neon light of the supermarket sign reflects across car bumpers and black puddles that Nita is 90 per cent certain are not water. A woman in a black abaya exits the store, glances over. Her eyes—the only part of her Nita can see, even her hands are covered with black gloves—are lined extravagantly with kohl and green eyeshadow.

At the far wall, two young men sit close together, their heads bent. One is squinting at the other's naked foot, trying to get something out of the sole while his injured friend winces and groans.

Nita watches. It's an old, old gesture, a scene that pops up across stories and art—Lakshmana extracting a thorn out of Rama's foot, Cupid doing it for Venus, Daphnis for Chloe, that look of concentration the same across centuries. She is analysing, she realizes, like the talented essay writer she'd been in college. Old habits die hard. Once, she could have written a paper connecting this gesture across time and culture.

What is the use of all that education now? says a voice in her head.

The man tending to his injured friend says something, alarmed and pointing in the distance, and when the other man looks up, he makes a quick motion with his hand, making him yelp. He has pulled a sliver of glass out from the wound. They both look at the piece admiringly—a small thing covered in blood that caused so much pain.

Nita looks on, fascinated, until the two of them spot her. A shutter falls across their eyes, their smiles evaporate as if they had never been. They watch her, stone-faced, and she, surprised, doesn't move away quickly enough. One of them shouts something in Arabic. She doesn't need a translation. They keep calling out as she retreats into the store.

She has been seeing the city in Rouhi's wake. In her absence, the veil lifts a little and Nita glimpses a different side. The word for 'stranger' in Arabic—*gharib*—is a chameleon, meaning both stranger and intruder, someone impoverished of friends and relatives. She feels the many shades of it in how these people see her.

Back in her room that evening, Nita tries to write a letter to her sister that doesn't go heavy on her anxiety. She tosses out a couple of early drafts. Why spend stamps on a letter weighed down with worry?

Despite her characteristic cheerfulness, back home she'd felt the loneliness of a young widow surrounded by families. She thought she'd escape that black solitary feeling by coming here, only to find it waiting for her like an old friend.

So she cricket-ball-tumours it, as usual. She tells her sister about the yoghurt in the shops here, so thick that a dipped spoon leaves a sharp indentation, how the carton milk is so dense it coats her tongue, how fresh, cold strawberries are available in the middle of the desert in such quantities that they are on buy two packs get one free.

She writes about cheeses she'd never tasted before coming here—feta, halloumi, cheddar—and the air-conditioning, set below 21 degrees Celsius everywhere, as if the city is trying to make a point, posturing before the ancient desert. She writes about things rather than people, because these despite their bewildering quantity, are labelled and explained and make a kind of sense.

If she could, she'd call them up. But while Rouhi has said yes, that she can call once a month for a few minutes, the phone is downstairs and the extension in Rouhi's room, and it feels strange to talk to her son with the two women close by. Besides, Ani doesn't say much on the phone. She can hear Divya prompting him—'Tell her about your new teacher! Ask her about the little girl!'—but he is monosyllabic and distracted. So she sends long letters instead that Divya can read to him, with little drawings of pomegranates, date palms, the people in the supermarket.

With the husband absent, one may have imagined that this houseful of women was an idyllic, happy place, which was of course, wishful thinking. The two cooks are distantly related to the husband and poor cousins of a sort, and he has given them much-needed jobs. They are loyal to him and somewhat contemptuous of their mistress, following her directions only reluctantly. Rouhi has to repeat her requests often, and often grows frustrated, sighing loudly after tasting a dish, pushing it away. They tolerate Saba because she is small and charming, and of course their cousin's child, even if only a girl.

The two cooks are stocky and of similar age, and the only differences that Nita can discern between them is that one has a waist and straight hair gone grey, while the other is built like a rectangle and has dark shoulder-length curls. In her head Nita thinks of them as the two-headed woman, because of their similarity and the way they talk to each other.

When they first met her, her greeting went unacknowledged. They looked her over before turning away. They ignored her but the conversation was all about her. They talked in an ongoing murmur to each other as they chopped and sliced and fried huge piles of onions. Their conversation in Arabic sounded like one run-along sentence, only parts of which she understood.

'I hope she doesn't start cooking curry in the kitchen,' said the first. 'Hmm yes, the smell will stick to us even after we shower,' the second agreed. They hovered together near two pots on the stove, one boiling vegetables while in the other, a goat's head simmered. The first murmured, 'Tsk you can see her stomach, you can tell she's had a child'—'but still thin, not enough meat on her'—'Back home, she wouldn't even get married with those feet'—'oversized, like a man's, such a pity, and toes like dirty potatoes—'

They went on and on, casting sidelong glances at her until she fled.

The ground floor smells of cooking despite the exhaust fan running in the kitchen all day. Rouhi sometimes spritzes the living room with an air freshener that says *Rose* on the can but smells like nail polish. Mostly, she doesn't bother—she prefers the small room upstairs anyway, reading or sewing with her feet tucked under her on one of the sofas that have been relegated there because they are saggy and scuffed. There is an old banged-up TV with no remote that Rouhi watches her shows on. Rouhi behaves like she doesn't really own the things in this house and is only an exalted caretaker, taking little pride in the crystals and furnishings that Haroun has accumulated.

One evening, Nita comes out of her room to find Rouhi waiting in front of the TV with a jug of Tang and two glasses on the coffee table.

'Come,' Rouhi says, 'we watch *Bold and Beautiful*.'

Saba is asleep and the house is dead quiet, as if it's keeping as still as possible so as to not wake the afreet.

A few weeks ago, Nita would have been unsure about befriending her employer. Down that road be dragons. Once, in the school she'd taught back home, the vice-principal tried out a new policy, mandating an entry and exit register in the teachers' cafeteria. They had to sign the register every time they went out or came back in, whether for classes, student consultations, bathroom visits, or even to wash their hands. It felt tyrannical, and Nita drew the short straw of talking to the mulish man, who she just happened to be good friends with.

She finally knocked on Dijoy's office door and went in like she always did, with two cups of filter coffee from the India Coffee House down the street.

'How is Gollum?' She always asked after his dog, an adoptee from the street who Dijoy had named after the *Lord of the Rings* character because of his bulging eyes in a skinny, malnourished face. Gollum stayed that way no matter how much chicken liver Dijoy mixed into his food.

'Ruining my settee, which means he's in a good mood these days,' Dijoy said, 'He shows me he loves me by destroying my things.'

'You have Stockholm syndrome,' Nita observed, blowing on her lukewarm coffee unnecessarily before she sipped it.

'I do and I love it. And how is Ani?'

'Not chewing on my chairs, but he might as well be,' Nita sighed, 'Small boys are feral.'

It was only when the coffee was nearly done that Nita brought up the register. Dijoy didn't react well. His face turned stony. 'Wait, did you come in here to talk to me about the register? Did the other teachers put you up to it?'

'N-n-no, of course not,' Nita grew flustered. So bad always, with confrontation.

Dijoy pointed at his coffee. 'This was a bribe? Talk about Stockholm syndrome.'

Nita tried to explain, putting her coffee down and her palms up, but he refused to hear it. Dijoy was prickly, introverted and prone to digging in his heels. It took a mass boycott of the register by the teachers for him to eventually give in. Their friendship never fully recovered.

Never make your bosses your friends, was the lesson Nita took from this. But she is a social creature, and in this house, there is no one else to talk to about subjects besides English tenses, *Spiderman* and the best chewing gum flavour (strawberry).

So she sits down beside Rouhi.

Rouhi is devoted to *The Bold and the Beautiful* on the theory that it helps her learn English. But she plays the show with the volume down and you can barely hear the dialogue. Nita has to follow the plot from the gestures and reactions of the characters. That isn't difficult—everyone's emotions are highly exaggerated. Someone is always bursting into tears, throwing a plate or shouting passionately; surprise is communicated with cartoon-shocked faces.

Each season sets up a series of standard love triangles, interrupted from time to time by people returning from fake deaths to complicate the plot. The ten or so main characters get paired with each other in turn, like a bored child marrying dolls. The women telegraph their level of villainy by the amount of cleavage on display, the violet in their lipstick and the height of their highly processed hairdos. For the fans, all of this is quite soothing—the outsize reactions to both small and big controversies (the wrong birthday present, a sister revealing she is actually your mother) makes it feel like nothing really matters. The kisses are close-mouthed, not that you will see those on this TV since the Dubai censors diligently edit them out.

Nita isn't complaining. It's the first time she is looking at a colour television. But the TV, she discovers, is an excuse. Rouhi wants to talk. As Nita sips the Tang (chemical, unpleasant), Rouhi tells her about her home. She hadn't seen her parents for three years when they died, she says. 'They would say they have no money to catch flight here, and their car is too old for them to drive so far. They want me to come there. I was always thinking "soon" and then it become "never". Just like that.'

Her father used to smell of dates and lemons, so Rouhi eats dates all the time, and sometimes takes out the lemons from the fridge and smells them. The well water at home was sweet like sherbet some years, a bit salty in others because of minerals from the rain. The water changed the taste of the fruit each season, she says. Her father could pop a preserved date from the farm into his mouth and tell them the year it was harvested, a kind of party trick.

Her parents died the same year as the riots in Cairo, so Rouhi couldn't attend the funeral ceremonies. 'I never saw body, so now I think they are still here. Desert has mirage, you know? I feel, they will ring my bell. They will call phone.'

Grief—so familiar. The same emotion Nita knows so well twisting someone else's face. She doesn't know which is worse, thinking your dead parents will turn up any minute, or having seen their (grey, mangled, unrecognizable) bodies.

New lines appear on Rouhi's face when she talks about her parents, and Nita reassesses her age. Beauty so often conceals age, temperament, intelligence. The big giveaway with Rouhi are her hands—her left hand is on the sofa, inches away from Nita. She studies Rouhi's long, slender fingers, the blue veins and thinning skin. This part of Rouhi looks older than the rest of her, as if age has started its work here, and in the coming years, will creep up her arms, taking her inch by inch.

Every night after that, Rouhi waits for her with Tang.

Before Nita, Saba was Rouhi's main audience, even though the little girl mostly uses her mother's voice as reassuring background music as she plays or zooms around the room. Rouhi's stories are set in Egypt's farms and houses, a way for her to talk about home. According to Rouhi, village grandmothers interested in magic aren't just cutting the necks of chickens to make sure they have grandsons, or buying powdered herbs to revive the limp sexual desires of their daughters' husbands. In Rouhi's tales, they are badass ladies who knock elbows with demons, speak with the spirits of their ancestors and fight evil djinns.

She tells Saba and Nita about a woman who lived in a falling-down villa with her cat Maitoo. The woman was a widow who lived alone, and over time, she noticed that her east-facing living room had a corner the sunlight didn't touch.

The woman also realized that she unconsciously avoided the corner, sweeping around it. This was very unusual for her—she had a penchant for tidiness. She'd been a schoolteacher and had managed to keep her classroom clean despite managing two dozen sloppy seven-year-olds every year.

'*I am seven!*' Saba gasps excitedly.

'Yes, that is amazing! You are also seven.'

Finally, Rouhi says, the woman decided to clean the corner. After postponing this plan for several days in a row for no reason at all, she walked over to it one morning with her broom and reached into the black space.

The darkness shifted and the woman saw the djinn crouched there for the first time—with its long, over-stretched limbs and claw-like fingers, its yellow-eyed grinning face looking out at her, its forehead wrinkled and bunched with strange growths. And in the next moment, the djinn transformed into her beloved cat

Maitoo, the cat that had come with the house and purred against her paper-dry legs on the first day.

Maitoo looked at her with his malevolent yellow eyes before doing a stretch on the rug, extending out its claws as it yawned.

'Then what happened?' Saba asks.

'Nothing,' Rouhi says, 'she and the cat went on as usual. She didn't try cleaning corner again. He behaved like cat and she pretended she was cat owner.'

'But the cat is evil!' When Saba is agitated, she reverts to Arabic, like now.

'The cat was always evil, yes? She just found out that day. By then she loved Maitoo too much, and she couldn't throw him out. Besides, Maitoo had never hurt her.'

Saba frowns, uncertain. Something is wrong with the story, but she can't pin down exactly what. 'She should throw the cat out,' she says finally.

'Shouldn't knowing the truth change your behaviour?' Nita asks later.

'Maybe,' Rouhi says, 'but does that mean everything before this didn't happen? The evil creature is the same one she loves. It sat in her lap and she scratched its ears. They belong to each other.'

'But,' Nita points out, 'the cat hid its true self from her.'

'Don't we all hide true self from everyone?'

Nita is silent. Rouhi has a point. And the need to be loved is often a winning argument, one that makes many people stay even when they shouldn't.

'I tell Saba my old stories as part of my fight against Disney,' Rouhi says. She pronounces it *Dizzy Knee*. 'Why stories must end same way every time?'

'Yes,' Nita muses, 'I can see *The Princess Dies in the End* becoming Disney's next big hit, if only they took the chance.'

Rouhi giggles, and Nita gets a little thrill at having made her laugh.

'We try to help our child. But we only make mistake, yes?' Rouhi says, 'One day Saba will shout at me, "Mama, you ruined my life with those horrible stories!"'

Nita tries to picture Ani in her sister's house. He doesn't have access to the cartoons Saba does, but he is fanatical about *He-Man*, which also ends with the good guy in the fur underpants winning every time. Perhaps he is such an optimist because everything he sees promises him a happy ending.

Divya, loving aunt and substitute mother, probably isn't following most of the instructions Nita gave her about Ani's love for fruit, or about taking him to parks, or to the post office for undeliverable envelopes that he could scan for good stamps—the things Nita can't be there for, because she is working here for the extra income. Maybe every parent is unforgivable, no matter what they do.

On the television, a large-chinned man and a blonde woman draw closer and closer to each other, and the channel cuts to commercial, the kiss edited out.

'Before I left, I was telling my son a story too,' Nita says, 'We had just started. Now it builds up inside me.' She pauses, surprised at this confession.

'What is it about?'

'Well,' Nita hesitates, 'Ani loves stamps from all over the world. So I started telling him this story about a sailor on an adventure, travelling to our home town. But we didn't get very far.'

'I am here, you can tell me.'

So Nita does, except this time her sailor is Egyptian.

4

213 CE
Darius

We burn a library at least every hundred years, Nita says. It's a habit that goes centuries back—these bonfires are bright spots on the human timeline, forcing us to start over. The bark-printed Mayan codices burned by the Spanish conquistadors. The Buddhist Nalanda texts destroyed by Bakhtiyar Khilji. The Antioch Library burned down by the Christian Emperor Jovian. Maybe among them are answers about the world we've lost forever.

But you cannot burn the stories people tell each other unless you burn every storyteller who remembers. So these are among the oldest things we have. We tell them over and over to turn back time. We tell them to turn trees into seeds, buildings into huts. We tell them as a river turns holy, a river dries up, a river floods. We tell them as the truth changes—the Earth is round and then it is flat; the Earth revolves around the sun and then the other way around. As the stars become gods, as do the trees, the wind and the mountains.

Rewind, rewind, and here we are, the place where Nita starts—a ship lifting anchor on a rocky, wind-blown beach.

The *Tefnut* sets sail from the Berenike port after the Dog Star rises—around 20 July on the Roman calendar, which the sailors are forced to use because the insurance men and lenders, all Romans, are unfamiliar with the Egyptian calendar, and unwilling to learn. Late July is when the monsoon wind arrives to assist the journey, providing enough momentum for the massive ships.

It takes a good amount of capital to put together a crew and ship capable of crossing to Muziris and back. But the trip to this port city on the Malabar coast is worth it.

The Roman Empire is at the point that future historians will call *late*—the sun is setting among the cypress trees, the provinces are beginning to rebel. But for now, the gold and silver still flow, and the citizens have enough coins to buy and fill their rooms with Indian cinnamon, African myrrh and incense (all the better to keep out the stink from the streets). They spice their dishes with lazer and pepper. The women wear sparkling topaz and lapis lazuli in their ears for winter night parties lit by candlelight. Pointed-toe leather sandals from China and imported malachite eyeliner are all the rage. Ships taking the trouble to bring these treasures from Eastern ports make windfall profits.

To sail to Muziris, the traders rely on the monsoon wind that pushes the wooden ships with lateen sails down the Indian Ocean at six knots and lands them at the port in less than ten days.

Darius is watching the grey horizon. Around them, a light rain falls. If this turns into a storm, it will make the trip over the next few hours extremely dangerous.

To reach the Indian Ocean, their ship has to first cross the length of the Red Sea, which is a temperamental strait of reef and rock. Tefnut is the goddess of the sea, but her namesake ship is receiving no kindness from it in the strait. When the captain comes out of his cabin and looks out at the grey sky and water, the corners of his eyes narrow with worry. Money causes wrinkles, Darius's mother liked to say, to comfort her son after they had lost everything, and this man Babu, the captain of the *Tefnut*, has both money and debts, and a face like the leather ball the port workers played games with during the cooler evenings.

Babu makes his nephew, the youngest person in the crew, sit up at the front of the ship and call out when he sees any large rocks sticking out of the water or close to the surface. 'Nothing beats the eyesight of a twelve-year-old,' Babu says. The high wind ruffles the boy's dark curls, the seawater splashes his feet and the rain slaps at his forehead. He wipes his eyes and every few minutes, shouts out 'right' or 'left', and the oarsmen swing the ship to one side or the other, no laughing matter for this heavy boat.

One of the crewmen is already green in the face, hanging over the sides and throwing up. Darius is thankful it's not him. He is young enough to still carry some residual gawkiness and is trade-sailing for only the second time in his life. His own sickness is for home. He is glad to be out of the Berenike port, which has unpleasant weather and is beset by scorpions and rats. One night, he'd woken up in the warehouse with a giant hairy spider on his face, which was followed by several sleepless nights lying on grain bags listening to fights outside between drunken men, or the sound of horse hooves on cobblestones, as Roman mounted police units patrolled the streets. He doesn't miss that place.

But he's left his mother behind, who is working in her old age at a caravan rest stop at a distance several *aters* outside the city, handing out water to parched travellers, when by rights she should be spending these years on a soft bed in her village. But since the *seyal*—the flash flood—swept away their home and killed his father and sister, the two of them have become wandering itinerants. Her only home is the place where she works, and his is what shelter he can find.

But at least he is young. It is the new age—213 CE. The Egyptians are now Roman citizens, thanks to the governor's decree two years ago. They still live under an unequal sun, looked down on by the central Roman provinces, and mostly find only hard, back-breaking work. But for a change, there is money to be made. Until five seasons ago, the closest Darius got to a ship was chopping the wood used to build them, and he had watched with mixed feelings as entire plains of doum palm were cut down and carried by camels and donkeys to the shipyards.

A year ago, a captain finally hired him as a cleaner for his ship. But the man fell ill when they were still a week out from the port of Adulis, where they were supposed to fill their hold with expensive tortoiseshell. The sea can be particularly unkind to some people—it takes them apart. The captain grew delirious with fever, calling out the names of gods and past lovers, and broke down weeping asking for his mother. Darius treated him with the twist of medical herbs he carried with him for seasickness and other ailments. When he recovered, the captain told everyone who would listen that Darius saved his life. Darius didn't think so himself but didn't contradict him.

He has a coveted spot on this ship's crew due to pure luck and a good word from that man.

'You like being on a ship, do you?' the *Tefnut*'s captain, Babu had asked when Darius first went to meet him.

'I prefer it to being on land,' Darius said, 'where I am poor and reminded of it every day. At least the fish are naked and don't move around in palanquins.'

The captain laughed. 'You will be able to afford a palanquin when you return, but I wouldn't recommend it. It's stuffy, bad for the back and if one of the men carrying you stumbles, you break your nose.'

The cargo they plan to bring back from Muziris will be worth around 200 million drachmas, give or take, and the captain will get a fourth of the profit after taxes. Darius, as the youngest of the crew, will get 1 per cent. If they fill the hull with all the pepper they can buy, it is enough money to build his mother a new house in town with cash left over for retirement. It would be more money than he's ever seen.

'I have to ask you this,' Babu said, 'I ask anyone who joins. Are you sure you want to do this?'

'Everyone in Berenike is dying to get on a ship,' Darius replied, 'so why wouldn't I want to?'

The captain was quiet for a moment. 'You are just a boy,' he finally said, 'I'll tell you something I wish I had known when I was as young as you.'

This man had thick, slumped shoulders and thinning hair. Darius couldn't imagine him young.

'Those sun and moon palaces that you see back home,' Babu says, 'the beautiful ones where our pharaohs lived. They look whole, like one complete building from the outside, don't they? But they aren't, did you know that? They are hollowed out from the inside into a maze of corridors. The rooms in the centre of these palaces are for dining and parties and meetings and fucking, but the walls are filled with secret passages and listening spaces. The kings and queens had no privacy.'

'This is what happens when you live somewhere not built by you. The building plans were made by the royal family's advisers, supposedly their most trusted men, who wanted ways to spy on the family and know exactly what they were doing.'

'But why would anyone agree to live in a place like that?' Darius asked.

'You stayed in the palace built for you, like your ancestor and your ancestor's ancestor. You had little choice. And the spaces were well-hidden, so the royals themselves didn't know that their home was tunnelled through.'

Darius waited for the moral of the story. Stories older people told usually had one.

And indeed, the captain leaned forward, his hands on his knees. 'We are now living in a world built by the Romans. Everything benefits them. They are the biggest winners from the ship trade. Yes, they pay for the ships. But they are also getting the bulk of the profits, while we ride the temperamental seas, go to strange ports, and risk disease, theft and death. This is not the short hop to Adulis that you have done. It's many days at sea, and then months in the port, and nearly every moment will be hard.' He paused. 'You will be richer at the end, but you have to live through all of that first.'

'All right,' Darius said.

'So you still want to do it?'

'Yes.'

'Fine.' Babu smiled, which somehow made him look completely humourless, it was just a straight-line grimace across his face with teeth showing. 'You have a young body that works better than mine and you need the work. So welcome aboard.'

Darius's recollections are interrupted by swearing. The rain is now coming down in sheets, and the captain is cursing at the sky. 'If I die here with this fucking ship's loans on my shoulders, my wife and daughters will have to join the whorehouses,' he shouts at the crew. 'There will be even worse waiting for *your* families. Let's try to get out of this strait as fast as we can.'

The ship groans as the sea whips it around, and the nephew abandons his post for fear of being swept overboard. They have no eyes and the wind howls in their ears. They steer and row blindly, staying awake through the night-long storm. At one point, it sounds like the hull has been breached—there is a ship-shaking thud and the huge boat leans terrifyingly to one side, but it uprights itself and when they go down to check for leaks, the holds are dry.

The *Tefnut* is built in the Phoenician style, and the method of sewing cedar planks together, rather than making the hull from a single piece of wood, is what saves them in this storm, allowing the ship to survive the occasional rock despite its weight and size.

The next morning, the six of them look out at a calm, endless grey under clear blue sky. The goddess, spent from her rage, is now asleep. May she wake up rested and benevolent, Darius prays. He spends the early dawn mopping the deck with the others. The wind picks up and the sails grow taut. There is some damage—one sail is torn, and the prow has a new crack running through it.

Darius is in the cargo hold, getting fresh sailcloth when the captain comes down to check once again for leaks.

'Will we make it out of the strait?' Darius asks as they go back up together. The captain points with his chin to the horizon as they reach above deck. Darius sees that the water has changed.

The distant shoreline is gone, the breeze is cool. The water looks darker, more ponderous.

It feels as if they are riding on the back of an immense, living creature. They are in the ocean.

'We always do,' the captain says to Darius, who has forgotten his question.

Darius walks to the prow. He can feel the ocean's seething mass underneath as the ship pitches itself forward. If the ocean has a will of its own, it is one that constantly contradicts the monsoon wind's, pushing back the ship that the wind pushes forward. While sailors have now been doing this voyage between Berenike and Muziris for hundreds of years, it is still a small number in total that have ever been out here. In this place, humans are forever outnumbered. There are gulls circling curiously above their heads and the water beneath ripples with life. Darius sees a large, snouted fish break the surface, leap back in. Then another, another. Travelling in groups, like people do.

The poor are invisible even to the gods, but perhaps Tefnut will notice him now as he rides her ocean on her namesake ship. Whatever gold he gets, he intends to take a portion back to her temple in gratitude.

Luck is a brand-new companion for Darius, meeting him post the terrible seasons of his teens and early twenties. His body is a testament to past suffering, scored by old farming bruises, including one unfortunate accident with a blade that nicked off the tip of his thumb. The usual badges of a hard life growing things. When his father died in the flood and they brought his body back with his head caved in and his face unrecognizable, teenaged Darius held his hands, with the callused fingers and cracked palms, the scar on the left wrist, the two ripped fingernails—all unmistakably his father's. Even in the darkest moment, Darius had recognized those hands by touch. The scars had defined him as much as anything else.

It wasn't just his father the flood killed. It took his beloved sister, and Roro and Tbiti, who he'd played Five Stones with and grew up alongside, and their mothers, who'd fed him hot bread with date syrup when he went to their homes. The flood took away nearly everything worth remembering of his early life.

Darius' body grew increasingly marked by later indignities—his back carries the raised, healed-over lines of leather whips from the days he chopped wood for a brutal camel transporter who treated the animals and workers the same. In the arch of his right foot is a cut from working at the storage sheds in Berenike, before his first sailing job. He'd already hated the seaport, with its all-pervading sour stink, the low-rent whorehouses, the lonely drunk men getting into fights, the smells of dead things.

This most recent injury was in some ways the worst because it had been careless and self-inflicted—he had stepped on a rusty iron chisel on the floor next to a pile of wood, and it cut deep into his foot.

The chisel on the floor felt like malevolence by the port itself, because no worker later claimed the implement as theirs. That injury was what had made him an expert in healing unguents and herbs. He needed his foot to heal in order to work, so he'd gone from doctor to doctor, accumulating enough tips to come up with a pretty effective salve, one that he applied for weeks before the wound closed. It was the same medicinal stash that helped him save the captain.

Darius is melancholic—if not naturally so then because of circumstances. He is the kind of person who, closed wounds or no, doesn't let himself fully heal, who looks back more than he should, who mourns the things that happened and the things that didn't, twin demons that eat him up.

The other men on the ship are sailing veterans and all older than him by at least a decade, save for the twelve-year-old boy. They've worked together before and have, if not a camaraderie, the kind of understanding that comes with familiarity. When they rise the first morning, they sing a sailor's song together, which by the second stanza, Darius figures is a litany of fellow men who died in past voyages. Jabeer of Alexandria, drowned at sea, Remy from Scythia, killed by a scorpion on the dock an hour before sailing, Lodo, dead of an excessive 'love' for women. And so on. The tune oddly cheerful and festive.

One of the men, Madu, licks a filthy finger and holds it up to the breeze. 'The wind is good,' he says, pleased. He has iron grey hair but a still-young, ruffian face, the kind of person, Darius guesses, given to tripping up authority for his amusement. But he and the captain seem to get along.

Babu calls Darius over, introduces him, 'This new fellow is a good worker, and more importantly, cheap,' he says. 'One of the things we will have to teach him is how to negotiate.'

'I hear you heal people, that you have magic fingers,' Madu says, 'But it sounds like the captain already picked your purse with his.' Laughter, thumps on Darius' back.

Ebo, the biggest of them, bare-chested and hairy, with a cleft chin and scary dark eyes, considers him. 'I have a sore on my backside I would like you to look at,' he tells Darius.

The others wait for his reaction. Darius frowns. 'This is a common mistake,' he says, 'That isn't a sore, it is actually your asshole. And to anticipate your second question, no, it's not going to close up.'

That gets more laughter and thumps on the back, including an extra-hard one from Ebo, and the breakfast meal commences with just the regular amount of attention paid to him. There is salted mullet and sardines out of wooden barrels, some bread, and even a bit of sweet bulgur cake that the captain unwraps from an oilcloth, 'celebration for crossing the Mad Strait'.

'For the first time in a while, I can eat without being told I am disgusting,' Madu says, cleaning a fishbone with his teeth, sucking the cartilage. 'Never marry someone above your station, my brothers. They will remind you of it when you bathe, when you shit, when you take off your clothes, when you suck a fishbone. They may forget it while you fuck but the children that come will be fresh reminders of your blunt nose and small forehead.'

The cake is excellent, but Ebo grumbles. 'We could do better than cake,' he says. He looks meaningfully at the captain, who sighs.

'How did you find out about the beer jugs?'

Ebo shrugs. 'You know that when it comes to the good stuff, we have noses like dogs.'

'If I find any of them empty—'

'Relax. Did you hear a single fart between the five of us? No raid has happened yet, but it will soon if you don't take one out.'

'I am saving some of it as gifts when we reach,' the captain protests, 'but one jug tonight, I promise.'

'Riding the sea is like sitting on a drunk camel walking sideways,' Ebo tells Darius, 'I have never been able to take it. Only the beer, which the captain tries to hide each time in a new place below deck, makes it bearable. I don't know why I do these trips. Yet I do one every year.'

'Who knows why all of us do this? The call of the sea is a sickness,' Babu says.

'We do it for the gold and the women, of course,' Madu says.

'I have enough gold, and I no longer feel the need for women,' the captain answers. When he smiles that cheerless smile, the lines on his face multiply. 'But I am still here.'

'Your wife isn't listening, my good man. You can admit it— that you can't wait to introduce your wares to the honey-coloured ladies in Muziris,' Madu waggles his head to guffaws.

'No, no,' the captain insists, not giving in to the levity. 'This is Tefnut's fault, for putting us under her spell. Admit it. Where else does this need to travel to strange places come from? We chase the chance to hear a different tongue saying the things we do. You know that joke our men crack at each other, "The rocking of the ship last night felt just like your mother's bed." I heard the same joke in Adulis; one of the boatmen said it to the other. When the local Egyptian there translated it for me, I couldn't believe it. Both places end up being like home—home itself and the places we reach. And yet, I am always eager to leave each one.'

'You might have something there,' Ebo says. 'Even on steady ground, I can feel the wind on my back nudging me towards the ships. When my daughter was born, the beach was one of the first places I took her to show her the sea. I couldn't think of anything more beautiful.'

Darius is silent, listening. He doesn't feel what the other men are talking about, this yearning for the ocean. Instead, the lasso of homesickness is around his chest, pulling tighter as the distance from Egypt grows.

He is certain—he won't be back on a ship once he has made his gold. These crewmen, he muses with contempt, have stopped thinking. Their emotions run their lives, like the monsoon wind in the sails of the ship. He, however, has a plan—use this trip to get enough to buy a farm and build a house.

They hear knocking and turn around in unison.

The response to knocking is wired in for humans, it's impossible to ignore the sound. But it's only one of the beams near the foremast that has gone loose and is bumping against the wood.

Tap, tap, tap, over and over: no one there but the wind, reminding them they are alone.

'You should answer it,' Nita says, pausing.

'It is so late!' Rouhi cries, rising from the couch. She opens the door that leads downstairs. One of the two-headed women is waiting, impassive, and she murmurs something to Rouhi.

Rouhi turns. 'Phone call. Must be Haroun.' She disappears down the stairs.

Nita isn't sure if she should wait or leave. It's past midnight on a school night. As a teacher, she's always had a school student's schedule and is used to sleeping early. Minutes pass. She gives up and goes to the room.

Just as she sits down on the bed, Rouhi opens the door without knocking.

'You are going to sleep?' she sounds disappointed, 'You were telling story.'

Nita's eyes are closing of their own accord. She tries to smile, obliging. 'I have to wake up at six to get Saba ready for school.' Rouhi, of course, knows this, but maybe she isn't totally aware since she sleeps in till eight.

'Oh ok, ok. But you tell me more tomorrow. How do you know so much about that time?'

'I studied history,' Nita says. Top of her class. Graduated in a dying market. Unemployed for six months before getting lucky with a job opening for a teacher.

Rouhi says something else, but Nita's head is somehow already on her pillow.

5

'Do the shoes look good?'

Rouhi turns—a swirl, a flash of ankles. The heels add three inches to her height and are bright purple snakeskin. Saba shows her mother an enthusiastic thumbs-up sign, but Nita hesitates.

'They look good,' she says finally.

Rouhi frowns. 'If I want lie, I can ask Saba.'

'The colour doesn't work—it's too much.' Rouhi doesn't need the extra height either. It's like putting a big house on stilts.

'That's what I think also,' Rouhi sighs, kicking off the heels. She looks at them with regret. She had come home with them earlier that week, the day after she had her hair cut in a feathery style with fresh highlights.

The phone call, it turned out, was Haroun telling Rouhi that she was invited to a company party for the merchant navy wives. All signs point to Rouhi not wanting to go. In the evenings, Nita notices that her employer is distracted, tapping freshly manicured nails against her glass of Tang while on TV, Ridge and Taylor sneak around adulterously in hotel rooms. She has

59

the nerves of an unprepared student before an exam. She is snide about the event, calls it 'left-behind women party'. The day before, Rouhi tells Nita that she will be coming along as well to keep an eye on Saba.

'We will take the good car,' Rouhi says.

The 'good car'—the husband's—is an SUV with wheels as thick as a truck's, and Nita is overwhelmed by the size of it. You have to climb on a step to even reach its body-swallowing seats. The steering wheel up front is massive. Rouhi rolls her eyes at Nita's tentativeness.

She straps Saba into a car seat in the back, much to the girl's annoyance.

'I am big enough to sit in front,' Saba whines. 'No, you are not,' Rouhi replies in what Nita privately thinks of now as The Voice, and Saba stays quiet. You don't argue with The Voice.

Rouhi looks good but scrubbed and polished to an unnatural level of gloss. Her lipstick is a brighter shade than usual, her eyelashes caked with mascara. The foundation flattens out her skin tone and the blush on top is inferior, Nita thinks, to her original colouring.

Rouhi's dress, however, is lovely, a peacock blue kaftan whose voluminous sleeves come down to her elbows. Silver bangles shimmer on her wrists. Nita is also wearing a new dress, a cotton one with cap sleeves and pink pinstripes. She had bought two dresses from the supermarket's clothing section, snatching them up in a hurry without trying them on. One turned out to be unwearable, its polka dot design clownish and the waistline hitting her at the wrong places.

She feels a little strange in a dress, with her hair combed out and curling at her shoulders, as if she isn't a mom herself but someone about to go to class. The only girls she saw in skirts back home were school students.

The car is filled with the day's stored heat, the leather seats almost too hot to sit in. The three of them break out into a sweat immediately. 'Some people put AC in car garage also,' Rouhi says.

'Put together crazy weather and crazy money,' Nita observes, 'I guess that's what you get.'

'You will see crazy money today,' Rouhi says.

Crazy is also how Rouhi drives, tacking uncomfortably close to the stereotype of the woman driver. She speeds out of the gate as if they are being chased. Rouhi always drives a bit too fast, but at least her small Honda hatchback is underpowered. This SUV is a monster, leaping forward as if ready for a fight. She decides to take a shortcut, and they exit the palm and bougainvillea-lined avenues of Al Qasm into the narrow lanes of the Karama residential area, speeding through streets crowded with Indian and Pakistani-owned businesses—Zam Zam Bakers, Chetty Chettinad restaurant, the Karate-Cum-Yoga Centre, innumerable juice and milkshake and kebab shops. They zoom past the low-rise housing for port and construction workers, with their cheaply painted, goose-pimpled walls, open stairwells and window AC units. The apartments look prematurely old while the stores around them, with their PVC signboards and cheap shiny fronts, look like they came up overnight.

They make a turn and hit the Shaikh Khalifa highway, and the city looks different again, with broad avenues and date palms every few metres, a line of high rises in the distance.

Rouhi rides fast while rarely honking, so people don't see her coming until she's overtaking them indiscriminately at high speeds from the right or left. She has good reflexes, which keeps them alive, but Nita can sense the outrage they are leaving in their wake. She grips the armrest on the car door as if it will keep her safe. She grows disoriented when they take the underpasses, which are softly lit, echoing spaces with colourful mosaic tiles on each side, a five to ten-second submarine-like experience from which they rise back up into the harsh noonday sun.

They enter the concourse, and the concrete and cement buildings disappear, replaced by glass towers. Giant billboards show them ads for BMWs, anti-ageing creams and Versace watches, all with white models who would burn in the Dubai summer within minutes.

They turn into Wasl Street and the grey-blue Arabian Sea comes into view, frilled by a crescent-shaped beach. The house Rouhi slows down at is iron-gated with two uniformed men out front, and involves a security process which has Rouhi looking into a camera before she is allowed up a winding driveway. At the parking lot, Nita understands why Rouhi chose this car. The Honda would have looked ridiculous here, among the Mercs, Jaguars and Bentleys. More uniformed men direct them to a parking space.

As Rouhi unbuckles Saba, she tells her, 'Remember from last time—Yanni is mean and Lila is nice. Stay with Lila.'

'Ok mama,' Saba says, but she is already sulky. Nita digs inside her bag and hands her a Capri Sun. It is Saba's favourite drink; it is marketed with a picture of fresh oranges on the label but the drink itself has only a passing resemblance to orange juice and is mainly sugar syrup and flavouring. It has an instant effect on Saba that is either soothing or electrifying depending on her mood and is Nita's fail-safe for Saba's tantrums—this kid's Bournvita on toast.

They go through the open front door of the house only to come face to face with an elevator in the foyer. A young Filipino woman in uniform, with her face impeccably made up and a hairstyle a lot like Rouhi's, appears and presses the button, and as they enter, she presses 2. She stays outside and watches the doors close.

When the doors open on the second floor, the same girl is already waiting to escort them, wearing the steadiest of smiles, as if she hasn't just run up two flights of stairs to meet them here. She ushers them into a hall where a long table is piled with purses and scarves. They pass through multiple rooms with walls covered in oil paintings of falcons, either mid-flight or perched in trees. Someone is obsessed, Nita thinks.

Large vases are filled with fresh flowers everywhere they look—roses and tiger lilies and magnolias—an astonishing sight in a city where none of these grow. They follow the sound of voices into a dining area filled with women and children. Despite the vaulted ceilings, the air here is near-sticky with the smell of food and perfume. The anonymous laughter makes Nita instinctively hug the wall. A panic response: *they are laughing at me*. Saba pulls her hand away and runs off in the direction of the kids. The women's eyes turn to Nita, assessing as they look her up and down—evaluating, dismissing. Nita knows at once that she is dressed entirely wrong, her outfit feels cheap and thin in this room. Rouhi, whose face had looked strangely over-made up back at the house, fits right in.

Rouhi walks into outstretched arms, kisses people's cheeks.

'Look at you, Rouhi,' the woman seated at the head of the table welcomes her, and it sounds like the beginning of a compliment but isn't, 'always the last to arrive'. The woman's silver dress technically covers her from neck to ankle. But it hugs close to her hips and breasts, accentuating her curves, not leaving much to the imagination. She gets up, taking her time, and gives Rouhi a hug that is all elbows.

This lady, presumably the host, has a great body but her face is vulpine, with a hooked nose that must have been subtle on a younger face. Lines are deeply etched around her mobile mouth. Her overarching characteristic is a tautness, of someone waiting to pounce.

Rouhi looks around, smiling her hellos. She gets a Schrödinger response from the others—friendly and also not. The slight pause around the table and the delay in the returning smiles are painful for Nita to watch. The politics of belonging is something she understands. Rouhi is far from the popular one here, and there are intersections of hierarchy and hostilities Nita can't see, with old arguments simmering underneath.

Everyone, including the couple of white women and the only Indian lady attending as a guest, is wearing large quantities of expensive-looking jewellery around their necks, wrists and most of their fingers, the 'three-piece rule' for jewellery not just thrown out of the window but chased out of the grounds.

Heads are bare, their outdoor veils cast aside. Hair is apparently a very big deal, done elaborately—dyed, highlighted and styled into updos, feathered bangs or big blowouts, decorated with silver pins and tiny tiaras. Almost every head is a small marvel in terms of effort and expense. Rouhi's hair, loose and down her back, is relatively unadorned despite the recent salon visit.

Even minus the head coverings, it is possible to tell which women are from the most conservative households—their black abayas, hung on the backs of their chairs, are plain and unembroidered, and their dress sleeves come all the way to their wrists and cinch tight. The tell is not just in the clothes but in the slight, nervous flutter of their gestures, as if they are about to be caught doing something wrong.

A couple of the women are dressed in traditional, sleekly cut linen pants paired with silk tunics embroidered at the collars and sleeves with delicate gold thread. Others, once their flowing abayas are off, reveal expensive Western fashion—high-waisted, hip-hugger velvet trousers and silk shirts, translucent lace dresses paired with leather belts, cutout tops and designer jeans.

The chatter is near code, all references and inside jokes. They speak in an English–Arabic medley, making it hard for Nita to follow. But it's quickly obvious that they are talking constantly about sex in allusions, insinuations. One woman calls a particularly promiscuous actress a walking fish market. When the salads arrive, someone jokes about eating the cucumbers whole.

The vulpine host, Mrs Sherri Nusseibei, delivers an extended riff about an acquaintance, an absent navy wife, who she says is always losing things. 'I saw her last week—she's lost some of her hair, but we know that's not the first thing she lost. She lost her purse a few weeks ago at Ghurair Mall when I was with her, but that's not the first thing she lost. Last month when I met her, I told her she'd lost some weight. But we all know that's not the first thing she lost.' The ditty gets laughs all around. Perhaps it's also a lesson for the attendees—turn up at the party if you don't want your reputation shredded.

However bawdy, to say the actual words out loud—*sex* or *fucking*—would be like a bomb going off in the room. Like the kissing scenes on television, these are fully excised.

The husbands' ghosts hang around the table. The shadow hierarchy here descends from the positions of the men, and the bosses' wives are the bosses here. The women seem aware that a wrong thing said at the table can filter its consequences down to the husband's career. In a way, the senior wives are the guards at

the gates, deciding whose husband is good enough company for
their own. Decisions are made in this room, and navigating the
fuzzy, unspoken social rules here takes skill.

Of course, they talk about the men on the ship. The work
on these ships is dangerous, and even senior marine engineers
and deckhands spend time around heavy machinery and inside
engine rooms. One snapped rope or machine strap is enough for
disaster, for a one-ton container to fly through the air and break
a spine in two.

There is an ongoing contest for who has the most homesick,
lovelorn husband—the rare man who is presumably immune to
the wiles of whores waiting to seduce him portside.

If Ahmed, Daya's husband, called her from the Jeddah
docks, Mahmud, Aisha's man, rang her from Aden, when the
ship stopped for twenty minutes for a partial refuel, managing
to sneak out to a phone booth in the local market even though
they'd been barred from disembarking.

Rouhi does not participate, remaining silent rather than
saying 'No, Haroun rarely calls.' She is losing points. She frowns
and raises her eyebrows at no one but is the subject of a few. *Does
she think she's too good for us?*

The food begins to arrive—heaping plates of it that keep
coming, dishes topped with herbs and edible flowers like works
of art. Somewhere in the middle of it all, a massive rack of roast
lamb turns up, the ears on its head crisp and intact, and everyone
cheers. The stomach and intestines have been scooped out and
cooked separately into a gravy you dip soft kuboos bread in to
soak up the juice.

By now they have shifted from talking about the men to
talking about what the men have bought them—brands get
namechecked around the table faster than in a rap song. The

intensity with which the women discuss their Versace jeans and Givenchy bracelets is to feel that to not own one is to be slightly depleted of life force.

It's not as if these women don't have more serious things to talk about. But those painful stories will not be lanced here. As far as this group is concerned, those things never happened—there are no children they dislike, no quiet affairs, no husband who punched them so hard their jaw dislocated, no late-term miscarriages, induced or otherwise. Perhaps, they are unable to perceive their suffering clearly. Their focus is instead this strangely superficial competition, and they go to war for nothing else.

A woman they call Fleury, whose real name, Nita thinks, must surely be something else, sits up with an exclamation as the servers circulate the table. 'What?' the others ask, 'What is it?'

'I am not sure,' she looks around, hesitating. 'I'm wondering if I left my hair iron on?'

There are groans across the table: 'Not again!' 'Fleury, you do this every time!'

But Fleury's eyes are round with panic in her small face. The outfit she's wearing is a pink and soft-looking wrap dress that can't be more than an XXS size—the whole of her is childlike, just like her name. Her nails, however, are long, painted red. When she puts her hands to her face, she looks even more like a bird, a thing with talons. 'I don't know, I don't know. Now that I am alone, I can't keep track of anything.'

'What happened to your maid, isn't she home? Maybe she can check for you,' someone suggests.

'No, I fired her. What happened to my maid is also why I had to drive myself here today.' Fleury lifts her eyebrows in that universal implication: *this is juicy.*

'What happened?' The hair iron forgotten again.

'It was the tomatoes,' Fleury says.

Fleury says both her maid and driver knew that she never came to the car garage in the evenings, but this time she went out there looking for the tomatoes she had bought that afternoon, which she figured she'd forgotten in the car.

'First thing I see through the car windows is my driver's big hairy butt, flat like a pancake, and it is moving back and forth, and I am confused, I don't even understand what it is,' she says, completely serious as some of the women start to giggle. Fleury looks around, anxious. 'What? It is the first male bottom I have seen, you know. My husband switches off the light and comes at me like a ghost. After seeing the driver's, I can understand why.'

'So I can't tell what it is and what he is doing. But one of the car windows are open and I hear my maid making these cat sounds. Only then do I realize.'

Her Filipino maid and her Lebanese driver were getting it on in the back seat of her car, despite them having no language in common. 'Well, which man needs conversation before doing it?' someone remarks, and there's more laughter around the table.

'The worst of it was, I still needed the tomatoes. So I made the two of them get out of the car with only their tops on so I could check the seats. In case, you know, they had squashed them. But the bag wasn't there. I had left it in the supermarket.'

Some of them are horrified. A good woman would have rushed back into the house and dealt with them once they had their clothes back on. But Fleury is Fleury.

A bit too risqué, this story, and the conversation is going quickly off the rails, so Sherri Nusseibei gives Fleury a pointedly ambivalent smile and changes the subject, asking the young, pregnant woman a few seats down from her how far along she is.

'Seven months,' she says, her hands going to her belly.

'It looks like more,' the Indian woman, Mrs Joji Chacko, says. 'Is it a boy?'

The mother flushes. 'A girl.'

'Looks like a big one,' the woman seated opposite her remarks. She has overlined lips and hair piled on the top of her head and held together with multiple jewelled pins. 'My second was very big. The effort it took to push him out.'

'Giving birth is horrible,' Sherri says, her eyes intent on the pregnant woman's face. 'Don't let the doctors fool you.'

This is all they need to come at the pregnant woman. They talk about bodies tearing themselves open, and frankly describe the vagina becoming a bleeding hole twice its original size, ripped open by both the baby and the doctor's scissors. The cuts extending to the insides of the thighs, and the months ('seasons, years') it takes to heal, if it does at all. They never pee right again. Sex, ruined. The flesh down there like a dress you put in the washing machine on too high heat, stretched out and never sitting right. Sad breasts, forever bad teeth, hollow bones, constipation until you die.

'There are no songs about this,' another lady observes. Her waist-length, side-swept dark hair is like a waterfall over her shoulders. 'But there should be.'

The doctors and nurses are no help, they say. They are the most jaded audience for your pain, especially after birth, focused more on the baby and making sure it is ok, because no one gets tired of babies but everyone is tired of the mothers even before they enter the hospital. And nearly all the gynaecologists are men.

Their own mothers are not much help either—they envy the painkillers, anaesthesia, antiseptics. They had home births in summers with no air-conditioning, without enough water to bathe the baby or mother. No, sympathy is as thin on the ground as the water used to be.

They try to place optimistic punctuations at the end of these stories. Maryam, who has just described how her left breast never returned to its original size after breastfeeding and now hung off her chest next to the normal-sized right one like a deflated mango, looks at her son, who is tossing Lego pieces at another kid, with affection. 'At least now I have Abdul,' she says, 'and hopefully will have five sons more.' The children they look adoringly at don't return the favour, engrossed as they are in their pursuit of taunt and fun.

'But why would anyone do this more than once, if it is so bad?' the mother-to-be asks reasonably, white-lipped with anxiety. She has dark, laughing eyes (quite serious now) and her face is flushed and bright with pregnancy hormones. You can't imagine her red and screaming while a doctor wields his episiotomy scissors on her.

The others cross their legs over their ruined vaginas and slack abdomens. 'It is what we do,' one of them says as the others nod. It is *maktoub*, destiny.

Nita should ideally be in the small alcove adjacent to this room, where the help is eating their lunch. Even as she hangs around here, eavesdropping, she is hyper-aware of her dress, her lack of jewellery—her *station*, as one might say in a Jane Austen novel. But she can't bring herself to go over. The caretakers and maids, a mix of older Filipino, Indian, Pakistani and Sri Lankan ladies, who are seated there, are deep in conversation about their own dramas. Nita has stranded herself in a no man's land between these two spaces, in a corner of the main dining room, between a tall rack of CDs and a very heavy-looking marble vase, which obscures her somewhat. She pretends to watch over the children, who are busy rehearsing the arguments and status-jockeying of the adults ('I have a Neo Geo and Nintendo at home, this place doesn't even have Sega,' one snotty boy is complaining to the others).

Nita has the hungry curiosity of someone who grew up living on the sidelines of a big, emotional family. After her parents' accident, she'd spent her childhood as a person with unclear status in her aunt's household—an impoverished family member, dependent on their good graces and therefore a fair target for her cousins. Her own sister already married and living in her husband's house. Everyone in her aunt's house knew she had nowhere to go. She survived by becoming the talker, the jokester, the 'fun one'.

Rouhi is clearly not the fun one here. She looks uncomfortable; her usual sangfroid is gone, and she is hunched over her food, barely making eye contact.

Watching them is like standing outside a beautiful, lit-up house, looking in. It is hard for her to imagine any of these women doing something ordinary, like cleaning a poopy diaper or trimming a plant. The heavy make-up also makes it hard to read them. It's like a whole new face painted on top of the original.

Nita's stomach rumbles with hunger, but she cannot tear herself away. Her attention keeps trailing back to Rouhi. The way she sits, raises her arm, lifts a spoon to her mouth, pushes her hair behind her ear, it all feels momentous to Nita. It pierces her—both her beauty and her vulnerability.

An hour passes. One of the servers stops on her way to the table. Nita prepares to be shooed away. Instead, the girl puts a large glass of soda into her hand. 'Drink it,' she says in Hindi, and

Nita looks at her with gratitude. She gives Nita a conspiratorial smile. 'I'll get you something to eat,' she says, 'but it may not be on a plate and it will take some time.'

She hurries off before Nita can thank her, her severe face back on. Over the next hour, she brings her two samosas—flaky spicy ones stuffed with mincemeat, that Nita eats as quickly as she can, wondering how she has never tasted ones like these before. The delight she feels is muted by the immediate worry that she will never taste these again.

After a while, the girl brings her some cold red cherries, a thing of wonder that has reached her fingers via transatlantic cold chains and refrigeration, a wedge of soft French cheese that has the salt-smoke taste of something pulled out from deep inside the earth, and a bowl containing a small cake in a pool of saffron milk. There is no spoon, so Nita pours it into her mouth, wanting to lick the bowl clean. It is a tiny hodgepodge of what is being served. She doesn't get a chance to ask the girl her name—she moves between tables and the kitchen like the superhero Flash in Saba's cartoons, too fast for her.

Flash Girl and the other server carry out a four-tiered tower of seafood—crabs, pomfret, salmon and prawns with their tentacles and eyes still intact, piled so high that everything trembles slightly, like the whole of it might collapse any moment. It sits next to platters of untouched roast chicken and goat stew gone cold.

Nita spots Saba hovering in the doorway to the dining room. She is uncharacteristically hesitant, tentative—usually all doorways are meant to be blazed through, doors pounded on until they open for her. It is near-impossible to use the loo with her around. Nita places her empty dessert bowl on the CD rack and walks over.

'Hey,' she says.

'We go?' Saba asks.

'Aren't you having fun?'

Saba squirms at the question. 'No. We go home? PLEASE.'

They are practising politeness, but for Saba these words—
'sorry,' 'please,' 'thank you'—are mainly punctuation for her
demands.

Nita looks over at the other kids. They are red-faced from
running around, but right now all twelve of them are tightly
packed in a circle rather than in separate loose groups. This
suggests one leader—usually not a great sign. Six-year-old leaders
can set up tiny playtime dystopias in the blink of an eye.

At the big table, Rouhi is nodding and smiling, making
conversation, but her back is stiff.

'Ask your mother,' Nita says, 'But you have to give her a
good reason to leave.'

Nita watches as Saba pushes her hair back from her face and
smoothens down her little dress before she approaches the table.
She is already learning the art of presentation.

Rouhi lowers her head as Saba whispers in her ear.
There is a small confabulation, followed by Rouhi shaking
her head and whispering to Saba. But Saba talks some more,
gesticulating, and Rouhi's expression changes to Mama Bear.
In a few minutes, she is getting up, making excuses and saying
her goodbyes.

'We should go shopping together,' Sherri Nusseibei says.
Her hair is falling across her face so Nita can't see it, but her
words sound venomous. 'We can buy you something less roomy
to wear next time! There is nothing wrong with some curves.'

'All of us dress the way our husbands allow us to, Shari,'
Rouhi smiles at her, pronouncing her name the Arabic way.

Saba breaks the uncomfortable silence that follows with a lilting 'Ba-bye'. The faces at the table soften as they give Saba that tiny handwave people use for children. The lady with the side-swept hair grins, 'It's time for Saba to have a little brother.'

'Haroun will have to get a second wife for that,' Rouhi says lightly. She leaves before their collective gawk blooms into something else. Nita darts out from her corner to follow her.

Saba trails Rouhi, dragging her feet now that they are out the door. She is sucking on a lollipop she has somehow procured during their exit, and the cheap food colouring turns her lips a bright red. She doesn't resist this time when Rouhi belts her into the car seat—her eyes are already half-closed. 'I wish I could sleep this easily,' Rouhi says, getting in. 'Nita, why don't you sit up front?'

The front seat is even higher, and Nita climbs in with as much dignity as she can muster. She waits for a scolding for having spent the whole time at the party sneaking food in one corner like a house mouse. But none comes.

'The boys were playing a game where each of them lick a girl's face,' Rouhi says, reversing the SUV rapidly even as a uniformed guy runs up to help. She lowers the window and tips the man with a folded note. She drives towards the gate with such speed that the guard hustles with the latch, as if he half expects her to ram through it.

She drives as if she could leave the humiliation of the event behind her. Meanness comes easily to some women, but this is something else, Nita thinks. There is some history here, as hard to miss as a dead cat under the table. But it is not her place to ask.

Gazing outside the window, missed opportunities nag at her. She wishes she'd asked Flash Girl her name. Or found out what the dessert she inhaled was.

'You know in Egypt, I had so many friends,' Rouhi says. 'I was, what is word? Well known?'

'Popular?' Nita suggests.

'Yes, *poplar*. I could make boys laugh also, not only girls, and in Egypt the boys try very hard not to laugh at girl's jokes. But here, they hate me from first day. And I hate them also. Except maybe Fleury.'

'Why?'

The corners of Rouhi's mouth pull down. 'I am shadow of husband for them. I do all this,' she gestures at her dress, her face, 'And they only see him. And they don't like him.'

Her driving slows. She glances at Nita. 'You had bad time?'

Despite the reality of her job, Nita had not felt truly like the help until this event. Back there in her cotton dress, and the way the women looked at her—it had made her feel small. Like she should know her place. Her cheeks are still burning from it.

So to get this cautious question from Rouhi, as if they are equals, is disorienting. It is dawning on her that Rouhi is the outlier. The shouts from the men at the parking lot, the looks from the women at the party—that's how she is supposed to be treated. This is a hierarchical place with many rules, and she is the inferior, her foreignness, her job and the colour of her skin mark her out as not requiring the usual courtesies. She is supposed to be one among the servants, maids, the construction workers living in crowded, cheap quarters.

But Rouhi is lonely, and maybe that is what puts Nita in the front seat of this car.

'That Shari?' Rouhi says, 'She is ship captain's wife, she thinks she also gets badge and is boss. When I came here, she was nice. Haroun and I went to their house, they give us tea, best biscuits, and nuts and dates that were not as good as in Egypt but still good.'

Rouhi drums her fingers on the steering wheel. The monster underneath her hands is now crawling, far below the speed limit on the highway. She is the one being honked at as cars swoosh past. 'Later, Shari call me. Says, we go shopping, I will show you city. I am happy, I think this is my new friend.'

'She picks me up in this car. Bentley Continental—Nita, that is top model, very expensive. She is rich from her family. House, cars, servants you saw? All is from her money. Husband paid for one kitchen sink she tells me. She make many jokes about husband, like we are best friends.'

'We go everywhere! It is nice, all these shops, I buy pretty soap, cream, perfume. Everything smell so good, but it is expensive. I buy a little bit while she shops like crazy person. If she like something, she will buy it many times. Three perfumes, six creams, four pearl earrings. There is man walking behind her carrying all the bags, also my small bag. She asks many questions, where I from, what my father do, and I tell her about my college and my friends, she not care. She wants to know my family. Who they are, what their name is. How much money they have.

'It is night by the time we are coming back. She tells the driver to take this road through Deira. The roads there have less light, it is old Dubai. The first Dubai. We are driving there when she says, stop here, and her voice is so different—it is as if all music is gone and only bark is left. I am confused, I say what is it, and she says she has dropped something in the car and wants me to get out so she can check where I am sitting. So I get out, and she throws my bag after me outside, closes the door. And the car zooms. They leave me there.'

She was on a side street, Rouhi says, dark except for the shop signs advertising car rentals and travel agencies. She walked for an hour, hoping to find a taxi. But it was late at night, there were few cars about and the road she was on kept getting narrower. On the footpaths there were only men, eyeing her as she passed. Garbage overflowed the bins in some places, a rare sight in Dubai, which made her even more nervous.

Eventually, she entered a small dry-cleaning store and asked the Thai couple behind the counter for help in getting back home. The man walked her to a taxi stand where she caught a ride.

'After few days Shari calls me to her house. I go, I am so angry I know exactly what I will say, and I walk in and see the other ship wives. In her living room. And before I say anything, she introduces me, this is Haroun's wife, she has come from farm in Egypt, her mother is so smart she can kill live chickens.'

'When she say "Haroun's wife", I am telling you, their eyes all turn to these slits. I knew, whatever I said, they will just—' Rouhi stops, gives an abrupt shrug. 'They don't see me. They only see Haroun who marry stupid farm girl.'

'That is horrible,' Nita says, 'Why do you go there anymore?'

'I go because that is my job as company wife. But it is same every time. They talk to me like I stole their goat. It would be *taraadin*—good for me, good for them—if I don't go. But I have to show face for Haroun.'

'They sound very unpleasant. And not at all fun, except maybe for Fleury,' Nita realizes as she says this, that she is speaking as if she was one of the guests and not the help.

But the put-down seems to cheer Rouhi up, so she continues, 'With all the money Shari has, you think she'd try buying something other than a falcon painting?'

'I know,' Rouhi rolls her eyes, 'I was surprised we were not also eating falcon.'

The party inserts itself into the rest of the week. Rouhi walks around the house, brooding, hangdog and quiet. Nita spends more time on the sofa with her, where they watch *The Bold and the Beautiful*. She worries that she is starting to like the Tang's perverted flavour.

Overall, the fiasco seems to have altered their relationship. Something added, something removed—Rouhi is more friendly, less peremptory. She sits closer to Nita on the sofa, and every once in a while as she speaks, she will put a hand on Nita's shoulder or arm. The touching is new, and frequent.

'Your story,' Rouhi says one evening, 'It is not like children's fairytale. Does your son like it?'

Nita smiles. 'I have been changing it for you. When I told it to Ani, the hero was the twelve-year-old boy. For you, I moved Darius from the back of the stage to the front.'

'And I didn't want to tell Ani a fairytale,' Nita adds, 'I wanted him to hear something real. Since I was small, I have watched all kinds of ships come to our port. I grew up hearing about the pepper trade and the wealth it brought us once.'

Even in its changed form, the story is a way for her to keep the connection going with her son. Back home, they'd slept on the same bed, bodies intertwined, his small nose tucked into the crook of her arm, or his head on her stomach. Here, she can't sense him at all, the mother's pull diminished by distance and his mute nervousness on the phone. It's a strange emptiness, and she finds herself walking through the house from time to time feeling like she's forgotten something.

6

Four more days to dock at Muziris and Darius is already losing some of his expected payout. It's a particular kind of stupidity, he thinks, to lose unearned gold, and an added humiliation when, after yet another bad game of Ur against Madu, he asks for a rematch and Madu refuses. Underneath that good-natured mien, Madu is relentless and an unexpectedly wily player. It's like he can sniff out Darius's next move before he knows it himself.

The captain had warned him. 'You are young, and that comes with stupid,' he said, 'Some people will see that and try to use it against you. Don't play Ur with Madu.'

Darius had bristled, and he didn't listen the first day, the second or the third. By the fourth, he is in that hole that both experienced and inexperienced players can find themselves in—playing only to recoup losses, hope puppet-mastering him through game after game.

He'd started playing to distract himself. The wind is high and strong this year, and there is not much to do on the ship besides adjust the sails, clean the decks and listen to the ocean. The deep ocean is not like the sea near the coast, where it loses strength against the rocks and beach. Here, its embrace is unchallenged, and the strength of its undertow slaps the ship constantly from side to side. It promises him a hug full of deep darkness. It has unnerved him thoroughly.

One afternoon, they spot distant grey clouds, with storms and lightning breaking over the water. 'Row!' The captain shouts, but he doesn't have to yell—the men are already racing to their oars. A storm in the middle of the ocean can tumble a ship upside down, turning it over as easily as a turtle. They row hard and fast through the evening and the night, and the storm never catches up with them, there is only a residual howling wind and thunderous waves that leave Ebo hanging over the edge of the ship again, throwing up both his breakfast and lunch.

The restless heaving of the ship has Darius asking the captain the next day about the sea monsters that the people in his village talked about—the fish women with many heads, large snakes with spiked horns that could break ships apart, the giant, tentacled squid creatures which blocked the sun when they rose out of the water.

'Those things exist only in silly stories,' the captain says, 'The real monsters are human. It's the pirates I fear.'

'So you've seen nothing?' Darius persists.

Babu pauses. 'The water stirs and shows you strange things sometimes,' he admits finally. 'Once, after too much beer, I hung around the deck looking out at the stars, missing my woman, the usual things drunk men do. Something moved and I looked down.'

Darius holds his breath.

'It was just blue against blue at first and then a large creature I had never seen before rose out of the water,' the captain says, 'It had a face—not like a fish but like a human's, with its eyes up front, rather than on the sides. And it was looking at me curiously, the way a person might. And then it dived away and I saw the length of its body—it went on and on. A gentle giant, I suppose. I never saw it again.'

'So yes, there are creatures in the ocean, and they keep their distance from us, probably for good reason,' Babu says, 'I've seen no monsters. Don't go jumping at shadows.'

But Darius is unconvinced and turns to Ur to distract himself from his terrors.

Darius has watched men play Ur from the sidelines before, when he was too impoverished to take a seat at the table. The rules are simple. Each person has five pieces. Madu's pieces are more unique than most, carved out of green stone and ivory. His board is made from a single piece of cedar, unlike the cheap hacked-together things you usually see, an unusual board in the hands of an ordinary sailor.

The game has fourteen squares for each player, arranged in a snakelike shape—at square four, you turn, and at square twelve, you turn again. The danger zone is in the middle when you hit the common squares, and the goal is to get all five of your pieces to the end and off the board before the other player.

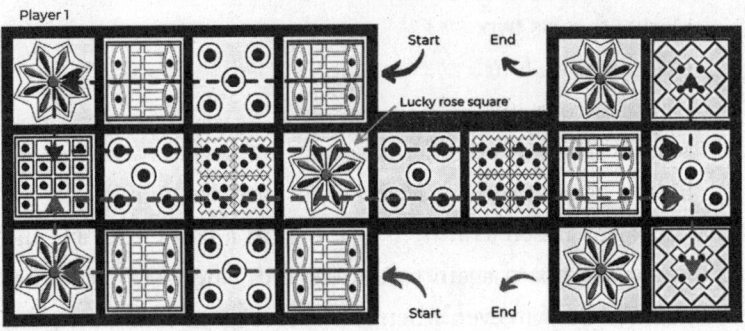

If your piece lands on the middle rosette square (the 'lucky rose'), you are allowed to occupy it as long as you like. Any opponent piece that lands on the same square while you are on it has to start all over again.

It seems like chance, it feels like chance. So Darius is optimistic at the beginning of each game, but Madu has beaten him every time.

When Madu lays out his board, dice and pieces, it is with the affection of someone who has won a great deal with this set. This board draws treasure and livelihood from others like a magic spell. Madu's pyramid-shaped dice—tetrahedrons—are eager to please their familiar master.

But in this particular game, Darius sees a glimmer of light. He has four pieces completed, and the remaining piece on the board is sitting on the coveted lucky rose.

Darius picks up Madu's beautiful dice and throws a three. He moves his last piece from the lucky rose, away from safety but towards the end.

Madu rolls the dice. His throw brings one of his pieces to the end, which grants him a second free throw. He throws and gets another piece to the end of the board. Each of them has one piece left, but Darius just needs a four to win.

Darius throws two.

Madu throws four.

Darius throws one.

Madu throws three.

Darius doesn't register Madu's win until the man stands up with his arms raised as if he is coming off a battlefield. He has to look at the board again to understand. The fact that he has been denied the win even when so close, suggests that maybe this game isn't for him.

'To be fair, those last throws were very good for me,' Madu says, 'I played like the god Thoth himself. I have yet to meet a player as unlucky as you.'

'Fortune draped herself over you today,' Darius agrees. He works hard to keep his misery from his face.

'Just like most women do. You want tips on that, come to me.'

He bends down and packs his pieces carefully with his board. 'So my take so far is one-fourth of your cut.'

Darius looks at Madu's bent head, digesting his words. 'No,' he says, 'you get 5 per cent of my cut, not one-fourth.'

'That's not what we agreed on,' Madu says, smiling. That smile, which looked so benign once, makes the hair on Darius's neck stand on end. 'We agreed that the take from each game was 5 per cent of your cut.'

'No, 1 per cent for each game. We've played five games. That's 5 per cent. Not a fourth.'

Madu hadn't struck him as an angry man, but it turns out he was wrong about that. A vein throbs in Madu's forehead, the genial face goes dark, the eyes flat. As he shifts gears, Darius finds himself backing away from him.

'Don't,' Madu snarls.

'Don't what?'

'Don't try to weasel out of a deal that we made.'

'I am not trying to weasel out of anything. You are trying to change the terms and steal my money.'

'A liar attempting to call me a thief. How priceless.'

'I am not—' Darius begins but Madu has already closed the distance between them and punched him across the mouth. He feels his lip breaking, a tooth somewhere at the back of his mouth loosening and he covers his face with his hands, pulling

away from Madu's reach. Madu's fist hits his ear, and the impact
makes him dizzy and he drops to the floor. He glimpses Madu
coming towards him to pummel him on the ground. He has only
one, quickly narrowing option. He kicks his foot up and makes
contact with Madu's groin.

Madu falls away with the yelp of a small animal. Darius rises
and tries to steady himself, gathering his hands into fists. His
head spins.

'It's a good thing that ships don't have doors to silence this
nonsense.' Babu is somehow here, glaring at Madu. 'I warned
you once.'

Madu stands up in a rage, although he seems to be wincing
a bit. 'This rat thinks he is going to cheat me out of my money.'

'Madu, I was there when the terms were discussed. I made
sure of it so that what happened last time didn't happen again.
When you are cured of your beer fog in the morning, you and
Darius can come to me, and we can discuss in the light of Ra
what he owes you.'

At this, the anger leaves Madu like air. A wily expression
replaces it. 'I'll see how I feel in the morning,' he says.

'Do that,' the captain says. He waits as Madu collects his
board and leaves. When they are alone, he looks Darius over.
'Not too bad, all considering,' he says, 'I hope you have something
on you for that lip.'

Darius can feel his lower lip puffing up like a gooseberry. He
has spent the last several seconds swallowing blood. 'I do.' His
speech is mildly impaired.

'Good. All I have is seawater.' The captain walks with him
to the corner Darius has chosen to sleep. 'I tried to warn you,'
Babu says, 'but experience is the only teacher young people seem
to accept.'

Darius has had his own encounters with bad guys, but none came to him before this with such a friendly face. 'Why do you have him on your ship if you think he can't be trusted?'

'Men like Madu can be useful, especially in unfamiliar places. Sometimes it takes the bad to deal with the bad.'

Darius wonders how much unpleasantness Babu lets Madu handle on an ongoing basis. Perhaps the captain hasn't come by his good-natured face honestly after all. Darius tends to take people as they present themselves. It's a blindness he's inherited from his father.

He waits till the snores of the crew echo through the lower deck. He goes up, taking his little medicine box with him. He sits near the stern and with touch to guide him—it is pitch dark up here on this moonless night—he reaches gingerly into his mouth and pulls out the loosened molar, swallowing his groans with the blood.

A cautious press with his tongue and fingers indicates a clean break, and he rinses his mouth with a little bit of fresh water from one of the jugs and applies the paste—a mix of honey and willow leaves—that has stood him in good stead all these years. He smears some of it on the cut on his lip. He has some oleo resin as well, but it is expensive, and the local healers are loath to part with even a little. He saves that and the opium for emergencies.

He'd never gotten used to the biting flies or the mosquitoes in Berenike, which swarmed up as soon as the day's heat subsided. Now he feels the ghost of those pinpricks in Madu's gaze, which stays on him as he works and cleans. He is a bad man to have as an enemy, that much is clear. With the false cheer gone, Darius glimpses Madu's inner malevolence. He is the kind of man born with a knife between his ass cheeks. He has not approached the

captain to contest the gambling arrangement again, and Darius
does not go near the Ur board.

One of the first things Darius bought with his earnings from
his first ship job was a small knife with a long tip, the kind used
to clean out cuts. It has a narrow blade to create small criss-cross
cuts near wounds to allow bad blood ooze and pus to leak out.
It was a pretentious purchase that cost too much that he carries
everywhere despite never having had to use it once.

He also has a small bottle of vinegar to clean the knife
itself, after which it goes back into its box, wrapped in linen.
But one morning, he leaves it on the mat post cleaning and
Ebo spots it.

'What is that for?' Ebo picks it up before Darius can stop
him. The man's fingernails are dark with dirt.

'It's a blood knife. In case anyone needs to have a boil lanced
or a wound cleaned.'

Ebo makes a face and puts it back on the mat. 'How do you
go near someone else's pus? My own sickness would disgust me.'

Darius shrugs. He may not have used the knife, but he's seen
enough people die. Pus is better than some other things the body
could expel. 'I have a better stomach for it than most. I suppose
we are all weak about different things.'

Ebo sits down on the deck floor beside him. Close up, despite
his size and good looks, Ebo gives off more of a cuddly vibe than
anything else. Perhaps being a big man makes it less necessary
to be vicious—one can be intimidating just by standing around.

'Your lip has already healed,' Ebo says. It's the first time any
of the crew has indicated that they know about the fight. 'And it
has healed right. So you must be good at fixing bodies.'

'It's easier to treat what you can see. The difficulty comes
with what is inside the body, like a broken bone or internal

bleeding,' Darius says. 'Suppose someone hits you in the kidney. Then only a surgeon can help.'

'Those men are butchers,' Ebo says darkly. 'I don't trust anyone who cuts a stomach open for any reason outside a fight.'

Many back home have at least one story where someone they knew died at the hands of a surgeon. Their reputation is not helped by the loved one's screams during even successful procedures. The only men feared more than the surgeons are the embalmers, who are suspected of seriously nasty stuff like necrophilia. When a young woman dies, the family keeps the body out in the sun for three days before handing it over, ripe and unfuckable.

'Look,' Ebo says finally, 'I am not good with words, but the captain is not going to say anything and neither are the others. We haven't been to Muziris as much, but in Aden and elsewhere, where Madu played Ur with a lot of the port and merchant folk, they called him 'Five Days Madu' because that's how long it took him to drain someone of all their money and sell their woman and children for more.'

Ebo rubs his chin. 'He tends to target the youngest shipmate for their share. It's good gold, you know? Near-guaranteed, and they cannot disappear after they've lost since they're stuck on the ship with him till the bitter end. Went through three of them that way, but I like you and I don't want that happening to you.'

Darius flushes with humiliation. He was the only one on the ship who hadn't known what was coming at him. 'The captain warned me, but he didn't tell me this.'

'Look at it this way,' Ebo indicates Darius's lip, 'That damage is easily fixed. And you haven't lost too much.' He then does that thing the crew dreads, slaps Darius on the back so hard his breath whooshes out of him. He strolls back up to the deck, the wooden stairs creaking under his weight.

Darius stays below, waiting for his feelings to subside. But they roil him, he can't sit easy. It gets hot and suffocating below as the day progresses, yet he still can't bring himself to go up. The crew's chatter and laughter leak down to where he fidgets, as they adjust masts and clean decks. The day is relatively calm, and they sound relaxed and unworried. He feels for the first time, like a real outsider to the lot of them. They probably see him as a village hick, bearing the marks of a hard life. People like him are easy, unthinking bait for those who make enough gold to be comfortable, to buy earrings for their wives and the best fish sauce in the market. Darius is someone they can rob without a second thought. Who can he complain to?

He sleeps fitfully that night, caught up in nightmares where Madu strings him up in a fishing net over the ocean and cuts the threads one by one as sea serpents with blood-red teeth circle below.

He attempts to call out to the others, but his dream voice is a croak. The sky above is purple, the sea underneath black. Where is everybody?

Celebrating. He wakes up to shouts and cheers from above. There is pounding above him—someone jumping up and down. He stumbles above deck, wiping sleep from his eyes, squinting as the sun hits his face.

The four of them are standing at the prow as the oarsmen row, all looking out in the same direction. Land. Any land would do, it's more home than the sea. 'Is it Muziris?' Darius says, croaking, but louder than in his dreams.

'Yes, my boy,' Babu grins, 'We can see the shore, and there are no pirates in sight because we are really early—those bastards are lazy and stay in the whorehouses till noon. We worked the oars hard and it was worth it.'

The oarsmen don't object to the captain's *we*, just row as silently as ever as the ship approaches land. Their arms are veined and dark from the exertion, and they are sweating heavily—they all are. It is as if the weather has changed overnight and thrown a sweltering blanket on everything. The wind has disappeared, as if it too is taking the day off after bringing them to their destination.

Darius spots fishing boats in the distance. The land, still a dark line on the horizon, inches closer.

'Why is it so muggy? It feels like Ra's armpit is in my face,' Ebo mutters.

'It's the start of the monsoon,' Madu says, 'the wind that got us here has also brought them rainclouds.'

'We come bearing gifts,' Babu says.

They fall silent as the shapes on the horizon grow larger, and the land takes on colour and texture. The only sounds are the creaking of the sails and flapping of bird wings as seagulls and herons draw close, watching them curiously and looking for munchies.

The mountains come into clear view first, their peaks shrouded by clouds. Darius can see green and red bursts of colour that begin where the sea ends. Green so green it stings his eyes after days of monochrome. Trees he's never seen before, with large enveloping canopies. On the ship, he'd gotten used to the absence of things, and now he faces a visual riot that is hard to take in all at once—the colourful tiled roofs of the port, a multitude of boats banked near the shoreline, people moving about on the beach.

Muziris, he realizes, is where a river meets the sea. The river is visible as a slender, green thread from here. A curled finger of silty green water extends several feet into the blue-grey sea before merging entirely. At the river's mouth is a jostling of small boats and canoes heading inland.

The crew gets busy around him, lowering sails and preparing to anchor. As they draw close, the smells hit him. Petrichor, rising from fertile earth. Moss, leaves, unfamiliar fruit and flowers. Something heavy and bitter riding underneath that might be some insect, or the scat of an unfamiliar bird.

He finds his eyes prickling with tears. Fortunately, none fall. He doesn't want to be even more out of place among these leathery men. This smell is different enough from how their farm smelled after the rains each year, but it's still a cousin of it— this sweet, strange wet earth—and it reminds him of the days he spent on the small yellow-floored verandah outside their home, watching the rain come down.

But then the sweetness of it all is ruined by a sudden, pervasive stink of dead fish wafting in from the piles of scraped-off scales and discarded bodies on the beach that the fishermen's boats have left behind. Reams of crows walk around on the sand, short, wide-legged and ridiculous, telling each other off as they pick out the fish heads, tails and entrails from the muddy mess. And then Babu is yelling in his ear, asking him if he is deaf and demanding help to unload the jugs and bags.

Unload it where? Darius wonders. They have banked far from the shoreline, and the water's deep. The captain picks up the wooden whistle hanging off one of the poles and blows. Soon enough, there are canoe-shaped boats heading towards them. The rowers are young men of a type— wavy-haired with wide beautiful smiles and curly sideburns trailing down their cheeks. Their arms are ropy with muscle, and when the crew unwind ladders down the sides of the ship, they swing up easily, shouting out Aramaic greetings before resorting to the local, musical tongue that only the captain and Madu understand.

The crew carry up the frankincense from the lower deck, the teal, patterned amphorae and the bags containing bright bead necklaces that the captain says fetch a good price here for their novelty. The beads are in small bags—with scarcity comes higher rates.

And then the captain's treasured beer jugs emerge, twenty-two of them sealed with cork. Babu supervises these himself and asks Ebo to go with the two canoes taking them to shore. 'Don't let them out of your sight,' he tells him, 'The local drunks know what these are by now, their noses find them a hundred paces away.' Darius doesn't think that anyone would dare—Ebo's beard has grown out, making his face fiercer than ever, and his hair is long and matted from the days at sea.

Darius helps bring the sacks up from the lower deck and watches the crew clamber down the side of the ship to the waiting boats. Now that they are here, he feels a deep sense of trepidation about getting off the ship. What could this place contain? New monsters, sickness, nightmares? Back home, every place he'd gone to had been worse than the last.

'Go on, then,' Babu says, coming up beside him. He's carrying two trunks by their handles—the gold coins they will use to buy pepper.

Darius glances below at the boat waiting for them. The man on it looks up at him, flashes Darius a grin. Shouts something.

'He promises to catch you if you prefer to jump,' Babu translates, 'Says he's used to coaxing young women off their balconies.' He lets one trunk down via a rope and descends one-handed down the side of the ship while carrying the second one. For a squat middle-aged man, he is surprisingly lithe. He lands on the boat, briefly creating a small splash as his feet hit the wood.

'Shall we just leave you there?' he shouts up.

Darius pivots himself out and goes down gingerly. The side of the ship is slippery from the trip. By the time he reaches the boat, he is out of breath and trying not to show it.

The captain and their boatman chat as he rows. Babu appears fluent enough in this lilting tongue that is so different from Fayyumic. The pitch of the boatman's chatter goes up and down, as if this too carries a meaning alongside the words. Babu wags his head in understanding but Darius bets he is missing some context too.

But then, Darius thinks, he's lost all his recent wagers, so maybe he should stay humble.

He leans over the edge of the boat and examines his wavering reflection. An inch-long beard is all he has managed to grow. His hair is a mess, his skin deeply tanned from the days he spent on the deck working, and his eyes are lit up with nervousness and excitement.

Their canoe heads for the river's mouth which is a loud one, with many small boats and coracles bumping sides and the rowers yelling at each other over the traffic jam. The other passengers are like them, wide-eyed with shoulders hunched while the boatmen chat, taking their time. Darius eyes the goods in the boats—sugarcane, spices, grain, strange gem-like fruit and flowers. There are also goats, calves, chickens, exotic-looking birds in cages, their nervous cries and chirps adding to the cacophony, and several locked wooden chests like the captain's that people have on their laps or between their legs.

The boatmen gossip and scold each other, this is their familiar crowd, while the passengers eye each other curiously.

There are many women passengers too, Darius notices, including a pair of women in the boat next to him, the younger one no more than fifteen, wide-eyed with astonishment, while the older lady, possibly the aunt or mother, sits with eyes like a hawk's, the heavy jewellery around her thick neck and muscular arms more like armour than decoration.

Finally past the chokepoint, the boatman rows them down a river that grows wider as they go in. The water here is alive in a different way from the sea—there is constant movement right below the surface from tiny, darting silver and green fish. Water lilies and lotuses grow along the edges, and in some parts, the river is heavily shaded by overhanging trees and creepers, green curtains that block out the sun every now and then. There is life in every inch of this place, including a greater variety of insect creatures than Darius has seen before. Water spiders skim on the river surface, blue-tailed dragonflies flit around his face fearlessly before they go about their business. A tree they row below is coated entirely with yellow and red ants, its trunk and branches seething with movement. He looks away with a shudder and sucks at the healing cut on his lip, afraid that some creature might be drawn to it.

The boatman reaches a long jetty, the entry to the port. Darius gets down as the captain pays. He looks back towards the ocean—their ship can no longer be seen. They are a long way in.

It is busy here too with boats crowded together. People are disembarking, or climbing on to go further downriver. The locals wear brightly coloured clothing—greens, yellows, reds. Bright shades are worn indiscriminately by all ages. Back home, the higher up someone is in the hierarchy, the paler their clothes, since it signals time and money available to keep things clean.

The shades of skin here range from a milky cream to the darkest brown, but a chocolate tan seems to dominate. Hair long, dark and curly, just like Darius'.

Madu and Ebo are waiting for them on the riverbank and Darius notices Ebo getting several glances from the people around him; some of the women look him over more than once.

Not that different from home then, this place. At least not different enough for Ebo to be ugly and Darius gorgeous.

Sometimes, a face is beautiful when taken out of context—that had been true of his North African mother, a woman his father met while working as a camel herder. People in his father's village admired her long neck, her slender feet. She shrugged the praise off—everyone back home, she said, looked like her, she was nobody special. Darius took after his father and hasn't found a place where he is special yet.

The captain is scanning the crowd. Darius thinks that he is looking for the rest of the crew, but Ebo is right there, unmissable, and Madu and the silent nephew are next to him. Madu smirks and nods at a woman off to the side. The captain spots her and breaks into a shy smile. His brown tan goes purple—he is blushing all the way to his distant hairline.

It takes Darius a few moments to understand that the captain, who had spouted all that stuff about his lovely wife and not needing a woman, has a lady here in Muziris. The crew must have gone and fetched her as soon as they arrived.

The girlfriend has a pleasant face, with large eyes and a full mouth that Darius has noticed on several of the women. She has a generous, wide-hipped body and has cinched her waist with a narrow cloth. She is wearing pink cotton shot through with gold thread. The fabric goes around her chest and pleats in complicated ways around her waist. Her calves are bare.

Her silver anklets are ringed with bells, Darius notices, as she saunters towards them. She watches with quiet amusement as the captain mumbles his greetings. A woman out of his league, Darius thinks.

Babu and the hot curvy lady look at each other for a moment before she turns to the others and hands Madu a small parcel wrapped in leaves.

'Sweets!' Ebo claps his hands like a child as Madu unwraps the packet, and they squat right there to eat. Darius thinks for a moment of the oarsmen left behind to guard the ship and how everyone, including Darius, is indulging in a deliberate amnesia about them. He is starting to understand his place in the hierarchy in the context of the people below him as well.

But here is a sweet cooked in a strange, nutty oil, made out of a grain he's never tasted before. He puts one of the pieces in his mouth and the mix of sugar, fresh coconut and millet causes him to close his eyes with a pleasure that is almost unbearable after so many days of dried sardines and bread.

He reaches out for a second sweet and finds all of them gone. The greedy bastards. No contemplative chewing for them. The captain is nowhere to be seen, having disappeared with his woman and the two trunks of coins.

He sits back, taking in the scene. This could be just him romanticizing the new, but the port looks better organized than Berenike. Fresh passenger boats arrive every few minutes, dislodging goods and people. The locals around him are calm and well-dressed, harried in only the usual morning way, and form mostly orderly queues without much jostling. It's the kind of behaviour that comes only with the easy availability of things. The place is clean, more or less, the soil a fertile dark red that sticks to people's soles.

Bullock carts wait off to one side to move unloaded goods, and an official-looking person with a dagger on his belt is positioned near a wooden gate that marks the exit and entrance from this landing point.

'Let's get these to the warehouse,' Ebo says. He gives Darius one of the lighter loads, the amphorae and the beads, while he and Madu carry the rest to the carts. Two bullock carts fill up with what they have brought with them.

The trip into town cuts through dense trees and bushes. Back home, everything has sharp edges—the Romans like their towns well-planned, and lay down roads and streets in grids of neat squares and rectangles. This street, however, curves around sprawling trees, rocks and occasional monoliths with etchings of text and symbols. The road itself is a casual mix of brick, flattened earth and multicoloured stones and seashells with the tops sanded down. All around is the scent of jasmine and palm and mango trees that provide the carts with shade as they go.

Ebo talks to the cart driver with far less fluency than the captain, but manages to convey where they need to go. They move down the road at a leisurely pace. Fruit and flower sellers pass by as they reach the outskirts, carrying fragrant baskets whose contents Darius only catches glimpses of. A couple of girls giggle at his appearance, eyeing his face and hair. He doesn't think he looks all that different from them—his hair has a bit more corkscrew to it, his skin is more tan. He watches the people with a neutral curiosity until he sees a young woman walking towards them.

She is dressed much like the other girls—in thin cotton fabric that is wound loosely around her figure, exposing her shoulders, arms and waist. Her hair is coiled at her neck, although tendrils are coming apart and grazing her shoulders. She carries a small basket heaped with fragrant red flowers and moves with a dancer's gait. The heady smell of her flower basket precedes her like a minor announcement, and he slows down as he walks beside the cart.

Thunderclaps and drumbeats sound in his head. All at once, he is in the throes of his first international crush. She looks at him curiously and then gives him a smile full of mischief like she knows what he is thinking. She passes by him as he attempts to get a second, third glance, a closer look at her figure, face, hair, elbows.

And just like that, she's gone. He faces forward to see two smirking men looking at him.

'He looks like he's gulped too much seawater,' Madu observes and imitates Darius's slack-jawed, goggle-eyed expression.

'Don't give up your heart so fast,' Ebo says, 'Believe me, you've seen nothing yet.'

The windowless warehouse has four thickly mustachioed guards at its massive doors. Black knives glint from cloth belts. They are bare-chested and have slicked oil over themselves to highlight their pecs and deltoids. Darius supposes these men are meant to instil fear—practically they are less effective than the bolts on the doors, but more theatrical. Ebo and Madu talk to them in pidgin Tamil as they unload the carts. One of the guards escorts them inside and points to a vacant corner.

When they are done moving everything—with Ebo fussing extra over the amphorae, 'One crack and the captain will take it out of our share'—Madu turns to the nephew. 'You'll have to guard this until one of the oarsmen takes over.'

The nephew flushes red and opens his mouth to speak for the first time. All three of them wait. Darius is nearly holding his breath. But he only says one disappointing word. 'Why?'

'I don't know what your uncle said in order to convince you to come along with him,' Madu explains, 'maybe he told you that you would have this great adventure across the sea, fight some pirates, ride a sea monster and so on. Well, the truth is that you make a great adventure possible for everyone else. Because you, the youngest, will sit here guarding these very expensive things until someone else takes over.'

'Remember your uncle is your ride back home,' Ebo calls over his shoulder, 'so don't disappear.'

As they walk off, the nephew yells after them, 'How long do I have to be here?'

'Don't worry,' Madu says, 'someone will come take over by sundown.'

'What's his name again?' Ebo asks Madu, 'I'm pretty sure Babu said it a bunch of times.'

'Who cares?' Madu says, and Darius would have judged him if he'd been able to remember it himself. He is belatedly grateful that the nephew came along—he has a feeling Madu wouldn't have thought twice about putting him on guard duty.

Eight days of travel and he is now in a different world, among the lucky few to cross the sea. Outside, there is a different, crystalline sun. It is nearing noon and the trees are glossy in the heat, and a high, warm breeze comes off the sea. Narrow, clean streets lead them to a central bazaar space and a wall of sound, from stalls selling everything from the useful to the nonsensical.

The sellers use their temporary shops as a performative stage, their promises growing exaggerated by the minute as they compete with each other, sweating for attention. 'Beads to cure you of any stomach ailment,' a portly seller insists over several jars of tiny glass beads, which if you are lucky, will go right through you harmlessly. 'A miracle herb to keep your woman happy every night,' another promises, indicating heaps of smelly, medicinal-looking leaves. A third hawks corked bottles containing a glutinous green fluid: 'Your child will stop crying with this or you get your coins back tomorrow' (this merchant is clearly leaving town at midnight). There are many impulse buys available of small wooden statues of local gods and good luck charms to string around your neck. Darius wonders if an extremely detailed carving of bull genitalia is a holy totem or a joke.

The more honest sales folk offer proven temptations—tart fruit wine made from a local pink berry and a hallucinogenic chewable herb called myrram. The food tents beckon with their intoxicating smells. Flies gather, fat and gleaming, on tentpoles and baskets despite the burning incense, feasting for free. Walking through one narrow lane, Darius smells the same kyphi incense—a mix of honey, wine, juniper and kanen flowers—that they burn back home during funeral rites, and is overwhelmed for a moment with severe homesickness and sadness.

He buys pepper lamb, which has been cooked over a fire and chopped into bite-sized pieces, and is handed to him on a banana leaf, and he gets his first taste of the spice he has come so far for. Here in pepper country, there is no miserly sprinkling—his bit of lamb has been marinated in it.

His parents never 'indulged' in pepper, saying it was too rich for the stomach. More likely, they couldn't afford it. He discovers that the spice adds both depth and texture to the meat. His tongue craves more of it immediately.

The shopkeepers are friendly, even though he understands nothing of the local lingo and has to point at the food and watch how many fingers they hold up.

They look at him curiously but without hostility. There are nods and smiles, a sense of welcoming. He soon sees why—this is a busy port with ships from across the known world, but the local people mainly trade among themselves with Roman coins. Muziris is flooded with money from his home. The arrival of more sailors like him on Roman ships is good news for them.

Darius is so overwhelmed that he buys nothing else. Straight off the boat, he feels like an easy victim for the avid bazaar sellers. The men and women on the other side of the wares are experienced at parting you from your money, all the while smiling at you and about you.

He circles back to the front and finds Ebo and Madu—Ebo with two bead necklaces around his neck, and Madu holding a bottle of berry wine. 'We are off to meet some ladies, and we are taking gifts,' Ebo says. 'Want to join?'

Darius' warehouse in Berenike had been close to the brothels, and he'd watched dramas regularly unfold between the women and their regulars—women whose feet were ridden with sores, men who returned screaming after their wives were taken with the same disease. He shakes his head.

Madu curls his lip at him. 'So women are not this little man's preference?'

'Not women I pay for.'

'Unfortunate. Because that means your particular beanstalk remains as undipped in honey as the day you were born.'

Darius blushes despite his best efforts. 'The honey you are after is the kind that will make your beanstalk fall off. But enjoy the paid pussy.' He walks off like he knows where he is going, hoping fervently that he's ruined Madu's experience for him. But no, two drinks in and picking out girls from a line, Madu won't remember any of this.

His absent-minded stroll brings him to a quiet street with homes on either side and gardens filled with a dense variety of unfamiliar plants. These brick and stone houses with tile roofs resemble the homes of the wealthier traders and merchants in Berenike. Here, the doors have been left open, and he can glance into the rooms as he walks past. It is afternoon now and people doze on mats on wood and lime floors, or sit cross-legged, heads together, talking in the afternoon dark. Through one doorway, he sees a fat, middle-aged woman oiling her arms and legs. The flesh of her thighs moves under her fingers like yeasty dough, and she looks back at him as she kneads with a placid, unsurprised gaze, like she's seen everything.

When he turns the corner into a dirtier, more haphazard street, he hears something unexpected. Fayyumic. He follows the conversation to a small dead-end lane, where a man sits, smoking. They look at each other—the stranger is tall and thin in a way that can quickly turn frail. Hooded eyes and a not-entirely masculine beauty. He is alone.

'Who were you talking to?' Darius asks him in his tongue.

The man nods at the ground. A honey-coloured cat is at his feet, washing itself. 'Does a Muziris cat understand Fayyumic?' Darius asks, bending to scratch its forehead. The cat has unusual yellow eyes.

'You could argue that she understands everything equally,' the man says. 'Have you just anchored here?'

'Yes. It's my first time in Muziris. Our captain disappeared with his woman, so I've been walking around.'

'That famous sailor's itch,' the man nods. 'There is nothing like all those lonely nights at sea to sharpen the need for a woman. I haven't been on a ship for eight summers, but I remember that if you wanted to start a fight, you talked about another man's woman. It blew things up like nothing else.'

He rises, stretches. Standing, he is a foot taller than Darius, and resembles the laklak birds from Darius's village, with his long, loose-jointed legs, bald head and wrinkly neck.

'What has it been like to live here for so long?' Darius asks.

'It's a port town, so the locals get used to anything fast. The ships bring a new marvel every week, but everyone is jaded—it would take a three-headed tiger, maybe, to get them to take a second look. So they don't mind me. But they won't embrace me either.' He shrugs. 'I am good friends with those with no family—widows, orphans, unmarried men, streetwalkers. The rest keep to themselves.'

'Do you like them?'

He frowns. 'They are not all that different from us back home. In both good and bad, they're more or less the same.' He scratches his chin. 'Except for two things. First, they've got rich very fast, because their crop is now like gold.'

He pulls out a pouch of tobacco and tucks some into his mouth before offering it to Darius. 'Second, they're used to fighting, unlike us, who for many flood seasons have been a Roman province. They're surrounded by bigger kingdoms who have slaughtered and raped their ancestors more than once. Lot of blood in this dirt.' They both look down at what, despite his words, is unremarkable-seeming mud.

'You are an odd cat,' the man looks back up at him. 'You didn't ask me my name, but you got personal quick.'

'I am sorry. I am Darius.'

'Faro. No need to apologize. I hate small talk and you skipped it entirely, so I like you. I live in the last house down this street if you need to find me. It's nice to talk in Fayyumic for once. There are some of us around, but most are not friendly. I guess the ones who've stayed here must not like our own very much if we put an entire ocean between us and home.'

'By the way,' Faro adds, 'there are men who track sailors who get off the Roman ships and will be looking to rob you of your coins. Be careful of those who want to be friends and pretty women offering a drink. Everyone here has a sharpened knife under their floorboards. *Everyone.*'

Darius nods, watches him leave. He imagines knives under the floorboards of the houses he'd passed. These people, calm as they seem, have gone through horrors. But isn't it better to fight an army instead of a flood? It gives your enemy a face and you half a chance.

7

Nita's room is at the far end of the second floor, the last and smallest of the three bedrooms. You have to look twice to notice her narrow door. She passes by Rouhi's bedroom every morning when she goes to wake up Saba for school.

This morning, Rouhi calls out to her, and Nita sticks her head in. Rouhi is seated at her vanity, wiping her face. 'I am about to wake Saba up for school,' Nita says.

'One minute,' Rouhi says, 'You come sit.'

There is no real place for Nita to sit on but the bed, so she perches on the edge. Rouhi's face in the mirror is pink from her bath, her hair still in a towel.

'I love how you paint your home in your story,' Rouhi says. 'It is pretty. It make me want to go.'

It's not really home, Nita wants to say, it's home as she imagines it hundreds of years ago. But Nita is distracted by how Rouhi is in two towels, one covering her hair and the other her torso. The second towel is not long enough for her usual modesty—her shoulders are bare and it stops mid-thigh. She's acting like it is perfectly normal for Nita to see all that skin, goose-pimpled and red from the shower.

'I left the mosquitoes out,' Nita finally manages. 'The mosquitoes are everywhere. Story versus reality.' By the evening, the mosquitoes would start swarming in from the ponds and the lakes, and she would hear their evil song as they approached, when she walked home from school. Even now, the memory makes her shudder, how they would make a beeline for her face, neck and arms. The desert has some upsides—no mangoes but no mosquitoes either.

'How is Saba doing?' Rouhi asks as she applies cream on her face and wipes it off with a little cotton ball.

'She's getting better with her English.' Nita picks at the edge of a thumbnail. The truth is that it is an uphill battle to teach an easily distractable Saba the rules of English grammar. She likes learning words, but the way she strings them together is pure chaos.

Nita tries to not look at Rouhi's shapely legs and shoulders, and keeps her eyes on her face. Rouhi looks different without her everyday make-up—her eyes are smaller, the transition between skin and lips less dramatic, the eyebrows faded. She is still lovely but in a less immediate fashion. She also looks vulnerable, somehow older and younger at the same time.

Nita's sister or her mother never did much as far as primping went, besides kajal on occasion and face powder in the summers. Rouhi on the other hand, always wears a little make-up even when she has nowhere to go. Now she begins a routine nothing short of elaborate. Nita watches with fascination as Rouhi releases her hair from the towel and mists it with a spray from top to bottom, filling the room with a sharp-sweet, ozone scent. She sniffs surreptitiously— it smells like hot iron on fresh laundry, vanilla ice cream.

Rouhi picks up a curler that's been warming up on the vanity table and begins rolling it through her hair. Nita makes to get up but she stops her. 'No, sit,' and Nita sits back down, anxious about the time but also tongue-tied. There isn't a clock on the wall here to tell her how late she is getting. The surface of the vanity is a mess of small, half-used or empty bottles of perfume as well as lipstick and powder containers, some of them with their lids missing. When Rouhi searches for something, moving things around, it causes a domino effect—a tall spray bottle falls on its side, a tube rolls off the table. She doesn't like anyone cleaning it, saying that she wouldn't know where her things are.

Rouhi's hair reaches her waist, and she works her way patiently from one side to the other. Nita considers the softening lines of Rouhi's arms and shoulders, her no longer entirely sharp jawline. A body going slowly out of tune. One foot is pressed against the stool she is sitting on. A peeling band-aid is on the back, the skin around it bruised.

Rouhi's curls are nearly done. They watch her metamorphosis together in the mirror as she runs a wide-toothed comb through what are now loose, shiny waves. Changed, Nita thinks, into one of those Disney princesses Saba is obsessed with. Except that this feels like adult Disney, with the smell of hairspray in the air and electricity in the room. Nita doesn't dare get up again without Rouhi letting her, but she pulls the edge of her thumbnail off as Rouhi massages cream into her neck, rubs lotion over her arms, as the air fills with scents—musk, lavender, cocoa butter.

Rouhi leans forward and applies lipstick to her mouth, a subtle pink that you almost can't tell is there. She opens what looks like a box of watercolours, and using a tiny brush, applies some on her eyelids and brows—first a white base, then brown shimmer across the entire upper lid, and then some green blended in, and finally, eyeliner along the edge, extending a little past the lash line. She dabs white highlight at the top of her cheeks and some colour below her cheekbones.

She has drawn close to the mirror, and Nita is leaning forward as well to see. Finally, she straightens, observing the effect. 'Now I look like Rouhi.'

There is some truth to that. The make-up accentuates her features and the result is an intensification.

Or perhaps Rouhi is recreating, reinventing herself each morning. A core of dissatisfaction lurks inside this process. Later, when Nita is hunting for Saba's *Words with Birds* book in Rouhi's room, she sneaks a look at the brown eye pencil that had changed Rouhi's eyes from human to cat. It was a dense brown MAC shade called Taupe—a colour that sounded about as romantic as a window curtain.

Rouhi turns to Nita. 'Get my green dress. The one like paper.' She indicates the cupboard.

Nita knows the lace dress Rouhi is talking about. She goes to the cupboard and pulls it open. The clothes inside are in small heaps, like they've been picked up from once-folded piles and then stuffed back in. The pretty outfit that Rouhi had worn to the party is rolled up in a ball at the back. She pushes the clothes around gingerly until she finds the green dress.

'This one?' she is holding it between two fingers, looking at Rouhi in shock.

'Yes. What is problem?'

'Problem is your cupboard. How is it such a mess?'

Rouhi shrugs. 'I am not good at folding.'

'How do you even find anything? Nefertiti's missing mummy could be in there and you would never know.'

Nita's shock has turned her into the scolding mother Ani knows well.

Rouhi starts to giggle, and Nita covers her mouth with her hand. 'Oh. I am so sorry, I didn't mean to talk to you like that—'

'No, is ok,' Rouhi snorts. 'Nefertiti's missing mummy!'

Rouhi's towel is starting to slip and Nita tries not to look. She places the dress on the bed and smoothens it ineffectually. It's lovely lace, but crumpled. Somehow when Rouhi wears these, they look fine.

A few moments pass as they look at each other. Rouhi raises her eyebrows. Nita belatedly realizes that she's waiting for her to leave so that she can put her clothes on. Blunder after blunder.

'Saba will miss the bus,' she says, hurrying to the door. It comes out disgruntled.

'It's holiday today, remember? It's Eid al-Adha.'

'Oh of course!' Nita almost smacks her forehead. Saba had stayed up past midnight yesterday, almost dizzy with excitement about the day off.

Rouhi smiles. 'See, I know you forget. I wanted to tease you, Nita, make you sit here while I talk when you want to be somewhere else.'

'I didn't want to be anywhere else,' Nita says, and feels her cheeks go warm as she hears how that sounded out loud. She goes downstairs to water the garden, an errand she's taken upon herself since she arrived.

'Garden' is an exaggerated description for the assortment of cacti that Rouhi has accumulated absent-mindedly over the years, most of which are still in the pots she'd bought them in. Cacti, the great water stockpilers, have enough resource margins in this place to be decorative, and these have grown strange waxy blooms, and party thorns that are yellow at the base, and red and orange at the tips.

There are more emotions than there are words for them, Nita thinks. The feeling in her stomach now, as she pulls the grit-covered water hose towards the plants, is like the sensation she had when she sat on a longboat in the backwaters for the first time. The boatman had pushed off the lake floor with a long wooden rod, and the boat had jumped forward with unexpected speed. Inside little Nita, something had twisted in surprise and pleasure.

If only she could untwist this feeling. If she is honest with herself, she has to admit that she came to this country only partly for the money. It was also to escape herself. This job is supposed to be her reinvention. Not just for her sake but for her son's as well—the marriage may have been unwanted, but she had very much wanted him.

Her parents' death was the wall between an ordinary life and a messy, unpredictable one. In the new school near her aunt's home, she was at first the friendless new kid. Over the next few months, she made friends with nearly the entire class. She was the one with the runaway mouth, who made people gasp before they laughed. Her narrow, pointed face could be a blank slate as far as beauty was concerned—pretty with some effort, plain in an instant with the right, exaggerated expression. She grew closest to two girls, Vani and Brijitha, sharing their lunches and walking three abreast to the bus stop after class.

Together, they could handle the drunks who bought their rum quarter-bottles from the kallu shaap down the road and turned up bloodshot-eyed at the bus stop to gawk and say lewd things to the schoolgirls. There was enough shared courage between the three of them to glare back at the creeps. Conversation that was tentative and awkward with the others was easy between the three of them—light and clever with inside jokes, and gossip about boys. Soon enough, they had to be shushed by the teachers for their chatter during lessons.

Brijitha was plump and wore her hair in double pigtails. She compensated for her weight and the slight fuzz on her upper lip with a kind of extreme girlishness in her gestures and a fervent crush on the Malayalam movie star Prem Nazir. They teased her about it, calling her 'Prem's second girlfriend', the one he might eventually visit when both his wife and his mistress had turned him down.

Vani was Brijitha's physical opposite—slight, tall and dusky, with thick eyelashes that Nita found mesmerizing. Sometimes when she laughed, she tucked her chin into her neck and looked upward at the person cracking the joke. Nita felt rewarded whenever Vani did that with her.

She found herself drawn to Vani—she'd always found introverts attractive, she thinks now, people who caged their feelings and were like puzzles, hard for her to figure out. The crush got air and space to grow as they spent more time alone, since Brijitha was on a different bus route back home. The hour every weekday in the back seat of the public bus cemented Vani and Nita's relationship, where they indulged in a shared passion for Kottayam Pushpanath's crime stories, especially those featuring Detective Pushparaj. They bought the serialized magazine instalments from the bookstall near the school and read them to each other—thirteen-year-olds voicing inappropriate dialogue from violent plots.

In one story, Pushparaj fought off three dogs and several men to get to some evidence in a house—a sari covered in blood. Nita read the story of the fight to Vani in a hushed whisper, recounting each of his wounds in a pained, sorrowful tone. 'Two toes and one finger had been torn away by the time the third dog was done with him,' she recounted, near tears. He eventually solved the case, bandaged and bleeding, and would have a permanent limp. Later, when Vani read the story by herself, she discovered that this was not the case—it was one dog and two men, and the wounds were manageable. Nita's version, Vani told her later, was worlds better.

The two of them would look out of the bus and invent dramatic, Pushpanath-like stories for the people they saw—the woman buying fruit buns at the bakery was planning to serve them freshly poisoned with the evening kaapi to her husband, as revenge for him having a woman on the side. The pre-schooler waiting with his father outside the nursery was actually the kidnapped king of the Travancore royal family, and the man he thought was his father was holding him hostage, waiting for the big payout. Sometimes they would argue about the characters long after they had left the hapless people they'd based them on behind.

Nita began doodling Vani's name in the back of her notebooks, a hot, unnameable intensity burning under her skin. She listened to her closely; every tidbit gleaned about her life was its own reward. What she ate for breakfast (idli or pongal), what her dad rode (a Bajaj Chetak), what she liked about her sister (she shared her earrings with Vani sometimes) and what she hated (she ratted out Vani to her mother often). She tried to read meaning into Vani's smallest gestures—an eyebrow raise, a sympathetic glance. Did she like Nita, did she not? Some days, she was certain Vani had feelings for her. On others, it seemed impossible.

What can Nita say? She was obsessed. In love.

She began to resent having to share Vani with Brijitha during lunch and school hours. The time spent gossiping about movie stars, the only thing Brijitha was interested in, felt tedious. Brijitha had amazing, poreless skin and a bovine expression. When Nita referred to her one day as 'that melamine cow' to someone in class, word got back to Brijitha pretty fast.

It was a small thing, that remark. But Brijitha, a big girl, was sensitive about body insults, and in a few days, things began to change. It was startling in retrospect, the speed at which a story concocted as retribution, spread.

Select thirteen-year-olds in class were sworn to secrecy before being told. But, of course, there is no such thing as a secret between teenagers, who are just beginning to understand the power of gossip and the rewards in social status for those who add to the information pool.

The story got back to Vani—a fetid, vivid piece of fiction about Nita and her kissing in the back of the bus, hands under skirts. The two of them had barely, maybe held hands. It was hard to trace the origin of the lie through the whisper network, but the source, Vani finally discovered, was Brijitha herself telling someone that her older brother had seen them at it. The brother in question was nowhere to be found, having conveniently visited a few weeks ago and now back to his college out of state.

For Vani, it felt as if someone had switched on a too-bright light in the room she and Nita were sitting in. The tale was outlandish and humiliating, but also an oyster around a dark mote of truth. Brijitha, for all her bovineness, had intuited that this friendship was not without sexual attraction. She knew that enough of the other students would believe it too.

Vani stopped speaking to Nita, and as with most high-school entanglements, there was no break-up conversation. None was needed since Nita had heard the story too. For Nita, Vani's withdrawal from her was the worst possible outcome. It wasn't just the ending of the friendship with the three of them sitting as far apart as possible in the classroom. The story also left her exposed to everyone as 'the pervert'. Vani's reputation was scarred by the story, but she had grown up here. Students knew her enough to give her the benefit of the doubt, and not cut her off entirely.

But Nita was frozen out. The classroom was segregated along gender lines, the boys on the left benches and girls on the right. Now, none of the girls would sit on the same bench as her, claiming it threatened their modesty. Nita kept her head down, tried to stay low-key, and waited for it to blow over. But while the initial storm died down, the cloud over her stayed. This was the only senior school in her aunt's town, so a transfer of any kind was out of the question. Three years passed like this and Nita more or less settled into the identity of the school pariah, doing everything alone. The girls tolerated her presence with stony silence while the guys sometimes left notes on her bench asking her, among other less palatable things, why she shaved off her moustache every morning.

And yet she still longed for Vani from a distance. She watched her grow pretty and shapely, the flat chest she used to complain about filled out, and she had to constantly fend off boys. Watching her every day, Nita began to understand herself.

It was only when she left for college that she could blend in again, and she tried to do everything right—be more girlish, dress in saris, talk softly, giggle about Prem Nazir and the young Mohanlal. She stayed far away from women she thought attractive. Even then, sometimes while chatting with someone, she thought she might betray herself, feeling that old pull of attraction, the stamped-out match catching fire. Her need like a brassiere strap peeking out of a blouse.

She said yes to the third young man her sister arranged for her to meet. After the marriage, there was routine, fortunately, abbreviated sex, and then there was the baby—which she embraced with a love she had been unable to summon for her husband. She thought she had put her past behind her. A college friend of hers who studied Biology—a degree with more reasonable career prospects, it turned out, than hers—told her once that the body replaces all its cells every seven years. She had found that encouraging. By then, seven years had passed since the Vani episode. So technically, she was a completely different person.

But it turns out that you fold up the past and bring it with you. It's easy to stay on the straight and narrow (even in her distress, she appreciates the pun) when there is no temptation. Today, she gave herself away at the first opportunity. She is shaken that Rouhi had tried to guess her secrets and at the first tug, Nita had revealed herself, her disguise unspooling.

In a way, Rouhi had revealed herself as well, letting Nita see her small vanities, the painstaking routine it took to bring the beauty back to her face.

When Nita met the man she married, he'd pierced her reluctance by complaining about the whole arranged marriage set-up—the formality of it and the absence of emotions from the discussion, the various aunts and uncles instead discussing the straightness of the nasal bridge, the fullness of the mouth, the thickness of the ankles. The over-sweet tea served to potential grooms. The clenched shyness and downcast eyes of the women he had to make conversation with—'How am I supposed to marry someone who can't even tell me what she ate for breakfast?'

She had agreed with him, and found his annoyance invigorating, honest. Later she discovered that it's just how he flirted—by looking for shared things to be irritated at. She watched him do it with bank tellers, the pretty neighbour. And she hadn't been jealous, only surprised that it worked so well. It had worked on her.

She prefers Rouhi's approach. That incautious, confident display of her body, short-circuiting everything else. She goes over that half-hour in the bedroom moment by moment.

She thinks of Rouhi's bare legs, the arched foot and the peeling band-aid, her shoulders, pink from the shower. Of Rouhi leaning close to the mirror and drawing kohl over her eye, looking at Nita and looking at herself. This Nita stores away to think about later, to consider the scene at leisure, to consider it threadbare.

Be careful, she tells herself. But she's always been impulsive, bad at listening to the parts of her that urge caution.

8

Nita wakes from strange dreams to noises outside—of morning routines happening a half hour too early. She checks her watch on the side table: 5.30 a.m. Usually, she's the first to get out of bed at ten minutes to six. She washes her face, smoothens down her hair and dress, steps out of the room.

Rouhi's bedroom door is half ajar, so she knocks before pushing it open. She is dressed and picking up her purse from a fully made-up bed—which is unusual because Rouhi never makes her bed. It's the two-headed woman downstairs who does.

'I take Saba to school,' Rouhi says, and then inexplicably, unfolds a dark blue hijab and puts it on. Nita stares. She's never seen Rouhi in a hijab before. She wears it expertly though, like she's done it a thousand times—folding it around her head and then tri-angling the fabric. With her hair covered, she looks different, older. She's made her eyes up today with green eyeliner.

'But it's early for school,' Nita says, puzzled.

'I know,' Rouhi says, 'but I am going outside, so I wake Saba also. She's eating breakfast. She's *ghadbana*, so angry with me, but she will be ok. You have surprise holiday.' She brushes past Nita in a rush.

'Wait,' Nita darts into Saba's room. She checks her desk, bed and then under the bed—there it is, her blue math notebook. Like mother, like daughter, when it comes to messiness.

'Why is it under bed?' Rouhi asks, watching from the doorway.

'She's struggling with carry-over multiplication,' Nita says, 'she finds it comforting to hide under the bed and do the homework.'

Downstairs, Saba is finishing the last of her milk and bread pudding. She is sulky and barely awake, and glares at her mother as she gets off the chair, 'Why can't I go on the bus today? Alma is bringing strawberry pop rocks. I'll miss it.'

'I'll get you pop rocks, whatever it is,' Rouhi says unconvincingly. 'You can choose car music, okay?'

This doesn't improve Saba's mood—it only confirms that she's being offered a raw deal. She drags her feet as Rouhi takes the car out.

Her mother honks twice while Saba dawdles at the front door, her arms crossed, trying to figure a way to get out of this.

It's November, but the season hasn't changed much. Hot has given way to less hot. The sky this early is still the colour of twilight. A hundred kilometres away in Ras Al Khaimah, two oil wells that accidentally caught fire are still burning twenty days later, throwing up plumes that coat people's skin and hair and throats. But here the air is clear, the stars bright.

Saba gives up and gets in the front. Rouhi doesn't insist on the car seat this time. Saba is finally getting to put on the grown-up person's seat belt. Another bribe. Nita feels a pang watching her—her routines are not yet her own, the adults around her can change them at a whim.

The last few weeks have marked a shift for her and Saba. Early on, Nita figured that Saba's problem was not intelligence but temperament. Longer assignments, the puzzling sentence structures of English or anything in math that took more than a few minutes to understand—all made her impatient and she lost focus. It was the overarching problem with tutoring Saba.

It came to a head with an assignment about time. The English teacher had assigned the students three pages full of clock faces and they had to draw the lines on the clock depending on the time mentioned in the text. 'Half-past six', 'The clock struck seven' and so on.

Saba found the whole thing tedious. She understood the numbers but couldn't map the phrases easily. She struggled with the meaning, for instance, of 'quarter to'.

'It doesn't matter,' Saba finally said, 'I only need to know it's near three.'

'It's important to be able to tell the exact time,' Nita said.

'But why? Why do I need to?'

'So that you don't miss exams, buses, planes. So that your friends don't get mad at you when you are late everywhere because you can't tell the difference between half-past four and four forty-five.'

Saba sighed and kicked the legs of her small table.

'You know, for the longest time people didn't even have clocks,' Nita said, 'They used incense sticks to measure time. And cats.'

'Cats?'

Nita told her about the monk Pere Huc, who while travelling in rural China on an overcast day, stopped to ask a young boy whether it was noon yet. The boy asked him to wait and came back holding a cat. 'No', he said, 'it is not yet noon.'

'How could he tell? The Chinese knew that as the day gets brighter, the pupils in a cat's eyes get smaller. They are smallest at noon.'

'And then as the day becomes evening,' Nita went on, 'the cat's pupils become bigger to get more light in. By midnight, they are at their biggest.' Nita makes a small drawing to illustrate:

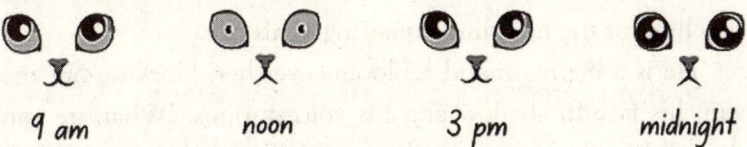

9 am   noon   3 pm   midnight

Saba takes Nita's drawing and studies it for a while.

'I would rather use a cat's eyes than a clock,' she says. 'People would have to carry cats everywhere all the time. Mama would have to get me one.'

'Yes,' Nita agrees, 'I would prefer it too.'

The stories make the lessons easier. And somehow over time, the two of them cross an invisible hump. Nita senses a curiosity building in Saba about her lessons, at least some of the time. She is frustrated less easily. Even the dreaded Wren and Martin grammar book, with its red cover, doesn't seem so intimidating any more. The spark that Nita hadn't been able to ignite in her tenth graders—she may have found it here. They are unearthing it together, bit by bit.

Today without Saba's morning routine, Nita is at a loss. The two cooks are busy in the kitchen with breakfast, and she wanders around the house, looking for something to do.

She finally goes out into the garden. Last week, Saba had helped 'design' it, putting heart-shaped stones around the cacti. Nita doesn't understand what it is with little girls and heart shapes. Saba and her friends like heart candy, heart stickers, heart pillows. They write each other's names on the backs of their notebooks and draw hearts around the words. No boys' names in there yet.

She rearranges the stones to give the hearts some symmetry. She's inspecting the smallest cactus, a hedgehog-shaped fellow, when a shadow falls over her. She looks up and that's how she sees him for the first time, squatting at his feet.

He is a big man, and he looms over her, blocking out the sun, his face in shadow and his voice furious. 'What are you doing?' he asks in Arabic, the tone full of menace, as if she's made some terrible mistake.

'Sorry, sorry,' she says, lifting her hands up, palms out. 'Nita?' she says, pointing to herself as he glares uncomprehendingly. 'I teach Saba? Rouhi's daughter?' hating herself as every word that comes out of her mouth became a question.

'Ah. You are the English teacher,' he says, relaxing all at once, even the size of his arms seeming to go down like they were air-filled balloons. Nita realizes that he'd been flexing them, ready to attack this brown person apparently trespassing in his yard.

He turns away and walks into the house, or rather, stalks into it. Belatedly, Nita realizes, *this is Haroun*. The man who'd been about to yank her up by her collar is paying her salary.

She waits for her heartbeat to return to baseline before she returns to the house. He's already settled in at the dining table, and the women are serving him breakfast. Their expressions are the same as always, stoic and unsmiling, but they talk to him as they take small steps to the table and back, chatting in that same looping way they do among themselves.

A different breakfast from the usual, it's being served in the bone china bowls that usually stay in the display cupboard because they are fragile and expensive. The two-headed woman brings in cuts of grilled halloumi, bread pudding in saffron milk, fried sesame pancakes with date syrup. Haroun eats it all silently, unresponsive to the chatter of the two ladies as he washes it all down with innumerable cups of gawah, the intense black coffee that Rouhi dislikes so much.

Haroun is tall, with a broad muscular frame that's softening into fat. He is beautifully dressed—his shirt is silk and his pants look tailored. Who wears tailored pants on a merchant ship? she wonders. His haircut is fashionable, the style perhaps on the younger side for a thirty-eight-year-old man. On the whole though, it looks like he's aimed for something and failed. There is a deep line between his thick eyebrows and his intense dark eyes look pissed off. The look stays even as he eats the incredible spread cooked for him in his sprawling house.

She hears Rouhi's car pull in. She enters, walks past Nita and into the dining room. There is a murmur of conversation.

Nita retreats upstairs, where she finds a half-eaten cheese and sugar sandwich under Saba's pillow along with some smashed cheetos, and is cleaning out the crumbs when Rouhi peeks in. 'Haroun sometimes in bad mood when he come home, so I take Saba to school early,' she confesses, 'I not tell you. Sorry.' Before Nita can answer, she goes into her bedroom and closes the door.

That afternoon, as usual, Nita picks Saba up from the bus stop, 'Your father is here.'

'Oh,' Saba looks at Nita. Always the social kid, searching for clues in other people's faces for how she should react. Nita keeps her expression neutral. *You aren't getting any pressure from me, kid.* When they reach home, Saba's father is on the living room sofa, the phone on the armrest, in between phone calls.

Saba greets him politely from several steps away. He nods, then interrogates her in Arabic. 'How are your studies, how is your English?'

'I am at the top of my class in Science,' Saba says, 'Near the top in Maths. Middle in English.' Saba's usually not modest, but in front of Haruon, she is muted. Still, Nita can tell that she's proud of how much she's improved.

'Ok,' her father said, 'you beat the boys too?'

'Yes.'

'*Wayed zain*. Very good, there is at least some of me in you then.' His pager chimes and he disconnects from them, checking the number and reaching for the phone. He's changed into a white thobe and traditional headgear. The black braided headgear is shot through with gold thread. Polished leather shoes, no socks. His calves are hairless, contrasting oddly with his hirsute arms. After speaking for a few minutes, he rises to leave, telling Saba, 'Tell your mother I will be late today.' He does not acknowledge Nita.

The house itself seems to exhale as the black SUV pulls out of the gate. 'Nita,' Saba shrieks, and for once, Nita doesn't tell her off for yelling at the top of her voice, 'Come play Throw Jaffa Out with me!'

Haroun leaves early in the mornings before Nita comes downstairs. In the days after, Nita doesn't see Rouhi at all—she takes her meals in her room as if she's in purdah. The cooks collect the plates from outside the door. Everyone acts as if this is completely normal.

No Rouhi with Tang, no *Bold and the Beautiful*: the evening feels like a yawning stretch of hours with nothing to do. Nita picks up her dog-eared copy of *Moby Dick*. She has read it so many times since college that she can open it to a random chapter and be absorbed in it with the comfort of knowing what happened before and after. The familiar lines reassure her. *I love to sail forbidden seas, land on barbarous coasts.*

The head of the household has changed and the routines now revolve around someone else. The food is spicier, heady with pepper and za'atar. Fewer raisins in the rice, more cashew nuts. The cooks are paying tribute to a different boss.

Nita eats dinner with Saba as always and tucks her in. Her young charge is stressed from the changes in her routine and acts up a bit more every day, like she is toeing the boundaries to see where the grooves are at. At her age, lying is like a portal to a more exciting world, and Saba fibs in the usual, expected ways for a seven-year-old—she talks about imaginary friends and things teachers said, about what happened on the playground.

But now the lying has amped up. She lies about the next school day being a holiday, hides her homework assignments, pockets any money she catches sight of, or anything shiny Nita leaves lying around, like hairclips or her supermarket earrings. She denies it when caught, even when faced with clear evidence, but she is not good at this, since her cheeks glow red. The giveaway is as bad as Pinocchio's nose.

It's obvious why, of course. These days, Saba gets to see her mother right before she goes to bed and rarely before. Nita sometimes stands outside Rouhi's door while Saba is inside, waiting to be called in. But Rouhi never does.

Nita wonders if she has put her off or angered her in some way. But she cannot figure out what she has done. Some people are just moody, changeable, blowing hot and cold. Maybe Nita did something minor that Rouhi disliked— perhaps she was the kind of person who is always on edge, her wounds reopening at the smallest injury, like the fairytale princess who found a single pea under twenty mattresses unbearable.

Nita circles over their recent conversations, looking for a wrong turn. She starts biting her nails. She bites them down to the quick, into reverse half-moons. They look mauled, like her fingernails in high school. Vani-era fingernails.

Haroun usually returns home after Nita has disappeared into her room. Once though, he comes up the stairs just as she's headed to bed. She smells his heavy, complicated perfume before he enters. It seems to get stronger by the day. The fragrance is layered and expensive, a musky-woody-spicy concoction meant to be part seduction and part announcement, and he wears too much of it. To Nita, he reeks of insecurity.

He steps into the living room and looks at her with his hooded eyes, saying nothing. His beard hides his expressions. Close-cut beards are in fashion, and the Sheikh himself wears a well-trimmed one to his public events. But few Emirati men wear the traditional white outfit with the headdress nearly every day, like Haroun does.

She walks past him in silence, trying not to hurry to her room. Haroun takes up a lot of space, nudging her to the corners of the house.

Rouhi finally comes downstairs for lunch one afternoon when Nita is midway through her usual late meal, which she eats at three after everyone else is done. She is on her second, guilty bowl of umm ali. The bread pudding is sweeter than usual.

When Rouhi enters the dining room, Nita knows at once that something is wrong despite the curtained windows and her turned-away face. She watches Rouhi reach for the walls and chairs as she moves.

'Rouhi,' Nita says, even as it strikes her that she has never called her employer by name before. Over the past few weeks, she'd adjusted her sentences to avoid saying *Madam*. When talking to Saba, Rouhi is 'your mother'. Using relationships as a moniker was what people did back home when hierarchy was uncertain or difficult to acknowledge.

The two-headed woman comes in and puts fresh grapes and dates in a basket on the sideboard.

Nita approaches Rouhi like one would a deer. She is gazing at the covered bowls of food on the table as if they are something new and strange. Her lips are bruised, her left cheek is swollen. Nita pulls out a chair for her. She sits and watches as Nita brings a plate and piles food on it—a bit of biriyani, fried goat brains, bread pudding. It's party food everyday with Haroun around.

'Please,' Rouhi finally says and gestures Nita away.

Rouhi doesn't eat until Nita coaxes her. Just three bites. Ok, two more bites. That's so great. Two more! Like with Saba and literally any vegetable—Saba can sniff out a vegetable nestled inside food like a bloodhound, so Nita puts tiny servings on her plate and talks her through them.

Rouhi eats slowly as if her jaws hurt. She skips anything too chewy and nudges the nuts out of the rice.

Back in the bedroom, Rouhi's face on the pillow—'Don't tell Saba.'

'Of course not.' Now that Rouhi is calm, Nita feels her anger rise.

'How often does this happen?' she asks.

When Rouhi hesitates, Nita squeezes her shoulder, 'Don't tell me the cleaned-up version.'

Rouhi smiles with half her face. 'Two times a week like going to buy vegetables.'

'I don't understand. Why does he get angry at you?'

'No, there is no "get", Nita. He angry. Always. Sometimes drunk and angry. He use this'—she gestures at her face—'to get less angry. So I say something in wrong voice or little loud. That is enough. That is reason.'

She shifts like she's trying to find a position that doesn't hurt, winces as she pulls the blanket closer—the air conditioning is turned up high, as usual. Nita is too cowardly to ask if the bruises on her face are the only ones she has. Instead, she holds her hand until Rouhi tells her to let up before she breaks her fingers.

Nita picks up the small pot of cold cream from Rouhi's dresser and applies it to the bruise near her eye. When she is done, she rests her hand against Rouhi's face. Rouhi is the kind of woman who, even in her worst moments, will pat talcum powder on her face before venturing outside her room. Nita's fingers linger against her powdered cheek. Rouhi looks at her with half-lidded eyes. Something rises between them, sharp and dangerous.

Nita pulls away. Rouhi closes her eyes, sighs.

'May he fall off ship,' she says, 'Get eaten by shark.' A woman giving curses because she can do nothing else.

Nita strokes her hand. Rouhi's French manicure is chipping off. 'If I forget everything, then I can leave,' Rouhi murmurs as she falls asleep, 'Cut him out of photo.'

As the days pass, the interactions between Saba and her father are reduced to polite greetings from her in the mornings and afternoons, which he answers with brief nods. He is uninterested, she, fearful. Her walk around him is almost a tiptoe.

They do building blocks and counting games in her room. Then they watch Channel 33 cartoons. The television—the

Fantastic Four in particular, Saba's favourite—is an excellent English tutor.

When she finally comes back downstairs, leaving Saba with her homework, the newspaper is on the coffee table. Nita reads it end to end. She hasn't had a new grown-up book to read since she came here. On the front page are the biggest crimes of state-sponsored violence—the war between Iran and Iraq, with the sympathy clearly tilted towards the latter, Sunni country. News of bombings in Gaza, followed by smaller murders and assaults on the inside pages. The United Arab Emirates is a tiny peaceful country, and there is rarely much to report. The crimes when they do make news, seem to involve people from Nita's country and other immigrants—mostly the men packed into cheap, overheated housing where they live atop stacked bunk beds when not working on the construction sites. *Look at them,* the pieces seem to say, *look at how violent they are.*

She reads about a South Asian cook caught pickpocketing and sentenced to fifty lashes. A man accused of assaulting his neighbour—a hundred lashes. And then oddly, a prime number— sixty-seven lashes for someone caught trying to smuggle gold bars, which were concealed in his anus, on to a flight.

You read something over and over, and you are apt to reach a certain conclusion. A bias growing roots until the shrub becomes a tree. A mud track laid a long time ago gets deeper and wider. In their own ways, humans are lazy and use assumptions lying around to build gospel.

One evening, the husband turns up early for dinner with two work friends. The cooks have prepared enough food to weigh down the table, covering it with party dishes including Egyptian favourites like muhammara made Rouhi-style, and local dishes like ghuzi, a dish very much like biryani, with lamb and vegetables in the rice. The ghuzi has roasted zucchini in the mix, another of his wife's variations. The men rave over it, suck the bones of meat and let the gravy drip down their fingers.

Nita has come downstairs for a glass of water, but the kitchen is on the other side of the dining room. She doesn't want to cross it. She nears the entryway, trying to decide.

Still out of sight, she can see the cupboard with its mirrored glass doors. The glass is diamond cut, so its reflection of the dining table splits the men into multiple tiny versions, all with wet, smacking lips, their eyes glued to the food. She observes several Harouns, a man of many heads like Ravana. The heads watch the guests eat the dinner quickly, competitively, as if the best pieces might run out, and the Harouns urge them on, laughing and expansive, wearing the costume of a generous host.

Right now, the Harouns are almost handsome, the hooded eyes lit up and the usual sour expression nowhere to be found.

The two-headed woman brings a steaming bowl from the kitchen and Haroun's face glows with pleasure. 'Look,' he says, 'this is made from the feet of the goat. The filthiest part of the animal becomes the most delicious dish.' Haroun's English, unlike Rouhi's, is accented but fluent.

The two co-workers with him are not Emirati. Nita knows at once that they don't have wives here—they are both dishevelled in that 'man living alone' kind of way. These men of a certain generation have been passed on from mothers to wives for caretaking, so in their absence they are helpless.

One is a red-headed white man whose skin is peeling badly from the desert sun, and the other a brown man from a country that Nita can't determine, with salt and pepper curly hair, deep-set eyes, and a generous nose and ears. His lips cured dark by too many cigarettes. The loneliness that wafts off them is as heavy as Haroun's perfume and Nita is sure he can smell it too.

Maybe he is the kind of guy who has a nose for the vulnerable ones. For both marriage and friendship, that is his style.

She is astonished by the charm, how Haroun switches it on. He is telling them a story about an aunt of his in hospital for a surgery, how the nurses kept rushing into her room because the monitor was throwing alarms that she was having a heart attack. And then they found out: 'My young cousin, who had no idea what that power cord was for, was unplugging her machines to switch on his tape player and listen to Najwa Karam's music!'

The aunt recovered, apparently none the worse for it. Haroun shrugs as they laugh, 'How can mothers compete with Najwa Karam when it comes to a teenage boy's love?'

The curly-haired man and Haroun gossip about the buxom Najwa, professing both desire and disapproval—what a voice, but getting a divorce of all things? A loose woman, they agree, their admiration sliding easily into contempt.

'What do you think of the soup?' Haroun asks the redhead, who is still taking careful sips of it even though it is no longer steaming.

'It's very good,' he says. His face and the scalp under his disappearing hair have turned red with the heat of it. 'But I can no longer feel my tongue.'

They laugh again—everything now makes them laugh, the food and the whisky helping things along. 'God, I miss my mother's bread soup,' the redhead sighs.

'Make it for us!' Haroun says, 'Feed us something from your home.'

'I can't just *make* it,' the man shakes his head. He dabs at his running nose with a kerchief. 'It's difficult, it takes an entire day.

My mutti would buy bread that was steamed over a hot spring—it made the loaf very tight and dense. Black bread. She'd soak it in lemon water and cherry jam for hours before boiling it with cream until it completely melted. Where will I get that black steamed bread here?' His joviality leaves him as he reminisces and he is now close to tears.

'Now, now,' Haroun pours out more Blue Label for them and goes to the cupboard to take out a glass for himself. Nita pulls back a bit from the edge of the door as he takes out a goblet and pours the whisky into it—the sound of liquid splashing makes her even thirstier. He sips very slowly, it is only his second glass to their third or fourth. The whisky seems to do something to these men. They grow pensive, emotional. Perhaps that's why they drink this strong stuff—so that they can shed their carapaces.

Their faces are sweaty now from the food and exertion. 'Did you fellows hear about the late-night meeting between the officers last week?' Haroun asks.

Even with the whisky, caution returns to the table. She can see it in their faces. Haroun lets the silence hang. And hang. The Irishman gets twitchy first and says, 'I heard some whispers about Rahim being in trouble.'

'Of course, you sit on the upper floors,' Haroun notes, as if just realizing it, as if this isn't why he is having the redhead over for dinner. 'What is he in trouble for?'

Haroun waits, only to be met with silence. 'Aren't we lucky,' he says, 'to have good whiskey, great food and such good storytellers around the table? I am so interested.'

'Well,' the redhead laughs, embarrassed. 'I don't know how good a storyteller I am. Most nights, the only audience for my stories are the roaches climbing out of my kitchen sink. How are there so many of them in apartments here? Marble foyers everywhere and cockroaches climbing over them.'

'Good storytellers are those who happen to be in the right place at the right time,' Haroun suggests, ignoring the attempt to change the subject. 'And you, my friend, are in the right place.'

The man shrugs. 'Finance doesn't know that much, we are at the far corner from management. But I hear Rahim is being interviewed over a container going missing.'

The curly-haired one bangs his glass down on the table. 'You cannot gossip about what happens on our floor, Phil,' he says.

'Gossip? Gossip is what women do over sewing and sweets,' Haroun waves his hand. 'We are talking about work.'

'But not your work. Haroun, this shouldn't concern you. We can lose our jobs for talking about this.'

'Well, I would like to know the danger my ship's captain is in,' Haroun says.

'Don't you know a little about it already?' the dark-haired one asks.

'What is that supposed to mean?' the first flash of anger from Haroun.

'Nothing, nothing,' the curly-haired fellow shakes his head, looks over at Phil. 'But we should go.' He gets up, clumsy from drink and nearly knocks over his glass of water.

Haroun swallows his whisky, turns his eyes away towards where Nita is standing. She is pretty sure she is out of sight. He can't see through walls, she tells herself.

She inches away and tiptoes cartoonishly towards the stairs. Like *Tom and Jerry*, another Saba favourite. She drinks the odd sharp-tasting water from the bathroom tap and gets into bed, her appetite killed by watching the men eat.

She pounds the pillow, imagining Haroun's moisturized face. She can't imagine how a man can mash his fist into a woman's body and then everything goes on as normal. His friends smile, his employees serve him his wife's recipes heaped on beautiful plates. He goes out in the world, wearing spotless white while his wife hides until she heals.

One late evening not many days after that meal, Haroun puts an open suitcase out in the living room, in the middle of everything, pushing aside the coffee table whose surface is now covered with overflowing ashtrays, cigarette packs, nail clippings and work files.

Over the next few days, the suitcase fills up with Haroun's purchases—new clothes, male toiletries, expensively wrapped chocolate, and delicate looking brown packages with tags that say Issey Miyake, Hermes, Fendi.

The pile in the suitcase grows, and Saba does not reach into it despite the fragrant shininess of some of the things. The self-control she displays in her mother's absence is impressive. When he is finally done packing, he can barely close the bag and calls the two-headed woman over for help. The long-haired one comes over and sits down on the top while he zips it closed.

The next morning, he is gone. Nita can tell as soon as she wakes up—it is as if a weight has eased off the house's roof, the crouching rooms have straightened their bent spines.

Just in case, she tiptoes down the stairs. The suitcase is gone, as are Haroun's crocodile leather shoes and balled-up socks next to the door. She stands still and listens to the sounds of the house—an open cupboard door's creaking hinge, the sigh of the air-conditioner upstairs, a drop of water easing out from a loose tap. Everyone is still asleep but sunrise is near. She goes back upstairs to the master bedroom and waits outside the door for a moment, listening. Still, but not too still. A rustling, perhaps.

Nita knows the old stories with a closed or locked door that is off-limits. 'Don't go in there,' the narrator is told. But, of course, they do. And it changes their life, usually for the worse. In a fairytale from her childhood, a girl forbidden to go into a locked room does it anyway and finds a jasmine plant inside in full fragrant bloom. She gathers the flowers and strings them into a garland, only for it to turn into a snake when she puts it around her baby brother's neck.

The student in her knows that the doors in these stories are about the price of desire. You are punished if you cannot control yourself. Restraint is a virtue, these tales make clear. But they also admit that humans cannot ignore their greatest desires—the person must turn the door handle, open it. They pay the steep price of entry.

Nita tries the door, and finding it unlocked, goes in, closes it gently behind her. The bedroom floor is covered in clothes, Haroun's pre-leaving mess—silk shirts considered and discarded, a lonely patterned sock, stepped-out-of and crumpled trousers. Her foot lands on a sharp, solitary cufflink and she muffles her yelp. On the table next to Rouhi are several cups. Downstairs, they are running out, left with Saba's cartoon mugs. Nita has been drinking her sweet milky tea in a glass.

Rouhi is on her side, facing the door. Nita climbs on to the creased, cushion-covered bed, over cotton sheets turned chilly from the air-conditioning, pushing several small pillows off to the side. She moves as gently as she possibly can, her heart thumping in her chest.

It is one thing to talk with your employer in front of the television and let a friendship grow.

134

DEVI YESODHARAN

Climbing into her bed, however—that is a vault over several red lines all at once. Even as she moves towards her, she is reconsidering and maybe planning to sneak back out, when Rouhi opens her eyes. Over the left eye is a different kind of eyeshadow—a bruise. Nita leans forward and touches it gingerly, certain that this part is going to be warmer than the rest, radiating purple heat, but the skin is cool.

Rouhi is quiet, seemingly unsurprised that Nita is there next to her. When she straightens her legs, she winces like a person turned inside out and raw.

Nita draws closer. 'Are you ok?' she asks.

'He leave me alone yesterday. He was busy planning trip.'

She doesn't know if this is a lie. Rouhi is a good liar but of a specific type—lying with omissions, evasions, metaphors, her stories full of buried hard-to-get-at truths. A woman who talks about djinn cats and beautiful orchards, building fairytale houses on top of her past.

Nita can sense her about to change the subject.

'You are relieved he's gone,' Nita says before Rouhi can start a joke or excuse. It isn't a question.

Rouhi presses her face into Nita's arm. 'Ertaht?' *Am I?*

'Aren't you?'

Somewhere in the room, an alarm clock ticks, impossible to spot in the mess.

'Say it,' Nita says, feeling a heat rise inside her. This is, she tells herself, anger. 'Say it to me.'

Rouhi lets her breath out in a long sigh. 'Yes. Yes, I am happy he is gone.'

Nita kisses the top of Rouhi's head like it is the obvious, comforting thing to do, and feels Rouhi relax against her, draw closer. Closing the gaps. The line of plausible deniability is fading with every moment. She moves her face against Nita's neck. 'You smell so nice,' she says, 'you smell of my favourite dessert.'

'Basbousa,' Nita says. A cake made of oranges. Rouhi kisses her.

She kisses her full on the mouth. Nobody sees or hears them, but Nita's ears roar with sound—an airplane passes over her head, a group of dancers pound their ankleted feet, a room of people break into song.

Beneath the thrill of it, she immediately thinks that this is a mistake, the worst one in her already error-filled life. The bed is a chasm that will suck her down.

And what about the chasm between them? Employer-employee, wife–widow, citizen–migrant. Nita still has the chipped sparkly green polish on her nails from a beauty salon game Saba played with her last week while Rouhi's is a French manicure. This is the last thing she should be doing. She is already in fragile territory, a misunderstood stranger in a country where she barely knows the language.

On the other side of the argument—how like butter Rouhi's skin is. Soft and softer, pressed against Nita's scratchy-elbowed self.

Rouhi reaches behind Nita and fumbles at her hair. The bun comes loose and her hair falls to her shoulders in curls. 'Yes,' Rouhi says, brushing the strands off of Nita's face, 'I saw you in dream. I didn't know it was you because your hair has been up till now.'

Another Rouhi tale, like something out a hokey romantic novel. This one isn't true either—Nita has sometimes worn her hair open around her shoulders. Perhaps Rouhi mythologizes as a precursor. To do the unthinkable, she must first make it a familiar story.

They kiss till the sun lightens the curtains, also lighting up
the unvacuumed dust on the floor. Nita gets up in between to go
to the bedroom door and lock it, and returns to the bed, pausing
only for a minute to look down at Rouhi's undressed body.
Purple, yellow and green bruises bloom like flowers floating
below the surface of her skin. It is worst across the stomach,
upper thighs and below her shoulders, places chosen for where
the flesh was tender and where others won't see. It suggests a
certain premeditation from Haroun, where he calculated for
both maximum damage and secrecy.

'Don't look,' Rouhi says. She pulls Nita into bed so that they
can lie there entwined. There is a hunger in Rouhi which Nita
finds herself responding to. Their hands and mouths hunt each
other's bodies for release, they tire themselves out.

Nita is at first embarrassed by all that Rouhi seems to
know. Her confidence that Nita wants her. Rouhi knew about
Nita's desires before she herself did. She had called her into the
bedroom that day to watch her apply her make-up because she
knew. The only one surprised is Nita herself.

Soon—too soon—Saba is knocking on the door, demanding
breakfast.

'Coming,' Nita calls to Saba, still looking at Saba's mother.

Nita dresses and takes a deep breath before she unlocks the
door. The afreet is freshest in the mornings, rising out of her
slumber with freshly sharp teeth.

She goes downstairs with her, gives her a heaped tablespoon
of Nido milk powder to eat while she prepares her breakfast. Over
time, Nita has begun to indulge Saba's food requests a lot more.
In the first months here, she'd seen her as a lucky, extremely
privileged kid. Someone who has things that Nita would struggle
to give Ani in even the nicest version of their future.

But increasingly, she feels sympathy. Saba is growing up with her gaze trapped inside concrete, a child who's never seen an owl up close, who has only known cartoon dragonflies and not the real thing with their vibrating tails and who has never felt mossy steps underfoot (best in the morning after rain when it is soft-spiky and only a little damp). Much of her life is this wall-to-wall, allergy-enabling carpet. Nita wonders sometimes if this will soon be everyone's life. Where they burn everything down and show you only the pretty pictures.

The milk powder is not meant to be eaten dry and things get messy fast, Saba's chin and face smear as she tries to lodge the entire spoon in her mouth. Meanwhile, Nita adds raisins, apple slices, apricot jam and salt crackers to Saba's oatmeal. She finishes it in a few short bites.

Watching her eat, the excitement of what happened this morning dissipates and is replaced with a heavy guilt. She wants to push the rewind button, turn things back as easily as one would with a VCR—the hands under clothes, the kisses. The sliding into Rouhi's bed. Entering her bedroom. Turning the doorknob.

She had chances to stop, pause. But that needs a different kind of person.

Not me, Nita thinks.

9

A story now punctuated with kissing.

Rouhi and Nita walk together with Darius down an ancient stone laid street. It is beautiful, this particular place in the before. The river is out of sight but audible—its murmur fills the air on this windy morning.

Parts of Muziris look transitory, especially the places where the visiting seafarers and merchants live. These have barn-like structures of three brick walls with the front open, the roofs straw, mud or terracotta, barely able to withstand one season of rain. But the main Muziris market has multi-storied buildings and wide, sturdy warehouses. It has its own temple with a stone idol of a goddess, where visiting merchants and travellers of all faiths leave mementos like good-luck rocks, Roman healing bones and small carvings that are offerings as well as requests to the goddess for help—the earring of a lost beloved by someone hoping for their return, the sculpture of a foot made by someone with an injury.

The market is mostly local, but there are some Romans and Phoenicians who have made permanent shops here, trading the bead necklaces, china and amphorae that the ships bring in.

Women and men move around them, harbouring thoughts and fancies that will dissolve like smoke by the day's end. The places they walk in barely survive much longer. History is full of this ephemerality. Very quickly—in less than 200 years—this place, like many others before and after, will disappear as if it has never been.

And with it will disappear, for a long while, women walking unveiled and decorated, their bodies eloquent and unsilenced, flirting and chattering with the men. This rare scene comes and goes quickly.

Freedom for women signals times of peace, when they don't need to be hidden and protected from strange men and marauding armies. Around Muziris, battles are far fewer, thanks to the wealth arriving by sea. Everyone has more than they are used to and for a while, they are content.

But peace and chaos are siblings, they walk hand in hand—after the first arrives, the second soon follows. Eventually, the ships thin out as the Roman Empire falls. The coins stop coming, and a warlord who calls himself king and fashions himself as a god is killed by another one who claims the same. As the fighting surges, Muziris sinks back into the mud, amid escalation, deaths, a terrible flood.

Beads from broken necklaces float in the backwaters for centuries, scooped up by children and adults a thousand years later when they go swimming over these buried cities.

Right now, however, people's eyes are shining with the promise of it all, their cheeks ruddy with health, their stalls full of items so coveted that people on the other side of the ocean have gone into debt to buy them.

Around Darius, the women strut while the men in the stalls offer compliments and commentary. These fellows do lay it on thick. Every woman it seems, has skin like honey, eyes like blue lilies and legs like smooth vines. Come marry me, they say to the women, and I'll give you a house for each of our children.

The women flirt back with insults, telling them that their beards are ratty enough for a bird to nest in, that their eyes are like the neighbourhood crows', round with their lechery, and that they would need to find money to buy onions first before they can buy any houses.

Darius walks, lost in the wave of Tamil, Chinese and Greek chatter around him, picking up snatches of Latin here and there. Someone is negotiating the exchange of a misshapen, unglazed clay bowl with a polyglot shopkeeper, for a basket of mangoes. A mango is something Darius tasted for the first time yesterday—a fruit with a golden inner whose green skin smelled of the forest and didn't foretell its taste, so that his first reaction was utter surprise and he almost dropped the fruit. He held it close to him after that like a prize he'd won and ate all of it, including the bitter-green skin. The seed at the centre was like a smooth tongue you could suck on for a while.

After the brown stink of Berenike and the grey of the sea, to be here in the middle of this strange green valley feels like he's been dropped into paradise, naked and trembling. He has the tourist's gaze that softens even the terrible details—the wounded, legless soldiers who sit together under the large banyan, drunk much too early in the day, are gallant heroes; the cheap cottons in the stalls are glamorous as silk, everyone's hearts are purer, their motives more romantic, their families happier than those he's left behind—he feels this to be true even though he knows better.

The pepper bales are moving fast—they can barely keep up with the coracle boats arriving riverside. He has been assigned the task along with Ebo of inspecting each bale they buy, its weight, health, whether it has been fattened up with useless stems and leaves. In the process, he has learned something about his own skill to spot the liars—he is very bad at it. The men and women who to him seem the most sincere, likeable and twinkly-eyed have something wrong with their cargo.

The pepper farmers talk to them in a broken patois of Latin-Aramaic-Min Chinese, phrases picked up from multiple seasons of selling to ships, a strung together tongue that is completely nonsensical to Darius. Ebo understands some of it, and critically, knows the numbers. But whenever a negotiation or conversation goes beyond the rudimentary, both of them are lost.

Many angry conversations are happening today around the rejected bales. After several of these, a young girl, dark-eyed, her hair in three thick, intertwined braids laced through with colourful cotton threads, arrives with an elderly one-eyed man Darius assumes is her father. Their small coracle is heavy with pepper. When Ebo examines their cargo, however, he shakes his head. 'It's too green again,' he says, checking the stalks, 'Babu will kill us if we accept these.'

The girl and her father shake their heads while they shake theirs—a mutual refusal. The girl speaks to them in rapid Tamil while they look at her in confusion. She becomes loud as the dad turns morose.

Ebo shrugs his shoulders and wrings his hands like a grandmother, regretful but stubborn. The girl says something to her father and stalks off as Darius and Ebo move on to another boat, but halfway through sorting these she reappears, with Faro of all people, at her side.

'Ah, the newbie sailor,' Faro says. He isn't smoking but smells heavily of the fragrant herb Darius had seen him rolling that day. A man constantly between puffs.

'Hello,' Darius says, 'Are you meant to translate her tantrum for us? I don't think it will do much good.'

'I thought she was going to punch me in the face,' Ebo agrees. 'But we can't take her cargo. The pepper is bright green. She plucked it too early in the season.'

The girl is looking exasperatedly at Darius and Ebo. Faro shows them his black teeth in what is supposed to pass for a smile. 'She was telling me in great detail that the two of you are very stupid, and have already rejected many bales of good pepper from previous boats, which they have sold downstream to others.'

'Well, she is welcome to—'

'Hold on,' Faro interrupts Ebo and bends over the bales in question. He straightens after a few moments and looks at them a little critically. 'How long has it been since you or your captain have been here?' he asks.

'Five summers,' Ebo says, 'not long.'

'The pepper farmers have been experimenting with cross-breeding since the piercing weevils attacked their crop,' Faro explains. 'This one here is a hardier variety, and the buds are bigger too. Look.' He breaks a stem from the girl's bale and crushes it in his hand. The smell of pepper fills the air. 'Can you smell it? It's a fairly simple test. These are ripe and good.'

'Even raw pepper can smell pretty heavy,' Ebo is defensive.

'Yes yes, but the seed would not be this tough when unripe, no? You are going by colour when you should be going by the smell and feel of the seeds.'

Faro nods towards the sacks filled with the pepper they have already bartered with coins and amphorae. 'You've been buying the older variety. The red and green ones are good this year, I'm pretty certain. Those on the other hand? You will have to go over the load to see how much of the crop has been hollowed out from the inside. The weevils are stealth thieves, they eat the berry inside out. A good bit of that will be tasteless dust.'

Ebo returns to the girl's haul and goes over to what they had already bought. After a while, he sighs and stands up. 'If you are right, we may be fucked,' he admits, 'We have already spent a fifth of our money.'

'Well, it's good this young lady found me, then,' Faro smiles. 'At this point, you have to choose your victim: you or your customers back home.' He says something to the girl. Both of them burst out laughing.

Darius' cheeks are hot. 'So we are the dumb sailors,' he tells Ebo.

'Could be worse,' Ebo shrugs, and he goes back to the girl and counts out the coins for payment. Darius knows by now that Ebo's cheeriness is an unreliable signal and possibly a nervous tic that intensifies in the face of bad news. The ship is insured, but it has big loans and bigger hopes riding on it. Every coin wasted is a little less profit for the crew. He eyes the bales they've bought over the past couple of days. Altogether, he calculates, they have over a hundred, easily a quarter of the ship's hold.

Ebo hands Faro some coins as well, and then tops the girl's money off with a few more coins in apology for the earlier argument, to Darius' irritation. With his charm, Ebo would probably do a lot better at selling than buying, he thinks. As a customer, he is a complete pushover.

'Listen,' Darius says, 'we need an expert opinion, not just some old Egyptian fellow telling us what is going this season.'

'I would agree.' Ebo ponders for a moment. 'There are some local Roman and Egyptian merchants in the market. It's hard to miss their scraggly black eyebrows and the whiff of fish oil.' They walk back to the market street, which is quiet in the early afternoon. Darius notices the increased attention from the crowd when he walks with Ebo. Ebo is a farmer's boy like him, but he was discovered early and offered better work from the start—rather than toiling like a donkey, he was sent by merchants to charm housewives into buying bead necklaces or persuade men into purchasing loans and shares in merchant ships. The work he did got better every year, so Ebo was able to save a good amount of money and even provide for the couple of children he fathered from willing women—women who were not his wives but not whores either.

At least now, Darius thinks, they are both in the same place. So maybe brains count for *something*.

At a spice stall manned by a gnarly Roman, Darius and Ebo put the stalks and seeds on a rough-hewn table. The two varieties, the dark red and the new purple. The man runs short, thick fingers over the seeds. He looks at them with one eyebrow raised. 'Where have you landed from?'

'Berenike,' Ebo says, 'There are five of us.'

'Big loans, I suppose, to sail all this way?' the man asks.

'Well, it's a big ship, and there are around fifteen wealthy men backing it. Including a tribune.'

'Ah. And they hired bright boys like the two of you, huh? Bright boys who couldn't find out what they should be buying before getting over here.'

Darius protests. 'No, that's not—'

'Too distracted by the local ladies' curves and their jasmine scent? Too busy checking out the local malt?'

Darius is about to shoot an insult right back at him, but Ebo shrugs and says with more friendliness than the man deserves, 'I made a mistake. I thought things were the same as five summers ago.'

'Well, things have changed, my young fellows, the future has arrived. The new seeds are what everyone is buying and you may have to pay extra for it.'

He fingers the fragile, old seeds. 'Look, you will be able to sell the old stuff; it's not a total loss. In a few years, the demand will completely fall off but for now from what I hear, there are still customers for this back home. Pepper is pepper.'

'But what about the ones with weevil bores?' Darius asks. He picks up a few old seeds at random, tries to break them between his fingers. The first two are good pepper. The third turns to dust.

'Yes, it's a problem, but your buyers are used to some shit in the mix,' the man says. 'Some of the farmers will have sold you a worse batch than the others, so check the seeds you've got in your sacks. Ditch the worst, keep the rest. Douse the sacks in camphor oil, so that the insects still in there die. You will be fine.'

Darius listens, wiping his forehead. The afternoon heat is intense.

Ebo is losing interest in the discussion. 'Look, he says it's fine,' he tells Darius, 'When we bought these last time, we got a good price.'

'Well, the weevils weren't this bad then,' the merchant says. 'This is what happens when everyone grows pepper, you know? It's good money, but the usual wild plants disappear and the insects and birds starve, and come after your crop.'

Darius tries hard not to look too dejected. If Babu finds the ruined bales, it would come out of his and Ebo's share. He can't afford to make mistakes, and here he is, piling them up. His stomach roils, and he feels like he might throw up the delicious fermented rice and meat soup he'd eaten for lunch.

The merchant is telling Ebo about a dance happening on the beach near midnight. No wait—*dances*, multiple. 'You are idiots if you are going straight to your beds after visiting the whorehouses,' he tells Ebo. 'Come by and see the women; the real women of our Muziris, those night flowers.' He says *our* like he belongs here too. 'Else the songs you miss will haunt your dreams.'

So even this man, who bites words off at the ends with his teeth, is susceptible to Ebo's charm, already inviting him to the local events.

Ebo leans against the beam, with arms across his chest, his biceps gleaming, his legs crossed at the ankles. He is not vain but ought to be. However he stands, it looks like a pose.

'What is this?' Ebo says, 'Not five minutes ago you were telling us that we had our eyes coming unstuck due to some full-bottomed ladies.'

Darius would have joined in on the ribbing, but his pidgin Latin gets in the way, and it doesn't help that Romans look at Egyptians and think 'barbarian', even though theirs is the richer province.

'What do you say, Darius?' Ebo looks over at him, inviting him along, just as Darius is working himself up to resentment. 'Shall we go charm the ladies this evening?'

'Sure,' Darius nods, 'if Babu is ok with it.'

'Don't miss the one-eyed lady with her fried fish stall,' the merchant calls out as they walk away.

'Bet that lady is his girlfriend and overcharges every visiting sailor,' Ebo whispers.

'Let's not tell Babu about the bad batches right away,' Ebo adds as they head back to the river, 'else he will put us under warehouse watch for the rest of the trip. Let's wait till the week before we sail.'

Darius agrees. He doesn't have the stomach for that conversation either. He hates the possibility of disappointing Babu, and also hates that he sees his father in every middle-aged man with wrinkles.

Their warehouse sits close to the beach, and under its high roof, the thundering sound of the sea is even louder, as if the ocean is at the door. On the way here, the captain mentioned that much of the port had been flooded decades ago. The people had to start over from bare sand, building further from the shore. Everything they see now is relatively new. It doesn't feel that way, though—the warehouse beams are rotting and already falling apart as the sea nibbles at the edges of everything.

Darius washes himself sparingly with the pot of fresh water they have brought in from the river, his first bath since getting off the ship. The people here bathe every day, Ebo had said wonderingly, another sign that despite what the captain claimed, all people weren't the same.

There is nothing much that needs guarding—the nephew is sleeping on the bales and Babu has disappeared with the coins, taking Madu along with him. They'd been uninterested in where Darius and Ebo were headed, which suits them fine.

They walk to the beach in the moonlight, the path lit by occasional temple-sponsored lamps and stalls still serving food. Darius manages to get a coconut shell full of spicy meat from a lady who has both her eyes.

The meat here has a different texture from the camel and goat you get back home. It has been marinated and has a deep, smoky flavour beneath the pepper. After the first burn and heat, Darius enjoys it enormously; Ebo is more tentative. 'Nothing beats the Flower of Garum for taste,' he insists.

Flower of Garum, the brand of fish sauce made from mackerel entrails, is the most sought-after sauce in Roman markets, and amphorae of it with its signature label sell out quickly everywhere in Rome. It has even made its way across the Mediterranean.

'I hate that stuff,' Darius says, 'It tastes like a fly died inside the bottle.'

Ebo looks at him like he has grown another nose. 'You prefer this over garum?'

'I would happily roll around in this if I could.'

'Ugh. Here, you can have the rest,' Ebo hands him his shell.

'Mmmfff.' Darius makes a closed-mouth sound of gratitude as he eats.

A crowd is gathering. It is a full moon night, the light turns the sand silver. Ahead of them are shouts, laughter, the beat of drums.

The dancers are already on the beach, ten women with painted faces moving sinuously as drummers circle them. They do a slow wriggle down to their knees, dipping their bottoms nearly to the sand, before rising back again with impressive control. Their arms rise to the top of their heads as they move up and down in a snake dance. The crowds hoot appreciatively and clap along, some offering weak imitations of the moves, and everyone is sweating buckets. Even at night the humidity is intense and makes the beach feel more crowded than it is.

Behind them all is the pounding of the sea, their source of wealth and suffering. And they embrace it like one would a mad family member, accepting both its gifts and its great punishments. The women's faces are deliberately grotesque—their lips and chins look like they've been dipped in blood, the eyes are outlined heavily in black. Their gazes move side to side to highlight the whites of their eyes. The sound of the drums is answered by a thrum inside Darius, a response that starts low in his stomach. He sees it mirrored in the faces of the crowd, all of them reacting as one.

And then all at once, it is over. No one cheers and claps—the crowd just waits for the next thing as if the intense spell of the last several minutes never happened. Some of them break off towards the stalls.

Ebo disappears and comes back with two tender coconuts, which they have all developed an addiction to. 'We will go get something stronger in a little while,' he promises.

Up next is a comedy troupe, in a performance full of local allusions that he can't understand. The crowd laughs obediently but there are signs that the act is not the best and the audience is waiting them out. The entry of a man wearing a tiger mask and a fake beheading with a stick get a smattering of cheers. Still, the beetle-browed jokester at the centre of it seems put out at the crowd's response. As they leave, he pulls off his lungi and moons them, shaking a surprisingly full, round ass. The crowd barely reacts. Public nudity surprises no one here—plenty of men wander around in just loincloths.

The crowd is moving now, single-intentioned, to a different spot on the beach. Darius and Ebo follow. They congregate around a boat, apparently the site for another performance. In the open air, the stage doesn't need to be in one place. He can sense anticipation building, a murmuring among his fellow viewers, particularly the men. Conversations in Tamil rise and fall around them, and Darius wishes once again he could understand enough to eavesdrop. They could be plotting the king's downfall or discussing what they had for lunch, he would never know, as clueless as the child he spots dozing on her father's lap, her tiny fingers in her mouth for comfort. Another similarity, he thinks, among all these differences. Do small children suck their fingers everywhere?

The crowd tenses and Darius looks up to see two women standing next to the boat, on either end. They are mirroring each other, one's face painted entirely black, the other's bare, with lips painted red. Woman and shadow, Darius guesses, the meaning of their singing lost on him. No, wait—maybe it is two lovers, as the black-painted one is dressed as a man. They approach each other. Their singing grows louder as their arms intertwine, their faces draw close. The drums thunder. The dance is now sinuous, suggesting, he guesses, the act of sex. Ebo sits down next to him. After a while, he exclaims, 'Hey, I can understand some of this!'

'Really? What are they singing?'

'Well, I can understand one line,' Ebo admits. He nods at the pretty girl with the painted lips. 'She is saying "The dawn is a sword" over and over. That's all I am getting.'

The two women dance libidinously—that style seems to be big here on the beach—moving in unison, close but never really touching. It's a dance like a taut string. Then the red-lipped girl climbs on the edge of the boat, facing them, as the other one climbs up the other side, her back to the crowd. They sway back and forth on the boat's edge, and then to his astonishment, the girl sways forward, like she is falling into the audience, sways back, and then again so far forward that the people seated in the front reach their hands out to grab her. She then raises one leg and sways forward again, as the audience gasps. She sings the whole while as if all of this didn't require incredible, acrobatic control.

When it ends, the audience cheers, including him.

The crowd disperses quickly after that towards the toddy and food stalls. Darius finds himself lingering, drawn to the girl. She is a local and no celebrity. No one is waiting around to meet her– her shadow has already left. She picks up the things she had kept to the side before her performance–a bead bracelet, a scarf wound into a kind of purse.

She smiles up at him as he comes closer. 'You are Egyptian? Come here for pepper?' she says in Fayyumic.

So he is a stereotype. 'Yes. You speak my language well.'

She shrugs. 'There are many of you staying here. Some have become our friends.'

'You lifted the crowd off the sand with that performance,' he offers.

She smiles. 'It's just a small dance I put up every full moon. Most have seen it before but there are always a few new ones in the audience.'

Eye contact with her has left Darius at a loss for words. He has just recognized her–she's the girl he'd seen walk past him on his first day here, the one whose gaze had been a punch in the chest. He is sure of it, even though he'd only seen her for a moment.

'You are gawking like a fish right now,' she straightens up, dusts the sand off her. 'Have you been to the river yet?'

He nods. 'We spent the day there buying up pepper cargo.'

'That's where the boats dock. Go down the bank, and you will find the spots where the washermen work, which are quieter. My sister and I used to go there all the time because she wanted to wade into the shallow end and pick out the stones that had been smoothed by the river water.'

'How bad is the current there?'

'You feel the tug but you get used to it. My sister would tell me it's like a grandmother's hug, tight but not dangerous. She claimed it's how the river showed us her love. It was only when I got older that I saw a man swept away when he was swimming in the same places we used to wade in. But by then, I'd learned a lot of dangerous things. What was I telling you about?'

'The stones your sister would pick from the river.'

'Right. My sister would pick out the smoothest, roundest stones—she was obsessed. The yard outside our house, where we grew gourds and spices, was covered with them. They all looked more or less the same, but every once in a while, she'd get a blue one, or something like the green crystals that come out of the mines, which the king wears around his neck. Pretty things are common. She was going for the unusual. And you have an unusual face even for a traveller.'

He blushes. He is glad for his dark skin and the night around them. 'No one has ever said that to me before.'

'Well, here I am telling you.'

'People from my village rarely went to the Roman ports. I may be the first of us on a ship.' He found it hard to meet her direct gaze. 'You are unusual to me too. A woman, talking to a stranger so easily.'

'We are less uptight than your people. And me more than most.' He notices how the moonlight glides over her shoulders. She's slender but ropy with muscle. 'Don't be fooled though,' she adds, 'it's not like we women don't have rules here. Wherever cattle are roped and horses are bridled, women are ruled. They won't have it any other way.'

She is more beautiful, he thinks, when she talks, her face full of fleeting expressions that are never there long enough for him to read them. She watches him as if testing him as she speaks.

'Are you hungry?' she asks.

He realizes he's famished. He hasn't eaten much besides the pepper goat. 'I'm starving. I heard there was a stall with a one-eyed woman selling fried fish.'

'All the stalls are closed now; it is far too late. But come with me.'

They walk down the now familiar market streets, the thinning crowds still exuberant and talkative, high from the food, dancing and toddy, and every once in a while, the girl with him—who has still not told him her name—draws a greeting or glance. Her hair is damp with the exertion of the performance, her skin gleams. He watches her sidelong, trying to figure out if she is indeed the girl he'd seen on the first day. He'd been so certain then that he'd never forget that face. In the interrupting shadows, as the moon dodges behind palm trees and clouds, her profile forms and reforms again.

They turn down into a side street and the atmosphere shifts—it's quiet and hushed, the crowd left behind. They are on a residential lane, the homes better than the ones he had seen during his first wander, built out of stone and dark wood. The top of the houses are tiled in well-cut terracotta. Some of the buildings have two floors, an extravagance of space, he thinks, for one family.

'You haven't seen the royal lanes yet,' she says as he stares, 'The temples here will make you fall to your knees, even if you don't worship our gods.'

He bites his lip, not wanting to brag about the sights back home.

They reach a house set a little back from the street and wind their way through a large garden whose trees are thick with jasmine vines. The windows and doors of the house are thrown open, but visitors announce themselves by the clatter of pebbles down the path as they walk. A face appears at the door as they approach. The girl calls out, waves. The lady at the door is slender in the bony way some women get in middle age and has a big hibiscus flower tucked behind her ear. 'She wears a new flower every morning,' the girl tells Darius as they draw close. 'Or it could be the same one that closes every night and blooms again the next day.'

He hangs back as they fall into each other's arms. 'Maderi,' the woman says affectionately as she hugs the girl, 'I haven't seen you for days!' The look the woman gives Darius is jumbled up, like the coins from different places mixed together in the money sacks of Muziris' shopkeepers—there's curiosity, suspicion, wariness. A teenager appears, possibly the daughter of the lady, and there is more chatter and hugs, and they hand Maderi two packets of palm leaves, nodding towards Darius and waggling their eyebrows.

Maderi rolls her eyes and says to him over their giggles, 'Come, say thank you. They have given me an extra home-made meal for you.'

He approaches, tentative, racking his brain for the greetings the pepper farmers and Ebo exchanged. 'I appreciate your cat,' he says in Tamil, 'I will now leave again.'

The three women laugh, and Maderi says something to them that has them still giggling as they go back up the street.

'What did you tell them?' he asks.

'I said that it's not as if sailors are chosen for their smarts.' She smiles at his stricken face. 'Don't worry. We are used to stupid men, and find them adorable.'

'You don't have family any longer in this town?'

'That's an accurate guess,' Maderi laughs. 'No, my home is elsewhere. My grandmother, who we used to visit here, died years ago. When we got older, my father brought me and my sister here to offer us to the temple. He is—or should I say was? I don't know if he is alive—a cloth merchant. My sister left the temple when a man offered her marriage. I work in the temple as a dancer, but since last summer, not as much as I used to. The new priests are difficult. I live there, but I spend the day wandering around town trying to understand what to do next.'

'Have you figured it out?'

'Besides the options of being a dancer, wife or mother? That is pretty much all I am allowed to do, really. I could join a whorehouse or cook in some rich family's kitchen. But I would much prefer being a sailor or a merchant, and I thought once that if I crossed the sea, I would be able to do that. But from what I have heard, I can't. In fact, it may get worse.'

'Yes. You're right.'

She sighs. 'All my dreams of battles and seafaring, I will never have any of it. I can only dance and sing of love.'

They have circled back to a different, wilder side of the beach. There are no boats in sight. The sea is impossible to see this late at night, it is all sound. They sit on the sand and open up the food, which is a strange experiential delight, a feast of gourd cooked in buttermilk and mixed with red rice. They eat mainly by touch since the only light is a sputtering fire lamp some distance behind them near the path. For a while, it is impossible to talk—his focus is the taste of rice soaked in the sweet and sour gravy, unfamiliar vegetables, fried fish whose flesh he has to feel off the bone, and too soon, it is done.

They eat to the sound of the sea's endless rant, a roar that started before them and will continue after.

She seems content to sit in silence as the heavy breeze winds its way through their hair. Here on the dark beach, she is letting her tiredness show. She digs her toes into the sand, leans her head against her arms. She looks like she is resisting sleep, like someone who doesn't want to go home.

He can't hold back any longer, 'What was the song you were singing on the boat? Ebo understood only one line.'

'It's a jingle about abandonment. But people think it's about love.'

'Can you translate it for me?'

'I can, but I won't be able to sing it.'

'That's all right.'

So she recites her doggerel for him, without intonation.

It's morning, and sadness rises in the east
You stir, and I want to rock you back to sleep.
Outside, the sounds and smell of morning life:
Buttermilk, jasmine, someone frying a pancake in hot ghee.
My leg cramps. I don't straighten it even as pain rises up my thigh
The pain of you waking up is worse.
The dawn is a sword. It tears us apart, but I am the only one bleeding.
I want us to kiss with the sun watching. But you hate witnesses.

The dawn is a knife. It tears us apart, but I am the only one bleeding.
The pain of you waking up is worse.
My leg cramps. I don't straighten it even as pain rises up my thigh.
Buttermilk, jasmine, someone frying a pancake in hot ghee outside:
The sounds and smell of morning life.

You stir, I want to rock you back to sleep
But it's morning, and sadness rises in the east.

It sounds like a song written with a particular man in mind. She'd said that it was not a love song, and yet Darius finds himself seduced by her voice and the words and the high salty breeze coming off the sea.

Nita and Rouhi watch him fall in love here in the dark, with a woman he cannot see clearly. Perhaps he mistakes her easy friendliness for affection. It is a common mistake among men.

He falls, perhaps presaging another fall—where his well-planned life, that he was clear on just days ago—comes apart. Kingdoms, cities, people can accumulate mistakes and survive. But then one additional error, seemingly tiny, topples everything—the wrongest wrong, in a way.

10

The Wrongest Wrong

For Nita, small regrets about her life crowd in with the big ones—tearing up her sister's school notebook after an argument. Losing her mother's bangle, which slid off her wrist while swimming in a lake. Leaving her son behind. That's a big one. And Rouhi. Is Rouhi a regret?

For the new lovers, stealth is hard enough with the four-eyed watcher in the kitchen. And then there is Saba who, like most children, notices disruptions in her routines at once. They have to be careful to not change anything, or act different.

This is difficult because infatuation is a quickening, one that drives them towards each other with a sense of urgency. Nita has to ignore this and sit across the room from her employer as she always has, and accompany Saba after afternoon snacks to do her English homework, leaving Rouhi at the dining table.

Rouhi spends this time reading her magazines, and listens to the women in the kitchen talk to each other in their usual circular way. 'He called me and said that I owed him a thousand dirhams—that's a lot of money, isn't it—yes, a month's salary right—not an amount you want to part with—absolutely, that's what I told him, I said why, that's ridiculous it's a month's salary—he said that my eldest had stolen his motorbike from his backyard—Mahmoud stealing a bike, impossible—yes, that is what I said, impossible, he said Mahmoud hot-wired his bike and rode off with it—that's a tall story, isn't it—exactly, that's what I said, a horrible lie I said—he said he saw Mahmoud from his window and ran out, I said you must be mistaken—of course he is mistaken—and he said Mahmoud is thin and nearly bald and has a mole on his left cheek, and I said now I know you're lying, my Mahmoud he has a mole on his right cheek, this is someone else—A disgusting lie, of course, it is someone else—'

—Until Rouhi thinks she will go mad if she doesn't get as far as she can from the two of them. Rouhi tells Nita this, and then confesses she is scared to be around them now. Afraid to be around Haroun's cousins, in his house and in love with someone else. Afraid to be longing for Nita in rooms that he owns, so it feels like his eyes are on her by proxy, every moment.

And yet. 'You are music after long silence,' Rouhi tells her. Nita has come to Rouhi after fifteen years of dread and pain.

Night comes, blindfolding everyone else. They whisper the other's name, run hands over skin. The bed is an unexplored country with Rouhi in it. The two of them could be anywhere—a bed of petals under a tree, a carpet out in the bare desert, a rope bridge high up, strung between mountains. It wouldn't matter, it would all feel like Rouhi, this woman of the shapely thighs and silver stripes across her stomach.

Rouhi's kisses lull Nita into calm. She can sense her wariness fall away. The way Rouhi makes her feel convinces her of the rightness of being here. The body's truths are hard to deny. The laws made by men are fragile deterrents against the much older laws of feeling—love, rage, jealousy, vengeance.

But several nights in, her body is also telling her something else. Anxiety slithers up her spine—there is danger coming. The dread in the pit of her stomach is like the ghost of future pain, a warning from a time not yet here.

But then Rouhi will turn towards her with her hair falling across her face, call her *habibti* and pull her into her arms. And she forgets again.

Nita doesn't get much sleep in Rouhi's room. When they are not making love, Rouhi wants to talk, swap stories. Rouhi tells stories about her lost family as a way to bring them back, raise the ghosts.

Rouhi's grandmother's house, she says, had a set of gold and green crystal goblets in the dining room cabinet. There were just three remaining from the original set of eight by the time Rouhi was grown up.

Rouhi's grandparents had six daughters, in the family's futile attempts to have a son, and Rouhi's mom was the youngest. One afternoon, the father, while drinking rose sherbet out of one of the goblets, looked out of the window where his daughters played and grew glum. Upset about the lack of a male heir, about how each daughter was turning out more expensive than the last, refusing to wear hand-me-downs, driving him broke, he made an announcement to his wife—each time a crystal goblet broke, he would marry a daughter off, no matter how young she was.

'What if the glasses never break?' his wife asked him. 'With these girls around?' her husband answered, gesturing to his shrieking, laughing daughters outside, 'their screams are enough to break them.'

Sure enough, the first of the glasses broke only a few months later, on one sunny afternoon when Rouhi's grandmother was cleaning the counters. Somehow, the goblet got knocked down, rolling over the edge as she grabbed after it. The oldest daughter was just sixteen, but their father was unpersuadable. A promise made was a promise kept, he said, he was a man of his word. The terrified girl was married off to a wealthy shopkeeper that their father knew, who lived close by in the next village. 'She's practically next door. You can see her anytime,' he told his wife and weeping daughters.

The next goblet broke just six months later. Rouhi's grandmother had placed the set in a locked cupboard, hoping that this would keep them intact, but one day the father insisted on them being taken out. It fell and broke when one of them rose out of a chair and bumped the table.

Their father ate lunch, and watched his wife and daughters pick up the pieces from the floor. We can glue it back together, they said.

He listened as they made their case. The mother pleaded as the girls sobbed. After a few minutes, he couldn't hold back any longer and started to laugh. 'I was only joking,' he said, spreading his hands. It had been about time to marry off the oldest, he said, and the breaking of the glass was just good timing, it allowed him to extend the joke.

The women were furious. Their father sat at the table in his usual home wear—loose, rumpled shirt, boxers with failing elastic, his fingers full of food. Rouhi's mother told her that she was struck even as a little girl by how undignified and ridiculous her father was allowed to be while retaining so much power over them. Their mother was always impeccably dressed—wearing kohl even in the house, while the family bully ate lunch in his underpants.

'We control nothing,' Rouhi's grandmother told her daughters and later to Rouhi. 'Whatever you need, you will have to steal it.'

'I never steal anything, until now,' Rouhi tells Nita, fingers tracing the curve of Nita's cheek, 'Maybe that's where I make mistake.'

Rouhi's own father was less troll-like. But it was her younger brother Femi who was the beloved one, more favoured than her. Her father was affectionate—generous with bear hugs and long stories, and praised Rouhi at every turn, so she didn't notice for a while.

One summer though, the news on the local radio was full of a lurid mass murder, where someone had poisoned the soft drinks in a school canteen with cyanide. Eight glasses of orange juice were spiked among the thirty-two served, big enough doses that killed all the children who drank them within the hour. After it happened, parents pulled their kids out of schools, school canteens across towns shut down, stores saw their ice cream and juice sales collapse.

Cyanide is tasteless, odourless, impossible to detect until an autopsy. It was also a poison with deep local roots in Egypt, once made by crushing apricot pits, and famous for having felled kings, elderly parents refusing to part with inheritances, unwanted spouses, recalcitrant business partners. Newspaper reports contained lurid descriptions of what death from cyanide looked like—convulsions, a frothing at the mouth and bruising across the face, bodies contorted in death like they had been swallowed by a large creature and spat back out.

Rouhi and her brother went out with their father to the fair a few weeks after the story broke. He let them ride the Ferris wheel four times. They were walking back when Femi started whining that he was thirsty. 'We are ten minutes away from home,' their father said, but Femi began to slow down, said he wanted a juice, that he was thirsty, thirsty, dying of it, it was so hot, his feet were burning, his eyes were melting in his head. He could be stubborn, his resistance like a deeply lodged nail, and their parents always relented in the end. 'All right,' their father sighed, to Rouhi's surprise and relief, and ordered orange juice at a stall close to their house. He handed the first one to Rouhi, who took a sip and then a long gulp, before she realized that her father was watching her closely.

'Do you think it's poisoned?' Rouhi asked him, remembering the news.

'What?' her father laughed with surprise. 'Of course not. There have been no cases since.'

'Then why didn't you give this to Femi first? He was the one moaning for it anyway.'

Her father sputtered. 'What are you even saying? I would only give you something if I was sure it was safe. You are my only daughter.'

'You were sure? Or you were 99 per cent sure but not 100 per cent sure?'

He looked at her, shocked. He believed his own outrage and hurt, but Rouhi had seen that cautious look on his face as he watched her drink the juice. The look of a father who loved his son at least 1 per cent more. She held the half-full glass, not wanting the rest of it while her father bought the second to Femi. She took a few steps away from them, trying to tamp down on her rising fury. Standing there by herself, she noticed that while the inside of the stall—the mixer, the glasses and the produce—was spotless, there were ants all over the outside of it and on its roof, marching along the edges in endless lines. It must have been hell to keep clean.

Rouhi and her father had a closed-mouth argument about this for the rest of their relationship. Neither of them brought it up again but she saw that one per cent in every conversation, everything he did.

The story stumbles out of Rouhi like she's saying it to someone for the first time. It costs her to talk about it, and the gesture wins a little more of Nita's trust.

Love leaks out of the room into the rest of the house. Rouhi will glance at Nita when Saba says something funny. Her body does this automatically, like goosebumps in cold weather. On the comics page of the newspaper, which she knows Rouhi always reads, Nita draws a speech bubble next to a cartoon girl and writes, 'You are 100 per cent for me.'

Rouhi buys semolina and oranges, and makes basbousa herself because she doesn't think the two-headed woman is getting it right. It is a surprise and Nita doesn't find out about it until it's brought to the table after dinner. Rouhi claps her hands together excitedly.

Usually, Nita eats alone once her work is done and after everyone else, but this evening, Rouhi insists that she eat with her and Saba and watches with pleasure as she spoons the hot cake into her mouth.

'Mama, this is too hot,' Saba whines after taking a bite from her bowl.

'Blow on it, habibti,' Rouhi says distractedly, her eyes on Nita.

'You have to be more careful,' Nita tells her later as Rouhi strokes her hair, kisses her shoulders.

Rouhi responds by kissing her on her neck, making her shiver. 'I am careful,' she says.

'You are not. You used to mope around the house. Now you are too cheerful.'

'Ok, ok. I will look sad,' Rouhi says, 'I will cry downstairs every day if it means more kisses later.'

Some nights, Rouhi opens up her dowry chest. It's a carved wooden box that doubles up as the seat in front of her vanity table. Out come old silk and chiffon dresses, completely out of style with their shoulder pads and gold buttons, wedding jewellery, and even her old school uniform, packed in brown paper. She opens it up to show Nita a shirt and a green skirt with an impossibly small waist, before folding it back along the same creases, as if she plans to replicate the experience precisely the same way later.

'I want to show you this.' One evening, she lifts out a small box, wrapped in soft cloth as if the container itself is precious. She caresses its walnut wood before handing it over. It has no visible locks—she shows Nita how to open it by sliding two hidden slats of wood at the front sideways, the grooves like butter and loosened with age. The lid snaps open, and rather than looking into the box, Nita looks at Rouhi, whose expression is that of a little girl opening something for the first time, not of a woman looking inside for the hundredth.

The necklace she takes out is gold but soft-edged like it has been held by many hands. The hinges are delicate, the sharp edges smoothed off. It has a large locket, as big as her palm, with two birds carved in vivid blue gemwork, perched on red gemstones. At the centre is a man in blue, and above his head, a scarab. 'Look,' Rouhi says, pointing to the red stones, 'Garnet. The dark blue, lapis lazuli. To fight evil eye. The two falcons guard the king.'

The necklace was meant to be worn by the king's sisters, Rouhi says, as a protection charm for him. It was buried with the pharaoh to protect him in the afterlife.

'Wait, this is real?' Nita stares at it. 'How do you have it?' She doesn't find it particularly beautiful—it is too old-fashioned and ornate The inky blue and red-brown colours were rare then, but are common now in imitation jewellery, the colours of lapis and carnelian easily faked with paint and cheap crystal.

Still, there is an aura about the necklace that transcends its design. Age is hard to forge. Its accumulated past gives the necklace a velvety texture and an inscrutable gravity. Nita can't stop looking at it, and she couldn't even begin to guess its value.

'It's royal necklace, but we are not royal,' Rouhi agrees. 'It came to us wrong way, but it's been in family for long time. Does that make it ours?' She shrugs.

When the pharaohs were around, lapis lazuli came from the Badakshan mines in Afghanistan, and everyone around the Nile wanted some. The mines were in a place of deep gorges and ravines, and workers suffered in the unfriendly terrain to extract the stone. Stories of their pain travelled with it, perhaps making it all the more valuable. The stone came in green, turquoise and in the most prized colour, like the ones on the necklace, royal blue.

When Rouhi talks in bed, she likes to lie naked on her side, propping her head up on one arm, in a pose that evokes many different women for Nita. Titian's generous-hipped Venuses, Cranach's potbellied nymph, Goya's hairy Maja—Rouhi in a pose so many women were painted in, because it was comfortable when you were in the studio for hours, and also for how it arched up the hips, coaxing an hourglass shape out of the body.

Rouhi herself is a fusion of the mother and the naked Venus, female identities that male painters preferred to keep separate but are a vision when brought together. Her hips are generous, rising out of the covers, the silver diagonal of her stretch marks just visible over the edge of the blanket. Her cheeks are flushed, her tousled hair falls past her shoulders.

According to Rouhi, three identical necklaces were carved for each of the king's sisters. The stones were sent to Mesopotamia, where the best artisans worked. The transport ferries were guarded by swordsmen with three proxy boats in case the flotilla got ambushed. But while returning, the transport was attacked, and the haul included one of the necklaces. Piracy was everywhere then—enterprising, opportunist gangs in junks and bigger vessels waited in the blind corners of the river, relying on the element of surprise and the bravado of many clumsy but willing-to-die young men. Swords and daggers were freely traded, and armed guards for precious cargo often got outnumbered, overwhelmed. Each time a boat was successfully raided, word got around and the pirates got more recruits.

The ancestor who stole the necklace apparently had a lover in another port, Rouhi says, and he'd stolen it for her. But it never reached her—perhaps he died before he could travel there. And it has been in the family since.

The necklace looks better with the story wrapped around it. 'Did you find out who this man was?'

'I go to so many libraries. I call history departments in Cairo colleges.' Rouhi had promised her grandmother she'd find out. She looked at old texts and maps—her grandmother was correct about many details like the Badakshan mines and the date of the necklace. But she could unearth little more than that.

Rouhi picks the necklace up again. 'This wasn't supposed to be for me, but for Femi. He was to get everything. But father gave me as apology when he married me off. Now, I think this wasn't enough.'

She puts it on, and it sits incongruously on her bare chest. She gives Nita a come-hither look.

'Why did your father have to apologize?' Nita asks later. It has been a few nights and she's waited for Rouhi to offer the rest of the story. But this time she hadn't.

Maybe Rouhi left that remark dangling as a hook, waiting for Nita to come back for it. 'We became poor because Femi burn down house.'

Rouhi smiles, but underneath it is the horror of the memory. 'It was mistake—I still think it was mistake.'

A stupid mistake, a lit cigarette left on a blanket. Rouhi's brother had become woolly-headed from the medication he was taking for his rages and psychotic fits, the traits his childhood tantrums and stubbornness had mutated into as he grew older. The fire spread from his bed to the curtains, and by the time Femi came out of the bathroom, holding a second cigarette that he thought was the first, all the bedrooms were on fire. They barely got everybody out. Rouhi's mother's clothes were burning, she was screaming in a way that Rouhi still can't forget. The first floor was gone by the time the family reached the street. Gone so fast like the house couldn't wait to burn.

The morning was full of fog, Rouhi says, so they couldn't even see the end properly. But the fire left a permanent note on her mother's beautiful face, where her cheek and ear had melted off. She told Rouhi she was sleeping when the fire came, and woke up thinking something was licking her face. In the first few moments, there was no pain.

'I cry so much but Femi is silent. Maybe Mama's face was medicine that finally worked. After that, he was only sad, never angry.'

Her tone stays light as she narrates the story as if she is reciting a fairy tale, but she takes Nita's hand while talking and puts the palm against her cheek.

It strikes Nita how little she knows this woman, even as she has grown familiar with her more immediate desires and scars. 'There was no home insurance in Egypt,' Rouhi said, 'When people have little money, insurance is joke. So we live in other people's houses. With my aunts and uncles.'

Among the things the fire burned down was the family pride. Rouhi's mother sold fruit and vegetables from the surviving garden, her father borrowed money at huge interest rates and even that was not enough for him to save the business. The farm collapsed gradually at first, with losses that were persistent but small, and then all at once. It was a shock for the family because the farm had always been with them, keeping them safe. They had to live on the kindness of relatives. 'It's like dream you have of standing in street with no clothes.'

'Father had to get me married in hurry, now that he was poor,' Rouhi says, 'For my dowry, *mahr*, I got two of Mama's gold chains and this, most valuable thing in bank locker.'

She smiles, 'Probably most valuable thing in bank. No one believed my grandmother's stories but me.'

'So this is the original?'

'Yes.' She had it assessed recently when Haroun was travelling. After a complicated phone call, a gentleman from Vienna flew down to take a look at it after she sent them photos she shot with her Konica. The Viennese were discreet because they had a lot of buyers for things of mixed provenance. Not the Egyptians—they would have demanded that she return the necklace immediately if they suspected it was authentic, maybe turned it into a diplomatic issue with the UAE. The Vienna

assessor examined it and decided to stay another week, and had
another assessor fly down for a second opinion. 'He ask me, loan
it to our museum so we can give "more thorough examination",'
she says, 'But I had feeling that if I say yes, I will never see it
again, or Haroun will find out and take it.'

'You could sell it. And then leave with me.'

'That sound like bad movie.'

'Why not?' Nita is irritated at this easy dismissal. 'What's
wrong with that idea?'

'Have you looked outside, Nita? Is there place for me?'

'If there is a place for me, there is for you. There is a place
for us.'

Rouhi shakes her head. Nita senses irritation. 'Why won't
you just think about it?' she persists.

'You don't know what you say. Stupid girl. It doesn't happen
just like that.'

'But it could. My country is big enough to disappear in.
No one will find us.' Rouhi doesn't respond and Nita tries to
control her voice so that she sounds less wheedling. She thinks
of things to say and crosses them out, but after three tries, still
says the wrong thing: 'Women leave all the time, Rouhi. You are
like a prisoner sitting next to an open door.'

Rouhi looks at her as if Nita has just called her a coward.
'You are so young, Nita. You have son, but you are young and
stupid. You think this is like one of Saba's cartoons where mouse
escapes through pipe?'

Nita feels her own face grow hot. Lying naked here and it is
still words that embarrass her.

She forces herself to be calm. 'I'm sorry,' she says, unsure
about what she is sorry for. A few moments of silence, as Rouhi
looks at the ceiling, completely elsewhere. Then she draws Nita

close. They lie together in the middle of the bed. They are at their best not speaking, skin to skin, intertwined, their hair tangling together.

But even as they try to be careful, they forget themselves. How can they not? The human animal is error prone—error is our default, accuracy is rare. With an accumulation of many tiny cracks, a fracture forms in their disguise—a shared look of longing that the four-eyed woman sees, igniting suspicion; a smile lighting up the face when the other enters the room, whispers, too much laughter leaking from upstairs, footsteps overhead in the middle of the night, a question from Saba to Nita about her tutor smelling of her mother's perfume.

It adds up, adds up and the picture begins to make a shocking sense to the women downstairs. First, there is disbelief and horror. Then comes the rest.

11

Madu and the captain have returned from their week-long trip, by which time Ebo and Darius have purchased most of the pepper bales.

The captain seems unusually close-mouthed these days, which has him worried. Perhaps Madu has talked him into giving him more of Darius's cut of the profit. If he finds out about the bad pepper stock, it won't help matters.

While washing his face, Darius decides that when he gets a chance, he will talk to the captain and clear the air. In the meantime, he goes out in search of Maderi. The morning breeze is high, rustling the palm trees, a relief from the humid, back-soaking weather of the past few days. The local birds and the rude koels have been joined by several migratory species recently, and birdsong follows him wherever he goes, like he's a heroine in some folk tale.

The air smells of both ripe and rotting fruit, something he still hasn't got used to. The stalls in the market sell fresh coconut water, bananas and mangoes all day, and throw the cut fruit in a communal pile off to the side where it lies all mixed together, drawing flies and fermenting in the heat. The worst fruit salad ever in history.

Overall though, the mood is quite romantic despite the stink, and he feels unstressed and calm even though he hasn't been able to find Maderi today in the usual places. They've been together several times over the past few days, first on the beach right after they finished their night meal the day they met. It'd been a surprise to him how easily she'd reached out for him, pushing him into the sand. In the pitch dark, unable to see anything, navigating only by touch and with the sea roaring, it'd felt like they were inside the belly of a beast. The waves crept in and brushed over his toes and feet as she moved over him, and the spray of the ocean soaked his face.

After they were done and she had caught her breath, she lay back next to him and continued the conversation they'd been having, asking him about his village and Berenike. He didn't know what to make of it.

The next few times had proceeded similarly—she'd taken him to the small quarters she lived in next to the temple, whenever the girl she shared the space with was out, and he'd finally been able to see her properly. Perhaps as a direct consequence, his performance was rushed and somewhat disappointing. She had a slender, muscular body that went from a dark tan on her face and neck to golden and light brown over her torso, and then dark again. Her belly button had an unusual shape which he found incredibly erotic, with a small scar she said she'd had since she was a baby. She seemed unfazed by his wanting to probe it with his tongue, which suggested that there had been other lovers who had felt the same way.

Nothing appears to disgust her, a change from the village girls he's been with before this. Her lack of shock has the effect of emboldening him, of asking her for things that he wouldn't have otherwise, and she obliges with curiosity, sometimes even enthusiasm.

He wants to see her every spare moment, but there aren't many of those because of the day-long work of buying and packing the pepper, and taking the crop over in boats from the warehouse to the ship. Sometimes, moving the bales to the warehouse takes all evening. By the time he is done, he is often too exhausted—his shoulders and arms sore, his fingers bruised from the stems and the coir rope—to do anything more than eat something from the stalls and sleep.

Today, however, is different—most of the buying is done, and Ebo has gone into a huddle with the captain and Madu. Rather than stay on the outside of whispered conversations, Darius goes in search of Maderi.

There aren't many days left before they leave for Berenike. The wind is picking up, and if they miss this sailing window, they will have to wait for at least a couple more moons. He has considered the possibility of staying here or taking Maderi back with him. He could, of course, go home, hand his profits over to his mother and come straight back here on the next ship that would take him.

But would she wait for him? He hasn't been subtle about his feelings, and it's early days. When she appears, his face rearranges itself into a puppy-like expression completely involuntarily. He agrees to everything she suggests. He finds her endlessly fascinating. But she doesn't react to him the same way. She embraces him and holds his hand with a revealing casualness, and sometimes pats his arm in an absent-minded way while talking, like she doesn't feel the electricity that he does.

Today, she isn't there at her quarters, but her roommate is. The girl shrugs at him impatiently, irritated with his illiteracy in her language. She says something rapidly and gesticulates towards the river, neither of which helps. He wanders over to the market street, notices that it's more crowded than usual.

It feels like a party. The people around him are dressed in silks and interesting prints, and the women have their hair coiled into pretty braids with flowers pinned in. They smell of rose, jasmine, frankincense. An unusual amount of perfume this early in the day. Many of them have anklets on their feet, bangles on their arms. Both the men and the women carry their children on their shoulders, tiny beings also decorated festively, with circlets of flowers on their small heads, their eyes lined with kohl. Everyone's faces alight with excitement.

He keeps walking to where the crowd is the deepest, knowing that Maderi, if she is here, would head there instinctively. She likes being around people, being recognized, talked to and drawn in.

And yes—there she is, in the midst of everything, in a knot of girls and drummers, dancing. The drummers are using their palms and sticks to pound out a rapid rhythm that beats at both the rim and centre of the drum. The beat is fast and the dances are random and improvised. The sweat has turned Maderi's hair damp and her face shines with effort and excitement. The crowd's eyes are on the dancers—why wouldn't they be—at these men and lovely women swaying and shaking their hips, obliging the crowd with winks and blown kisses when they call out their names.

He doesn't feel jealousy, not exactly. How do you feel jealous about something that barely belongs to you? She is very much a flower of this place. No matter what she says about her alienation, of wanting to climb on a ship and join a sailing crew, it looks to him that she has flourished in this city's sunshine. People get themselves wrong all the time, their own soul a stranger. Obvious truths about themselves are often more visible to others. He would have to come back here to see her—taking her along with him on the ship would end very badly, even if she had affection for him. The realization depresses him a little.

The excitement here is infectious. He watches, claps, shouts along as more people join in.

She spots him and breaks off from the circle, disengaging herself from the embraces of the women. 'What's happening?' he asks. Her eyes widen. 'It's the day of the boat race,' she says, as if he should know this. 'It happens before the first harvest. The king will be coming by soon. Everyone is waiting here for him, and then we head to the river.'

'I see.' He is a bit surprised at all the excitement. This king here is more like a tribal lord, easily accessible to the populace. Over the last several seasons, his star has also dimmed somewhat. The success of pepper over conquest and war in making Muziris rich, has poets singing songs verging on the seditious:

The farmer's basket is the true sovereign and throws a large shade over the ringing green land. The king's parasol is a pale shadow.

Darius has seen the king from a distance a few times. He's a dark-skinned man, slight but muscular. He sometimes walks around the beach and market with several guards, wearing nothing but a loincloth and a choker of gold around his neck, his every move a necessary strut in keeping with his position. But despite the posturing, he'd seemed at ease with the merchants, sailors and priests who approached him. His subjects appeared only moderately obsequious compared to what Darius witnessed back in Berenike whenever anyone more senior than a Roman legionnaire deigned to visit.

They buy snacks. The king is late and the people grow distracted, crowding around the stalls, wandering off to the beach, and splintering into groups that squat around, eating and gossiping. Maderi stops from time to time to chatter quickly—to other young women, to couples where the men gawk while the women on their arms either glare or roll their eyes. Darius feels like a bit player in the local story, a late entrant, but is happy enough to be included.

They run into an older couple with their children. Maderi greets them like she knows them both, but it quickly becomes clear she knows the husband a lot better—he gazes at her from under caterpillar-thick black eyebrows without restraint, as if his wife and two teenage children aren't standing right beside him.

'You are a sight to behold,' he says, watching her hungrily.

'How nice of you to say that,' Maderi responds. She turns to Darius. 'Narven is a timber merchant. It's easier money than most things.'

'Money is hard to earn and easy to spend,' Narven remonstrates, as if Darius is some layabout, and waits as if Darius is about to contradict him. He looks at Maderi, 'But the money I gave your temple was very easy to give.'

His wife sighs and steps a little away from him. She is tall with white in her curls and sharp grey eyes. She watches Maderi and her husband almost anthropologically, with neither envy nor disgust. Darius feels a twinge of sympathy. She'd been married off to a womanizer, probably without much input on the decision.

The children, on the other hand, look humiliated. Their eyes don't leave the ground.

'I have been thinking about you,' Narven continues, oblivious, 'and that vine-like figure of yours.'

'*Your* figure is very much like a water pot's,' Maderi observes evenly, 'and it's gotten only more so.'

There is a bark of laughter from the wife and the colour on Narven's face deepens. He mumbles something about seeing her soon and the family decamps.

The wife turns to Maderi as they leave. 'I like your necklace,' she says.

'He would have undressed right here in front of his children, if you'd suggested it,' Darius says, watching their departing backs.

'They are not all like that, but he was one of the worst.'

'Was he—a paramour?' Darius asks.

'No, but he was an aggressive pursuer. There was a lot of gold and forever lamps gifted to the temple, along with a clearly expressed preference that I dance for him every night, and then he would push for more.'

'Your necklace *is* beautiful,' Darius says. She is wearing a large green stone around her neck on a slender thread. It has no elaborate setting but doesn't need it—it shines with its own dark amber light, like a tiger's eye.

'She didn't mean what you think she meant,' Maderi says. 'This was a gift from the king. It's his usual gift, I would say, for his favourite consorts. Most of the stones from the beryl mines up east are traded, and they have made him very wealthy. But he saves some of the best emeralds for himself and his women, and he gave me this a few summers ago.'

So Narven's wife had been acknowledging Maderi's royal connection. She looks a little downcast while telling him this, like it's a relationship she finds difficult to talk about. There are residual feelings there. It's hard to love someone whose own affections are not exclusive, who has queens, concubines, consorts, the pick of an entire city, probably anyone he locks eyes with on the street.

The crowd around them grows animated and then reacts like one large animal—a hundred eyes turning west, discordant conversations going silent. Muscles tense, necks crane and a cheer rides the crowd as the king appears on his horse. On an elephant, he is out of reach; this makes him more accessible and allows people to touch him as he moves past. Some of them try to kiss his feet, usually missing as their lips land on the side of the black, sleek Persian horse he is on.

Someone holds their kid up, the combined height just about reaching the king's waist. He ruffles the little boy's hair and people shout their approval. Darius sees others pushing their teenage daughters and sons to the front, perhaps hoping for the king's notice. Offering up their children, in the ultimate sacrifice—more concubines, more soldiers and miners.

Darius doesn't notice Maderi moving to the front. As the king's retinue draws closer, she calls out. 'Behrooz!' The king turns his head and laughs at the sight of her.

'You remember the horses,' he says, slowing the steed down. 'Outside the stables, even most of my palace can't tell the difference.'

'She has a white star on her side,' Maderi says, stroking Behrooz's neck. She looks up at him. 'I wanted to give you this.' She pulls at the locket around her neck and the thin chain breaks. She holds the stone out to him.

He pulls at the reins so that Behrooz slows, but doesn't stop. Maderi is still having to walk beside him. 'That's meant to be insurance for you. Security. Keep it,' he says.

'I don't want it.' But then she corrects herself. 'I don't need it.'

He takes it from her with a guileless smile.

No residue there, no pain. He can be friendly. Everything she's just said lands on him with the power of the blunt side of a knife.

She reaches out to stroke Behrooz again, but he speeds the horse back up to the ceremonial pace and leaves her behind.

Darius doesn't hear the conversation but understands her gesture, this giving up of both treasure and privilege in such a public way. It's an emotional decision, he thinks, not a logical one—maybe incited by what Narven's wife had just said to her. Perhaps she wanted to hurt the king or prove to him that she didn't need his protection, neither of which Darius thinks she succeeded at.

Darius doesn't dare hope that she did it for him.

They follow the crowd to the river, where the boats have lined up for the competition. By now, everyone's festive wear and ribbons and flowers are drooping in the heat, even though the sun is not yet at its highest. The rowers—twelve to each snake-shaped boat—are standing beside their long thin oars, a brief cloth wrapped around their torsos, their bodies bare and gleaming. Darius is not unfit, but these men exhibit a different kind of masculinity, their shoulders broad and their bodies tapered, muscles sharply defined down their arms and backs. Even some of the older ladies, the grandmothers in the crowd, jokingly whistle and hoot.

Each long-necked boat has a different creature painted down its side—an elephant, a horse, a fish with bloodshot eyes, a snarling tiger, a periyar kite with a bloody beak.

Darius is about to exclaim how wonderful it all is when Maderi sighs, 'I have been to so many of these. They are exactly the same every year.'

'Except who wins, right?'

Maderi rolls her eyes. Her earlier enthusiasm has wilted. 'The winner is almost always the team that the king favours because it draws the best riders. This year it's the boat with the elephant, the Adheerans.'

'It looks like the whole town is here.' The riverbank is crowded, and the people at the edge are slipping in the mud. A few lose their balance and fall in amid much commotion, and one young woman who emerges back out, dripping from the muddy water, provides amusement when she finds a small fish wriggling about in her blouse. She's unfazed but her mother is mortified.

'Let's go,' Maderi says.

'What? Why? The race hasn't even started.'

'I have watched it too many times. If you come with me, I'll show you something that you won't get another chance to see.'

She sees Darius' expression and rolls her eyes again. 'Is that all you can think of? I don't have a second hidden pussy, I promise you.'

Making it out of the crowd is easier than getting in, but pushing through the mass of hot, sweaty, close-together bodies still leaves Darius feeling violated in some inexplicable way.

Once they have extricated themselves, Maderi takes his hand and guides him through now-empty streets. Shouts and cheering rise from the riverbank and fade away. The lanes feel different without the hum of people—their steps echo in the narrow stone streets, and the sound of critters and frogs is clear in this silence. The injured soldiers, the fish sellers with their smooth fibs ('yes, freshly caught this morning'), the grandmothers sitting on steps making jasmine flower strings with arthritic fingers, all of them evaporated. People have left the doors of their homes ajar and gates open, giving an eerie feel to the temporarily deserted streets. One of the stalls has some puffed rice left out on a pan, which he scoops up with one hand as they walk past—it is still crunchy and warm. They reach the bazaar he'd visited on the first day, and he follows Maderi down its lanes to the king's stalls—the jewellers and artisans favoured by the court. The short gate in front is locked but unguarded. There is no one around.

Maderi smirks at Darius. She clambers over the gate, whose spikes are sharp but spaced at a manageable distance—the real discouragement to trespassers has always been the scary-faced guards. Once in the compound, they walk past empty shops whose displays have been completely cleared out. But Maderi seems to know where to go, and they hurry past the knife and gem stalls without a second glance, and into a roofed inner compound, where an entire section is curtained off. Behind the curtains is a small square space with a bench. Here too, the displays have been removed. Maderi bends below the bench and moves two floorboards, pulls out a locked wooden box.

'What are you doing?' Darius hisses.

'You don't have to whisper. Everyone is at the race,' Maderi says and takes out the small knife she wears at her waist. She fiddles with the lock and it falls open after a few moments. 'I knew Shiva was always overconfident about the security here, but this is an especially badly made lock.'

Inside the box are three pendants, each shaped like a different beetle. The jewels seem to catch some hidden light in this curtained room and shimmer as she moves the box. Maderi picks out the most beautiful beetle, whose eyes are fire opals, green wings garnet, its body flaming blue amethyst. Its six gold legs are carved so carefully that the artisan has even detailed the segments and joints of each one.

'It's beautiful,' Darius says.

'Now, look,' Maderi presses something at the beetle's base, and the legs begin to move in the same crawly way of all insects. It happens so quickly that Darius jumps back, thinking that the creature has come alive, and almost falls over the table behind him. 'What kind of dark art is this?' he says.

'It's built like that, you silly man, it has wheels inside it that make it move. It isn't alive.' Maderi's eyes are on the wriggling pendant. She presses the base again and the movement, thankfully, stops. Darius can't stop staring at it, however—the way the beetle moved had unnerved him thoroughly, upending his ideas of what constituted being alive or not. Maderi closes the box, puts it back in the hollow space and arranges both the boards on top of it. She gets up with the pendant still in her hand.

'You're taking it.' It is not a question.

'Yes.' They hurry out the way they came.

'But why?'

'Well, why not? I am sick of these men thinking that they can tie me to them, Darius, for a few weeks or months with shiny gifts. I am sick of men donating bronzes to the temple of women naked except for their jewellery and me knowing that's the only picture they have in their heads of me. I want to take something that I like, without that exchange. So yes. I am stealing it.'

He follows her out.

'But what does any of that have to do with this man and his shop?'

She ignores his question. 'Come,' she says, when they are outside the market. She tucks the beetle into the cloth around her chest and they run together through the still-empty streets, reaching beach sand warmed by the afternoon sun. It burns the

soles of their feet as they run into the water. The waves foam
around their legs and she pulls him deeper in until the water
reaches his waist and the current pulls hard at him. The sea
surrounds them, tugging at their bodies, willing them to go
deeper.

Two temptresses, he thinks. He does not know how to resist
Maderi. Until he met her, people had usually bent him to their
will using coercion, money, the occasional whip. She, on the
other hand, does not need to convince him of anything. He
goes along with her even as he recognizes her as his opposite—a
creature of impulse, who feels her way towards momentous
decisions.

But Nita suggests that maybe Maderi wasn't this way at the
beginning. Perhaps she lives fully in her present because she's
been given no choice in the matter, since others have decided
everything for her—her father gave her away, men commanded
her to dance, and even her lover, the king, took what he wanted
and left her.

And so it became her nature—live for the day, because she
has no idea what is coming next. Perhaps it is better to live in
the present as she does than to be a woman who's lost control
and chooses to stay in the past, reminiscing among her family's
old treasures.

Nita says this ruminatively, maybe carried away by the story.
She does not intend to wound (or does she?) but Rouhi stiffens
beside her, staring at the ceiling, and says nothing.

12

'Once you start, you cannot stop,' the man says. 'Each training session is a power play, so if you give up in the middle, you lose.'

The camel trainer fascinates her. He's probably in his mid-fifties, Nita guesses, and his brown skin is stretched tight and thin across a high-cheekboned face. He has a beard that has been grown inattentively and is scraggly, and his eyes are narrowed out of habit, even when there is no sand blowing. He's speaking in a rapid, impatient chatter that Nita struggles to follow. He is supposed to be a guide for the tourists who visit here but he seems, at best, ambivalent about his job, rushing his introduction and frequently lapsing into Arabic. Overall, he looks pained and likely prefers camels to people.

Nita can see why. They are a group of seven—Rouhi, Rouhi's childhood friend Huma who is visiting from Cairo, Saba and her, together with a couple of chatty Australians, who are sandy-haired from top to toe, and therefore blend in quite nicely with the dunes, and a lone, stout British man, who works at a telecom company and is perspiring heavily. It is hot, even in the shade, and the British guy, Dave, has a large handkerchief that he is mopping his face with over and over in a distracting way. Even in this startling place, it is possible to overly focus on this minor detail.

The camel camp is located in an oasis. They are surrounded by desert, but here there are two natural pools, the blue so striking that Nita wonders if something has been added to the water.

Palm trees and dry brush stretch outward from the water bank, before hitting some red line where they stop and it's just sand stretching into the horizon. There is grandeur here, but it is not hard to miss the danger of this place, and perhaps Salman, their middle-aged, striking Bedouin guide, cannot mask an inherited disdain for these soft-elbowed, round-cheeked visitors, who are dressed all wrong for the desert despite their attempts to follow instructions to wear 'loose, airy clothing'. They were driven to the camp in an air-conditioned Nissan minivan with tinted windows. They fit in here about as much as a herd of seals.

The camp is divided into two pens, one for camel training and the other for pasture, almost like a school and playground. The pastures have the thick, wiry plants that the camels typically eat, their guide tells them. 'We keep them on their natural diet,' he says, 'no grain, no packaged food.'

'That is diet I also need,' Rouhi whispers to Nita. Her face is chubbier these days, her stomach softer—it's the daily desserts she's been making, supposedly for Nita to sample.

The guide now takes them to where the youngest camels are. On the way is a 'camel refreshment stand' where they can buy snacks like carrots and wilted lettuce heads for the animals. None of them are allowed to carry bags into the camp after the one time a teenager sneaked in a can of soda which he fed to one of the calves, who drank it enthusiastically, the guide says, and fortunately, till date, has suffered no ill-effects.

Nita and Rouhi both buy carrots and lettuce before heading into the pen, where the calves are already galumphing around, waiting for snacks—new human faces mean food. The snacks disappear quickly, maneuvered through their agile mouths. Nita cannot call the calves beautiful—to human eyes, their mouths are too big, their lips are massive, dangling pouts. Their buck teeth are large and yellow. They look somewhat lecherous.

But they are keen creatures who stare insolently at the new guests and quickly choose their favourites. They seem to regard themselves as the observers rather than the observed, and after snatching up the food, they use their tongues, noses and mouths to examine the humans, sticking their faces right into armpits and chests. No respect for personal space. A young calf necks Nita without warning and licks her ear with its sandpaper tongue.

Too soon, the guide moves them along to the training pens where the older camels are. These are over three years old, the guide says, the equivalent of human teenagers in age. There is a training session ongoing, and the camel is snorting in an annoyed fashion as the trainer—who looks like a teenager himself, with a unibrow, a supermodel waistline and downy cheeks—places a weighted blanket on its hump. The moment the trainer lets go, the camel kicks out with its two back hooves, and if the young man hadn't jumped back in time, he would have been thrown across the field. The group gasps, and two pairs of eyes turn to them, human and animal.

Their guide glares at the women, Rouhi, Huma and Nita, although the two Aussies had been the loudest. 'Please don't interrupt the training, the animal may get agitated,' he scolds them.

But it is the trainer who seems upset. He retreats into a shed and returns with large steel shackles bound with rope; he approaches the camel carefully this time, making clicking sounds with his tongue.

The camel blinks lazily. It's got eyelashes worthy of a mascara ad, the kind that the women on *The Bold and the Beautiful* would pay good money for. It seems to have forgotten its earlier tantrum. The trainer bends down to snap the shackles onto the camel's back ankles. As soon as he is in position, the camel kicks out again, this time timing the assault perfectly and making contact with the man's chest, nearly throwing him across the field. He lands sprawling on his butt and lies perfectly still.

This time, no one remonstrates them when they gasp and shout—the guide is busy opening the gate and rushing into the pen. The guilty camel is already making a getaway, moving with remarkable speed towards the far fence, the blanket still on its hump. Running, it's a graceful creature—although it lacks a horse's muscular silhouette, it moves in a swaying, hypnotizing motion. Their guide is leaning over the trainer who is sitting up, looking none the worse for wear, save for the colour that is high in his cheeks from his embarrassment.

Salman returns, apologizing for the group not getting to see 'a real training session', but the excitement is high among them now, and the men thump him on his back and everyone tips him heavily. The group chatters among themselves; sharing something unexpected together has drawn them temporarily close.

The vans drive up to carry them back to the city—the city which feels much more like a mirage from here, deep among the sand dunes, on the hem of the evening, the sun blazingly beautiful as it sets in the far horizon, the orange glow of it awakening long shadows across the desert.

Nita waits till the van has dropped them off to Rouhi's car. She then asks the others if they thought the whole thing an act.

Huma and Rouhi stare back at her from the front seats. The perfume cloud enveloping the two women up front wafts to Nita and Saba in the back of the car, clashing scents of sandalwood, musk, lilies and lavender.

'What do you mean?' Rouhi says, 'Didn't you see that boy fly?'

Nita tries to explain that when the young man had bent down to put the shackles, he had hesitated a beat, like a bad actor waiting clumsily for his cue. He'd also been sweating heavily in a thick jacket that none of the other trainers were wearing. The camel was also younger and not as muscular as the others. It's almost as if the whole thing was a regular pantomime for extra-large tips.

But her explanation only seems to make it worse, and the two women exchange a glance, after which Huma rolls her eyes and ignores Nita completely. In the silence, her words hang, sounding either foolish or unkind, or maybe both.

Rouhi and Huma resume the discussion they were having— Huma is trying to resist desserts after getting elevated blood sugar numbers in her recent health check-up. It is the conversation of women being edged out of their prime despite their soft hands and red lips, women who are still full of desire and wants but are also aware of the sickness that now comes with it. Desire still has the upper hand, however—the conversation quickly degenerates from advice to a listing of their favourite dessert items. Arab delicacies are heavily debated alongside modern temptations like pistachio gelato and Magnum ice-cream bars.

Saba leans against Nita's arm and asks her to make her a cat's cradle, but her voice is dozy. Nita stays very still until she falls asleep.

Nita gazes out of the window as they re-enter the city, the buildings and the bustle rushing back at them until they are once again enveloped in its concrete embrace. Many of these buildings are over fifty floors, as Dubai struggles to accommodate an ever-growing population into the small space it has tended into liveability. Thousands of lighted apartment windows flicker past her, each with their own particular story. How small are her concerns compared to those?

Rouhi's laughter brings her back. She and Huma are busy reminiscing about sneaking out of the house as teenagers one evening to go to a nightclub. Despite the inexpertly applied, grown-up make-up, they weren't allowed in, and they had to sneak back home fully sober. They talk about it like it was their greatest adventure.

In a minor epiphany, Nita realizes that Rouhi would have reacted very differently if Huma had been the one to suggest that the aggressive camel was part of an orchestrated hustle. She would have considered it seriously, been ready to believe it. Nita's comments, when received in the presence of outside company, were treated as inferior. Nita is Scheherazade, lover, companion. But is she an equal?

Sometimes, Nita can glimpse a future where she and Rouhi are a couple. It is hard to knit together even in her head, but she manages a few scenes—the two of them at a table in a small kitchen, holding hands. Driving Saba to a school that looks a lot like the one she had taught in, back home. Going out for a movie together. But it is all very fuzzy, without detail, and the promise of it flickers in and out. From a distance, an oasis and a mirage look the same.

Soon, Haroun will be back, and she can't imagine living in the same house with him while in love with his wife. What is she supposed to do then? She could ask them for her passport and leave. But her emotions have handcuffed her to this family.

Under her hand, Saba's little body is warm. She's had a mild cough for days, which the doctor said was nothing serious but still prescribed a cloudy pink syrup with an awful taste and grainy texture, and it is a battle to get her to drink it every evening. Nita has to pin her down while Rouhi nudges the spoon between Saba's clenched teeth. Saba weeps the whole time in an agonized way and Nita's heart catches like it used to when Ani was unwell.

On the outside of the syrup, it says, unbelievably, *strawberry flavour*. Saba's favourite rendered unrecognizable, like some Frankenstein version. Anyway, Rouhi says, 'Strawberry flavour is big lie for anyone who has eaten real strawberry.' This is more like what one might imagine liquid cement tastes like. Vile and unswallowable. Nita is already dreading the dose before Saba's bedtime tonight.

Huma comes back with them to the house for tea. The fondness Rouhi has for her guests is measured in the chinaware she puts out—for her favourites, like now, she takes out the pretty blue and white Corelli cups and saucers from the 'display cupboard'. The biscuits have been baked that afternoon out of whole wheat flour, carom and sesame seeds, and coated with a mix of sea salt and sugar crystals. Nita eats two—it's the first time she's tasted these—and is stopping herself from taking more. Two is borderline, three would be too noticeable.

When guests are over, Nita doesn't sit in the dining room; rather she hovers in the neutral territory that is the doorway between the dining and the kitchen, one foot on the white kitchen tiles, ready to duck back in case of signs that she is unwanted.

Huma has taken off her headscarf, revealing a rash around her face along the scarf perimeter. It is angry red from fresh irritation. She runs her fingers gingerly over it. The spots are raised and glowering, and some look about to burst.

'I tell the husband'—instead of 'my', Huma uses the Arabic 'the', 'al' for her spouse. As if there is one husband to rule them all. 'I say to him that the scarf is making me a bad Muslim because I cannot pray, cook or think from the itching when I am wearing it.'

She counts out her interventions. 'I changed the detergent, the fabric conditioner. I bought different material. Pure cotton, pure silk, pure linen. I bought one scarf with such a high thread count, I wept tears of blood at the price. I changed my face cream. I stopped wearing cream! Nothing works.'

'You can't stop wearing the scarf?'

'I put it on for the first time after marriage, you know? I argued about it with the husband, I said, listen, some women like the hijab, some women don't, and I don't like it because of the itching. Then he said, "The rash is not because of the scarf." So I put it on in front of him along the rash that is now like a dotted line for "put scarf here", yes? So perfectly, it matched.' She shakes her head. 'But the husband then says that the rash is because of my impiety. It is *my* punishment for being a bad wife. His ruling now is that I cannot take off the scarf when I am outside anywhere. He says if I am a good wife, it will heal. Otherwise the itch will spread and I must allow it.'

Huma sighs. 'When I was a teenager, we all thought husbands would be like lovers in films, didn't we? Admit it, Rouhi. We thought we would walk by their side, not crawl behind them. How I would like to make a big sail with all my headscarves and float off on a boat in the Arabian sea.'

'We are like their camels.'

'Donkeys, Rouhi! We saw that a camel can attack and run away very fast.'

They know that even the princesses can't escape the hardcore 'my word is law, your word is shit' logic some of the husbands here have. A couple of princesses, since they are not allowed to divorce, have tried to escape their airless marriages on boats, beating against the influx that is coming into the country. But they are extradited back to the UAE by countries they land in claiming asylum, by governments who fear their relationships with the ruling princes and kings will get ruined if they don't.

This must be how Rouhi feels. If a princess can't escape, how can she?

Saba has been fidgeting at the table, playing with one of her dolls—Skipper, Barbie's forgotten sister, a mistake purchase by Rouhi that had triggered a whole afternoon of tears. Apparently having not-Barbie was worse than no Barbie. But after a few days, Saba went and fetched the doll from the corner she'd thrown it in and started playing with it as if nothing had happened. But Nita has noticed that she plays with Skipper fairly violently, dunking the doll's head in water and twisting its limbs out of proportion. Skipper looks like she's been through war, her hair frazzled and her face marked and dented. Now, Saba spreadeagles Skipper on the tabletop. Then she sticks one plastic foot up her nose.

'Saba!' Rouhi yells, reverting to English, 'Take leg out of nose!'

'My nose is itchy,' Saba complains.

'Then use tissue, like normal person.' Rouhi looks at Nita, who fetches a tissue for her.

'I'm sorry, Mama,' Saba says, reverting to Arabic, 'I won't be a *kahba*.'

She sees her error immediately on Rouhi's horrified face. It's not just Rouhi—the word detonates and completely changes the atmosphere in the room. Huma looks down at the table. No one moves.

'Where did you hear that word, Saba?' Rouhi asks, 'Did someone say it to you at school?'

Saba darts a questioning glance at the two-headed woman refilling the teacups, who in turn, involuntarily shoots a look at Nita and then at Rouhi, and it is in this web of gazes that Nita realizes it. The knowledge is like a firework lighting up the sky, showing you what you were surrounded by but couldn't see. Whatever the word meant, she and Rouhi have been discovered.

'No, no, Mama—I don't remember,' Saba says, her face growing pink.

'What do you think that word means?'

'It means a person who is . . . not clean?'

'Oh habibti,' Huma says, 'that's not what it means. It's a word people use when they want to talk bad about a woman.'

'Let me clear this table for you madam,' the shorter of the two-headed woman picks up plates and the small bowls in a noisy clatter, as if to drown out something she doesn't want the rest to hear.

Huma takes this as a sign to take her leave.

The two of them kiss each other's cheeks at the doorway. 'Children,' Huma sighs to Rouhi, 'what can you do when you start letting them out of the house?'

No, Nita thinks. Saba heard that at home.

Kahba, Rouhi later tells her, is the Egyptian word for prostitute. The word sounds like a cough because streetwalkers were forbidden from dressing the part or wearing make-up. So they drew attention to themselves by coughing as men walked past.

'They know. They know,' Nita interrupts.

'What? Who knows?' Rouhi asks.

The nickname sticks in her throat. Instead, she says, 'Aliya and Reema.'

'Them?' Rouhi does not automatically dismiss her worry. 'Why you say this?'

'When Saba said that word, they looked so nervous. And then they looked at me, and then at you. Both of them.'

Rouhi pushes aside the blanket—a thick, cosy thing printed with the faces of two tigers, a leftover, Nita figures, from one of Haroun's shopping sprees—and sits up on the bed so high that her feet dangle off the side. For a moment, she looks hopeless, despairing. But when she glances over, her face is calm.

'If they know, Haroun will know soon enough,' she says, and her expression is so in contrast to her words that Nita bursts into terrified tears. For the first time perhaps, she feels real fear.

'Oh no, no, no,' Rouhi's arms are around Nita, 'But my Nita, now that they know, his two mad cousins, would you not come to room? Would you not be with me?'

The tears continue to fall. 'No,' she says with resignation, 'I cannot stay away from you.'

Rouhi draws her close. 'We can't stop train with our hands, habibti. They do what they do, yes? We do what we do.'

'And what about what your husband will do to you? And to me?'

Rouhi is silent, and then says, 'We will see. First, I find your passport.'

But Rouhi can't find the small dark blue book anywhere. Cupboards, shelves, long long-forgotten suitcases are all opened and turned upside down. She finds the keys of locked drawers and searches in them too. Some long-lost jewellery is rediscovered. An old photo album where Rouhi is a teenager, lithe in silk shirts and bell-bottomed jeans. A beloved frog toy that belonged to Saba, aged three. No passport.

The day of Haroun's arrival draws close. For Nita, it feels like an incoming, obliterating event—a brooding volcano in the horizon, a tsunami's approaching mouth. She wishes each intervening day longer. Waiting in the mornings at the bus stop with Saba, she is of one mind with the pre-schoolers, hoping for stalled traffic, a late school bus. May the sun smoulder, not burn. She wants a deceleration of everything. Or even better, as she had hoped for before, a second chance, where they walk backward, unpreparing meals, unsleeping, unwaking, unloving, unkissing, all the way to the day Haroun left, so that she can stand again, outside the closed door.

Instead, time rips past her in a hurry. It is almost as if the summer is speeding things up instead, heating everything to a new intensity. She thinks about her passport, disappeared somewhere by Haroun, probably hidden away in a bank locker. The option for escape gone.

This is not the story she'd expected to be in. She'd started with simple goals (don't we all)—a not-awful job, some savings for her son.

The story she is in now feels like one of those old folk tales that Rouhi likes to tell, where the ending is pre-written and known, and casts a shadow over the entire tale. The story speeds towards it, the choices are already made and all that remains to be told are the precise details of the events.

As the months before the circled date shrink to weeks, the cooking becomes slipshod, unserious. Rouhi does not hold back on the scolding and correcting, she goes on as if everything is normal, as if her authority hasn't been tarnished. But it's as if the two-headed woman does not hear her, they barely acknowledge her beyond half-audible *mm-hmms*. They wield the knives like weapons, talking and pointing, make curries like soup, lay down the cutlery on the table with a clatter at mealtimes. There are no leftovers, they eat it all.

It gets bad enough that Rouhi throws them out of the kitchen after a particularly disastrous undercooked chicken that is still pink beneath the roast skin, and begins cooking simple time-saving stuff herself like tabbouleh and chicken baked with garlic, turning the bones back into a broth that she uses to cook rice the next day. She discards carcasses only when they have been boiled clean of everything edible. 'If you live on a farm, you waste nothing,' she says, 'You know the chicken since it is small, you know the real price.' She is a messy cook, just as she is with everything else. Her fingers get sticky, along with the kitchen counters. The jar of oil becomes slick and slippery as she opens the lid multiple times with fingers coated in sauce or labneh, and she leaves spoons and ladles teetering on the edges of the counter or sliding into simmering pans. Things barely in balance.

Nita still comes into Rouhi's room—just later than she used to, as if that makes any difference. When they lie quietly together, they can hear the small bedside clock ticking—towards dawn, towards the next day, towards next week, tipping them towards some longer night. They don't comment on it but hug each other closer, and their intimacy is full of urgent effort, as if they can pack more of it into the time they have, like overstuffing a suitcase.

'I can't feel my lips,' Nita says late one night, after a marathon kissing session. 'If I touch them, they feel like someone else's and twice the size.'

Rouhi has to kick her out some mornings, she doesn't want to go.

She reaches her own bed exhausted and her emotions raw. She is full of unsaid questions. Rouhi calls her habibti. One night, especially tender, she told Nita she was her *muqallib al quloob*, a controller of hearts. But she has never said she loves her.

Nita can't say it first, not in her subservient role. It would, she feels, worsen her position. Instead, she uses Darius as her stand-in, the narrator of her yearning. But Rouhi sympathizes with him as if he is an entirely different person.

Nita tries to figure out how Rouhi feels about her in indirect ways. 'If you could be anywhere at all in your life, where would you be?' Nita asks, and instead of saying *here, I want to be here*, Rouhi says, 'In my home before it burned down. Fourteen years old and watching from window the good-looking boys and girls from school walk down the street.'

'Put on my bra,' Rouhi says to her one night, and she does. It's too big for her. The hot pink lace trimmings, the underwire all feel like too much. Overwrought, like her insides.

One night, Rouhi tells her that Haroun will be back in three weeks. He hasn't fallen into the sea after all, as Nita prayed for, and his ship will first dock in Fujairah, where he wants to spend some time 'with the team', before coming over. 'He'll arrive smelling of cheap rose perfume I smell from three rooms away,' Rouhi says. 'His *team*, they are wearing so much of this perfume.'

She is so calm, Nita can't stand it. 'You talked to him on the phone downstairs?' she asks.

'Yes. Two-head must have heard.' Rouhi also uses the nickname now.

'They will be sharpening the knives.'

Rouhi is silent for a moment. It is the kind of pause that feels like something more, and it puts Nita on guard. Rouhi is about to say something that will hurt her feelings.

'We should go to embassy,' Rouhi says, 'for your passport.'

'Ok,' Nita says, buying time to think, 'Don't they need a letter from the sponsor of my visa? That would be Haroun.'

'I—don't think so,' Rouhi says, 'but at least we can do check.'

'And then what? What happens if they give me a new passport?'

'Then you go home, habibti.'

'Oh. But I cannot leave the country without my visa stamp, right? How will they know that I didn't come here illegally?'

'We go to embassy and find out,' Rouhi says with finality. 'I think you should not be here. When he come.'

'Rouhi,' Nita says gently, 'It will take them a lot more than three weeks to give me a new passport.' She isn't certain of this, but she knows in general that the Indian bureaucracy can be a foot-dragging pain. What she does know for sure, is that after all these days and weeks of worrying about her inability to leave, she can't bring herself now to just *go*. If she has more time, maybe she can persuade Rouhi to go with her.

'We still try, yes? You can apply,' Rouhi says, not relenting.

'We can try,' Nita pretends to agree, '*if* they accept a lost passport application without the sponsor involved, and *if* they do it without notifying Haroun.'

That as she expects, discourages Rouhi. She falls quiet, brooding over it, rubbing her face with her hands.

'Once Haroun is back,' Nita says, 'ask him for the passport. Until then, I'm the omelette stuck to your pan.'

Rouhi doesn't say anything for a moment. She gets up. 'Ok. But you get ready.'

She walks to Nita's room with Nita trailing behind her. 'You have suitcase?' Rouhi asks. She sits on Nita's narrow bed and waits as she takes out her small suitcase from underneath. Nita opens it and the zipper gets stuck in its usual place, where the teeth are warped. She usually packs and unpacks through the half-open mouth. Rouhi bends down and tugs at the zip. But it stays jammed and half open, the only thing respecting Nita's wishes.

'This zip, it is sticking,' Rouhi says. 'This bag is so old. Let me get you one.'

'No,' Nita says, 'The bag is fine. I have had it for years.'

'Yes. I can see,' Rouhi says before she can stop herself, and Nita looks at her, hurt, 'I'm sorry. But I can buy you new one? Or give you bag I have.'

'No,' Nita says, and this time, she is on the verge of tears. Why is Rouhi insisting on this strange performance, like she has to depart tomorrow? 'You can't make me take your stupid bag. I won't.' She sounds like a child. Rouhi glares at her and after a moment, leaves the room.

Alone, Nita lets herself cry in that angry helpless way she hasn't cried in years, the way she cried outside in her aunt's garden when she was fourteen, her back to the mango tree and her butt in the mud, after one of the girls in her class said things to her about being *filthy*, hissing it out as if it was full of poison. It had struck Nita with all the meaning that the girl could not bring herself to explicitly say. Usually gifted at clever retorts, she hadn't been able to snap back because nothing had been said really, only implied.

She knows how much of adult communication is similarly unsaid, and that as a grown-up, you have to still respond to it somehow. But now, the same emotions of rage and helplessness have come roaring back. Rouhi seems desperate to have her gone, and she is doing everything but coming out and actually saying *I don't want you here.*

She looks around her room with new eyes. She'd noticed Rouhi's embarrassment when she walked in. In all these months, Nita has somehow failed to properly notice how tiny her room is, how thin the mattress, how the cupboard has a bent hinge so that the doors don't close properly. A dismissiveness is inherent in the furnishings—the room has been filled with barely usable discards, it's one level above a shed. It's a place of scuffed corners and rounded shoulders, full of small indignities. It comes with judgement, a low assessment of the room resident's worth. How much had Rouhi been involved in setting it up?

Her tears dry as her anger grows, and she thinks, *yes I should leave, leave all of this behind.* She feels that momentary rush that comes with imagining escape, the chance to be back with Ani and Divya, before remembering yet again, that of course, she doesn't have her passport.

The door opens before she is done composing herself, and she wipes her face quickly, the mess of tears and snot, on the sleeve of her dress. Rouhi comes in with one of Saba's bags. It's kid luggage in primary colours, a knapsack with three laughing kittens wearing flower crowns on their heads.

'You can't refuse bag from Saba,' Rouhi says, holding it out.

Nita is too exhausted to argue at this point. She takes the bag and keeps it on her bed. 'What's the point, anyway,' Nita said, 'of a new bag without a passport?'

'I'll find out where he keep your passport,' Rouhi says, taking Nita's hand in hers.

'I thought you cared about me,' Nita says. She has never raised her voice at Rouhi, and is aware of the tightrope she is on with this accusation, 'But now you can't wait to get rid of me.'

'Oh habibti, no,' Rouhi looks stricken. She takes her into her arms. 'Nita, I am scared. I am very scared. I want you to go so Haroun, he won't hurt you.'

'Will you come with me, then?' Nita asks. She searches Rouhi's silent face. How could she possibly want to be with this man instead, who leaves the marks of his fingers on her throat?

Rouhi doesn't say anything. Instead, she squeezes Nita's hand, but this time, Nita pulls away. Maybe this at least, is something she can withhold. The rules seem to be that Rouhi can ask for things and Nita cannot.

'I'll see you in the morning,' Rouhi says and leaves.

13

A bird sings clear: *today she will love you.* Or maybe, *today she will leave you.* Darius chooses to believe the former. Every morning, he wakes up as hopeful as a lamb and every evening, he retires to bed with his dreams slaughtered. There are only a few days remaining before they depart from Muziris, but he has done nothing to further his relationship with Maderi besides memorizing a few choice Tamil phrases he murmurs to her in bed, some of which he suspects he mispronounces. Her sighs could easily be a smothering of giggles behind her hand.

He knows the words to confess his love—he learned them from Ebo and confirmed them with Faro. But in the evenings when he finally sees her, the words stay packed away behind his tongue, lodged there more thoroughly with each passing day. Saying them out loud feels like a joke. At night, coming from her bed, he lies on his back in the damp warehouse, his skin itchy with mosquito bites and regret. Once on the ceiling, he spotted a bat contemplating Darius's cowardly body upside down. What was right side up for a bat? Which way did it prefer the world?

Was it certain about its own viewpoint? Darius thinks that he himself probably sees everything the wrong way round. Not just with Maderi.

Again this morning, reliably like the sun, hope rises. He is cheerful over his desultory breakfast of leftover fermented bread from the day before, which he eats with some honey.

The others know he is in love. On their way to the ship—much of the buying is done and now the work is packing things into the hold, and bartering and purchasing interesting knick-knacks that will get a good price back home—they tease him. They speculate about Maderi's weak eyesight, which is the only possible explanation for Darius' success, his hopelessness in bed ('she probably has to hold it up for you, doubt it stands on its own'), and her lack of interest in anything but his money ('wait till she finds out the only shiny thing you have is the sparkle in your eyes').

The townspeople are used to them by now, and the stall sellers, knowing what they want, shout customized temptations at them—spices, touristy clay and metal carvings of local trees, animals and fish, perfumed oils. Stock Latin and Fayyumic phrases are thrown at them: 'A favourite among Roman girls', they say, as they hold out their 'today only' deals.

He knows them a little now and the sheen of romantic foreignness has faded. These people contain the usual percentages of some honest men, some a little bent and a few outright blackguards, all mixed up together and occasionally shading from one category to the next in their dealings.

This morning, he spots Maderi buying flowers for the temple. It's a task rotated among the temple girls, and each has their particular preferences when it comes to the mix of yellows, reds and white blooms. The crew gets louder on seeing her and

she looks their way. She doesn't blush or dip her head at the
sight of him among the other men; she has never been that kind
of woman. Instead, she grins at him guilelessly and studies the
others' faces. It's he who does the blushing.

He meets her later, with the birds roosting in the trees. There
is an impatience in their song by evening. They are probably
arguing about badly built nests, wasted days, hungry children,
uncaught prey. As it is below, so it is above—it's just that they
fight in tune.

He is exhausted because Babu has been especially harsh
today, having found one of the bales with bad seeds, the dust
falling out of the cloth they've tied the crop in. He gave Darius
and Ebo an earful. There are ten more bales just like that one
packed into the ship's hold already—he shudders inwardly at
the possibility of discovery. They only need to reach Berenike,
he thinks. Then the bad pepper will become someone else's
problem. Probably.

He relaxes when Maderi opens the door to her room. The
roommate once again, nowhere to be seen.

He wonders why if she doesn't fancy him, she agrees to
see him day after day during these past few weeks. Perhaps it
is because of his undisguised feelings for her—he hangs on to
her every word and brings her small gifts of food, sweets, clay
carvings he likes. The heat of his infatuation and the intensity of
his kisses are flattering even for a beautiful woman.

And the fact that he will leave soon—that there are not many
tomorrows left in this relationship—is probably his greatest
attraction for her. His love a tree providing sweet, temporary
shade.

They lie later side by side on her narrow mat, catching their
breath as they watch the fading light slide into the room through

the wooden planks of the wall. This housing section has been sloppily built, with plenty of space between each wooden slat, and there would have been no real privacy if it hadn't been for the dense trees outside. There is a flash of movement in the foliage and he glimpses a kingfisher among the branches— impossibly blue, its belly orange, beak tinted red. A bird forever dressed for a party. But it's no dilettante—he recently saw one turn into a blue streak as it dived into the river, and emerge almost immediately with fish in its beak.

'Your fellow sailors,' Maderi is saying, 'I have been hearing some stories about two of them.'

He looks at her, his interest snagged. 'Your captain and Madu,' she adds, 'have been emptying the purses of the local gamblers.'

He props himself up on his elbows. 'Ur?'

She nods.

'You play it here too?' he asks. How strange this world is, he thinks, where a game of dice can cross oceans.

'They play it everywhere. The ships bring the game with them to the ports. You can find local boards here, and some local dens play it daily with stakes of gold and silver. But it looks like your crew was a bit much for them to handle.'

'Madu is a dangerous player,' Darius concedes.

'Not as dangerous as me,' she says with a sidelong gaze.

A surprise every minute now. 'You play?'

'Pretty well—the king would have me beside him in some of his games with merchants and sailors. He plays anyone with something valuable enough to barter. It was especially easy with men like you coming in on ships every week. I'd give him suggestions in Tamil and he would pretend I was flirting with him. I would say, wait for a three, and he would snap at me like I had asked for a trinket and then he would wait for a three. They had no idea what we were doing.'

'I thought it was a game of chance, but I changed my mind after Madu won every time.'

'Yes, it's not all chance,' she says, 'Things rarely are, even when it looks like it. You speed up your pieces first and block the good squares.'

'But you need to throw high numbers, right?'

She looks at him pityingly.

'Madu took some of my share of the profits with the game,' he admits, 'Now if Babu finds out the bad crop, I'll probably end up with half of what I was supposed to get.'

Maderi is silent for a moment. 'You want me to play him for you?' she asks.

The thought, even though she just said she's very good, had not occurred to him. She is lying beside him, her face taut, her body glistening, her hair loose and lush. Like the kingfisher, she too seems like something delicate, made to be watched. But he can totally picture her wiping blood from her mouth.

'Yes,' he finds himself saying, 'I want you to win it all back for me.'

The one advantage for women, Maderi says, is that most men don't see danger coming. Darius only has to mention it casually when the men are bedding down in the warehouse that his girl likes to play Ur and that she's really good at it.

He follows the comment up with a line she's suggested.

'I don't think I have met a better player,' he says, 'she offers up her pearls and emeralds as bait, and wins it all.'

'Oh *ho*,' Ebo says, becoming Darius' unasked-for accomplice, 'Someone is a better player than Madu.'

Madu, who's already lying down on the far side of the warehouse—Darius tries to sleep as far apart from him as he can—lifts his head. 'That's not possible.'

'It very much is,' Darius brags, 'she's won games for the king.' He adds, with what he hopes is a studied casualness, 'The king has gifted her his emeralds in appreciation of her skills.'

Ebo whistles. 'Bet those are bigger than the ones you and the captain won from those small-time merchants, Madu.'

The comment lights a small fire in the dark about what Babu and Madu have been up to. It hints at why the captain has a sociopath like Madu on the ship, a dangerous man fast with his fists and rich in cunning. Madu is an instrument for enrichment, which Babu benefits from, even as he claims distance from the man's misdeeds. Madu is a golden goose that sometimes bites.

Speaking of geese and sitting ducks, Darius knows Madu can't resist a player that looks like an easy target—like a woman with emeralds to spare. Darius had been one himself. But Madu says nothing, only rolls to his side and goes to sleep.

When he sees Maderi the next day, she embraces him with more than her usual enthusiasm, and his hopes rise, that some late fervour has come to her, that perhaps her slow-burning affection has finally ignited. But she whispers in his ear that Madu is skulking not a short distance behind him. He follows her lead and does not look back. Instead, they walk arm in arm towards the beach, waiting him out.

The sea comes to them, quieter today evening, the waves lapping at their feet like a friendly creature that knows them well, the white lips of the waves curling back as they kiss their toes. He spots something that he thinks is a crocodile, which turns out to be an algae-covered rock. It is Madu that is the most dangerous thing here, easily.

Maderi times it perfectly. She turns her face, the hair fanning over her cheeks as she glances over Darius' shoulder and spots Madu, as if for the first time. He sees that small notch appear at the corner of her mouth, the only sign of her amusement. It's her hidden smile, one that he's grown incredibly conscious of over the few weeks he's known her: *am I the punchline?*

They watch Madu's short hulking figure draw close. He's smiling, wearing what Darius now thinks of as his public face (he has seen Madu's private one and Madu knows it too, and lets Darius see it sometimes, like a warning).

'We have met each other from a distance,' he greets Maderi.

'Most of the time, you are cracking a dirty joke about me,' she says, giving him her sweetest smile.

'N-no—what?' Madu looks at Darius, thinking he's tattled, but Maderi says, 'I have good ears. Everything worth learning is from overheard conversations.'

'Is that how you learned Ur?'

'I see Darius has been bragging about me,' she smiles up at Darius and he finds himself blushing.

'Care for a game? I have plenty of treasure to wager.'

'Everything except my body is up for grabs,' Maderi says.

'I am not so sure,' Madu replies evenly, 'When people are losing, everything is up for grabs. Something happens to their heads.'

'I wouldn't know,' Maderi smiles, 'I never lose.'

'Madu says he never loses either,' Darius says.

'Sometimes, you just need to meet the right person,' Maderi answers.

'That's some talk from a woman I have never played,' Madu says, still keeping the charm switched on.

'I am only warning you.'

'Consider myself warned,' Madu smirks. 'So how about a game?'

'My condition is to have a neutral observer, because of how men become when they lose to a woman,' Maderi said. 'The natural choice then would be the playing site on East Street, where they have two attendants who monitor and manage the wagers. If you are fine with that, we can play tomorrow after sunset.'

Madu shrugs. 'You can have all the observers you want. Keep in mind though—if you want more than one game, I play for big sums. Most temple women can't afford that.'

They watch him leave. 'He likes to have the last word,' Darius says. From behind, Madu looks like a water barrel on legs—his legs are short and hairy, and his upper body a squat square. Darius knows that most of it is muscle—he can throw bales across the length of the lower deck—but the form is unattractive. At least the knave isn't a seductive one.

'He's very aggressive as a player,' Darius tells Maderi, worried now that the game has been arranged. He briefly imagines Maderi impoverished and washing clothes to get by.

'Aggressive players are the best, Darius,' Maderi says, 'They cannot control their anger, which makes them lose.'

She's being quite breezy about the whole thing, and Darius hopes this isn't another kind of weakness, the opposite of his anxiety but just as dangerous.

He doesn't see her all of the next day. He's busy loading the last of the bales and getting the ship sail-ready. The sewing implement he is using to repair the holes and ragged edges in the sails is both sharp and rusty, and keeps catching in the cloth. Babu is intent on setting out by the coming full moon. He's consulting the wind maps available at the bazaars, comparing them to his own, riding out with the local men on the fishing boats to get a sense of how much the wind is picking up. The date he's chosen to sail feels depressingly close to Darius—just three days away.

He finds Maderi in the late evening at one of their favourite food stalls. The place makes a goat curry with a tamarind base that Darius is sure he will dream about for years, and that he might miss almost as much as Maderi. By the time he gets there, she's licking the last of her portion off her fingers, and he orders his own.

The moonlight casts shadows of palm fronds over her face, splintering it into light and shadow. Her eyes, lined with black and malachite, are bright with anticipation. She grabs his hand on their way to the gaming square and kisses him full on the mouth, and he resists that old hope rising again. This is just transferred excitement. He knows this—he is safe, temporary, he's the amphora she's poured her feelings into for now.

The air smells of roasted coconut and freshly baked rice cakes, and somewhere someone has cooked fish heavy with spices, wrapped in banana leaves over a wood fire. Just as he is about to say something about how lovely the evening is, a giant green night stinkbug flies very close to his head, dousing him with its signature oily smell. He lets out a yelp before he can stop himself. 'Don't worry,' Maderi laughs, 'They really like to announce themselves but don't do much damage. Just like your friend.'

'You know he's not my friend.'

'Since you are leaving soon, I want to tell you something,' she hesitates, and Darius' traitorous heart (never give up, its motto) rises once more before she dashes it to the ground by saying, 'I want to give you some advice.'

'All right?' He imagines something utterly devastating—he is terrible in bed or his breath is unbearable.

'Quiet people have loud heads,' she says, 'And yours is especially bad.' She turns him toward her and runs a finger down the line between his eyebrows. 'You are breaking your face with all your worrying. You should worry less.'

Her finger is now tracing the side of his face and jawline. He wants more, he wants her to draw closer. With her, he's a fish on the line.

'And how can you hear what's inside my head?'

'I can't hear it but I see it, Darius. You know, when you are sitting or lying next to me, you shake your foot so hard that your whole body jumps. You frown all the way from sleep to waking up. When you talk to me, I can tell you have already considered and discarded two earlier comments because you don't know what I'll think of them.'

Darius, mortified, gawks at her like one of those red-backed baboons back home. He had not known that he was so abjectly transparent.

This late, there are only three or four games still going on around the stone tables in the square, with a thinning crowd of spectators and hangers-on. All seem like locals, and they eye Darius and Maderi briefly before they turn back. He feels a little judged for his lack of jewellery and clothes without a gold thread in sight.

With its many pieces and dice, Ur is a game difficult to navigate in the moonlight. Several lamps burn around them, leaving a heavy smell of oil in the air. A young man and woman wander around, checking the oil in the lamps from time to time, and pouring out fermented jaggery brew, which is sweet and not too threatening to the faculties unless you go all in with multiple jugs.

Madu is nowhere to be seen. 'Let's sit,' Maderi says, making a beeline for a space in the sweet spot of enough lamplight but not too much of the smell.

Darius takes a seat beside her, notices that she scoots slightly backward. 'You are the main player,' he pointed out, 'why are you sitting behind me?'

'If you are confused, he will be too.'

'Do these little mind games ever work?'

'You would be surprised. One of the players here—his game is Senet, not Ur—used to apply a thin layer of honey behind his ears so that flies flitted around his head constantly during the game. It drove his opponents to distraction, at least the first few times he tried it.'

'That sounds very unpleasant.'

'There are all kinds. One player used to feed the crows on these grounds, so they became his coven and attacked his opponents whenever he got tense or nervous. He didn't last long though. It's civilized here, no one likes actual wounds in this place. That's for the battlefields and taverns.'

'Any place that Madu likes hanging out in isn't civilized.'

It's as if his name summons him—there he is, striding in. The beautiful boy and girl attendants do their usual check and make him hand over his knife. The young man even opens Madu's game box and looks inside, his fingers going over the pieces and dice. Madu looks at him as if he is running his hand, uninvited, down his backside.

He hands the box back to Madu with a smile he must have smiled a hundred times over the day and still looks earnest. Madu snatches it back and stalks over to the two of them. 'Look who's here.'

'Got here early to find a good seat,' Maderi says.

'Honestly, I would like to sit elsewhere,' Madu says, probably just to be annoying. 'I find this one a bit drafty.'

They look around, but the tables are all, to Darius' surprise, now occupied. This is one of the few pastimes available to people after dark when much of the town is asleep, Maderi says.

'Their brew is popular. And,' she adds, indicating the smooth, too-young faces of the men and women around them, 'it's served at night, when the parents and the older siblings of the drinkers are all asleep.' That also explains the dense tree cover around this space, an additional shield against the town gossips.

Thwarted, Madu has taken a seat and is unpacking the board, ignoring Maderi's chatter.

His face is expressionless as they prepare to play, but that itself is telling. Usually, he is expansive and happy—a man used to winning.

They roll the dice, and they serve Madu well in the first throws, giving him high numbers to move quickly down the board. He likes to play as many of his pieces as possible at once and four of his five have already reached the common squares.

'I heard you went into the palace for a couple of games,' Maderi says.

'Oh yes,' Madu agrees, 'we had a couple of big ones in there. Cleaned them out.'

'Did you play with the golden-faced one?' Maderi asks, using one of the popular euphemisms for the king.

'Wouldn't you like to know, now that you no longer play there?' Madu smirks.

'Hmm. How many doors did you cross inside the palace?'

'Doors?' Madu says, before recovering, as it dawns on him what she's referring to. 'I didn't count, but the room we played in had a golden door.'

'Not that far then,' Maderi's smile is all sweetness.

She turns to Darius, 'If you go to the kingdoms out east, you'll find elaborate palaces and kings who say that they are gods. But our king likes to present himself as a man of the people. From the outside, his palace is a mix of ordinary brick and stone, quite plain. Barely any carving besides the wooden tigers at the entrance.

'Things get more ornate as you go into the inner rooms and closer to the king. First, the doors turn silver, and then gold, then covered in gemstones, and then—' she turns to Madu, who's listening intently. 'But wouldn't you like to know?'

The play proceeds, and to Darius' surprise the game becomes just like his own games with Madu: Madu's pieces fly down the board uninterrupted, occupying the lucky rose square, finishing early while Maderi's pieces are backed up in the early spots, with only one done. Her game looks flat and passive.

Madu is trying to subtly charm Maderi even as he wins. Against his coin, she's staked a ring with an emerald stone— much smaller than the one she returned the king—and he leans forward to take a closer look. 'The workmanship on this is beautiful,' he says, and indeed it is. The design is two delicately carved fish in a circle, with the emerald framed between their open mouths. 'You must be quite a dancer to receive gifts like these.'

Maderi shrugs. In the moonlight, her skin is silver. Darius remembers the dance at the beach and how she'd waved off his heartfelt compliment after.

'Ah well,' Madu says, 'Men earn things, women receive them as gifts. I'm not surprised you don't know the true value of it.'

'The value of a beautiful thing is partly about having others covet it.'

'Fighting words from a loser. You know, I have seen men die while holding their swords tight in their fists. They are still dead, though.'

Two people trying to puppeteer each other's emotions with words.

The second game begins as someone comes to refill their cups with brew. Only Darius' cup needs topping off. Madu, probably suspicious, hasn't touched his, and Maderi has only taken a couple of sips from hers. The tables on both sides are filled with people turned giggly and happy from the drink, but here, the mood is ice.

For a game space, this one is loud. Fermented drinks and young people are a potent combination, and the sound within these walls goes up, up, up, as the night deepens. While some tables are quiet and focused on the board, most are raucous, with argument ('the dice bumped into your cup, it doesn't count'), negotiation over stakes ('this is ivory, I promise you, not bone') or with the game as background for the real business of drinking, gossiping, flirting.

Game two feels different a couple of throws in. Maderi throws fives and sixes and takes the lucky rose immediately. Madu finds himself bottlenecked—putting multiple pieces in play now is risky, since if a throw lands on the occupied lucky rose, he has to go back to the starting square. That's what happens with his second and third pieces, much to his frustration.

One way to disentangle chance from skill is in the decisions the players take with their hidden throw, which you are allowed once you get all your pieces on the board. The hidden dice throw lets you throw your dice in a box, out of view of your opponent. You announce your number, and if they challenge you while you are telling the truth, their piece that is furthest ahead on the board goes back to the start. If you are lying, it happens to yours instead. The hidden throws are opportunities for players to gain or lose the edge, throw sand in the other's eyes or reveal themselves. Darius had never lied on his, and had challenged Madu on his throw once and lost.

'My hidden throw,' Madu says. He has already got his first piece off the board to Maderi's two.

He plays the dice into the box. 'Six,' he says.

'Show the dice,' Maderi challenges, and all at once, the two smiling, golden-skinned assistants are beside them, looking into the box. Madu looks at them in astonishment. They seem to have come out of nowhere.

'It's to ensure that the dice doesn't get "accidentally" knocked over by the player when they get challenged,' Maderi explains. 'A real danger with these triangular pieces.'

The dice say three, not six. It's the first time Darius has seen Madu bluff.

It makes Darius wonder about the shape of Madu's tetrahedron dice, how each face is so narrow. A small flick of the wrist can move the face.

When caught, Madu loses his bluster and his anger, like it was all a front. Or perhaps this is the front—the sheepish grin he gives Maderi and Darius, the ah-well shrug of his shoulders. 'This gives you a free turn, doesn't it?' he says as if he is still figuring out the rules of the game.

To win, Maderi needs a four. She plays, but she gets a one, the second dice showing the blank jackal head, and Madu clucks his tongue and gets his fourth piece across. He proceeds swiftly, starting with his fifth and final piece. By the time Maderi finally gets the three she needs and wins, he's only a couple of paces behind. She'd nearly lost her advantage.

Watching them, Darius realizes he has a lot to learn about people. If he'd been in Madu's place, he would have been still steaming over Maderi's insults, unable to concentrate.

A good player has many faces, like the dice. Maderi uses mockery, misdirection, taunt, boredom. Anger is the place luck goes to die, and that's what she tries to stoke on the other side.

Seduction is something Maderi doesn't seem to prefer while seated across a board. Probably because she thinks men expect it and steel themselves against it. Still, today she has deployed her beauty subtly, wearing yellow, her best colour, tinting her lips, the curls of her hair perfect, the kohl on her eyes a sharp line. It helps that beauty is a clouded glass, making it harder to see the emotions underneath, especially when it is a man doing the reading. The king must have used her to great effect for his games, letting her draw the attention and heat.

Even at 1-1 now, with one game to go.

Maderi's moves in this final game are even more aggressive than the last. She proceeds as if a win is almost a foregone conclusion. Madu's rolls come up short of the numbers he needs, and he throws his dice with a new vehemence, which only give him worse and worse numbers. Maderi clucks at his plight, 'That's a strange run of bad luck right there.'

At the embarrassing end of this, Madu says, 'I suggest one more game as a decider.'

Maderi leans back and looks at him. It is so late now that the dusk is lightening a bit. They are the only table still playing in the courtyard. The young attendants have the slightly slack expressions of people trying very hard not to yawn or nod off. The woman's bun is sliding down her head. In a few hours, the breakfast carts, temple workers and washermen will fill up the streets, shaming them with the scent of their baskets and their fresh faces.

'That's not how this works,' Maderi says, 'I have already won your money. We are not negotiating.'

'No, of course,' the almost believable smile is back. 'I can offer something new to stake. You still have the ring.'

'I am tired, and we have played all night. So let's just—'

'Why don't you first take a look? Let me go get it. There are several lucky trees here, underneath which I have buried some of my recent winnings. The particular one I have in mind is close by.'

'You better be quick,' Darius says, but Madu doesn't even glance at him. His eyes stay on Maderi, who finally nods. He leaves at once, before she can change her mind.

Maderi yawns without covering her mouth. Two of her back teeth, Darius notices, are missing. He feels a twinge of surprise, like he'd expected her to be perfectly built through and through.

'Perhaps I can get hold of everything he has, and leave this place on a white horse bought with his treasures,' Maderi says, as she rubs heavy-lidded eyes.

'I doubt he is that irrational. You know, for someone with a temper, he seemed strangely in control of his feelings during the game.' Maderi glances over at him but says nothing.

The trees rustle around them. Some early risers among the birds are moving about in the branches, cheeping. How do you open your eyes before dawn every day and make music? It must take a great deal of optimism. He listens to the insomniacs, trying to identify their song and failing, and he realizes that he too is drowsy. In this state, names and ideas slip away and break apart before they can come properly together. It would be very nice, he imagines, to climb into a tree right now and sleep in its branches under a dark canopy.

Someone is shaking him awake. He startles up, disoriented. 'Here,' Maderi is saying, 'drink this.'

Madu is back. They are waiting for him to resume the game. It's ostensibly in his name after all—the king standing at the back of the army.

He drinks it obediently. It is warm, spicy, full of malt. Not a punch but a slap, yet still barely enough to keep his eyes open. Sleep is a hard lover to refuse. His eyelids hurt as he resists.

Madu is the one being the sore loser now, trying to renegotiate terms, win it all back, not realizing he is in danger of being emptied out. It's a position usually familiar to his opponents.

'You called yourself a master of Ur,' Maderi observes, 'but at some point, the game masters you. Are you really sure you want to continue?'

'Yes. And I don't think you will need much persuading,' he says. He lays a cloth on the table and unfolds it, revealing a necklace. He lays it out like it's a newborn creature, like he is in love—of course, it's all pretence and flourish, because Madu could never be a man in love.

Still, Darius can't help but lean in. The silence that follows is not the usual kind. Unstill, full of emotion and unsaid words. The shine of the gold is unmistakable, as is the stonework. The lapis lazuli, ruby and garnets in this have been polished to a high shine.

(Nita's audience catches her breath at this tribute. Like when a ghazal's verse has the name of a lover, who is present and listening in the crowd).

Darius recognizes the symbols: the scarab, the two sideways figures seated at either side of a lapis lazuli cat, the king at the centre. Tomb jewellery, dating back to Old Egypt. This had been made for a Pharaoh. He looks up at Madu. 'You stole this.'

Madu nods, 'There is a crime in there somewhere, but it's not mine. I won it from a trader who arrived here from Adulis.'

'This necklace,' Darius says. 'To barter this, is sacrilege.'

Madu sighs. 'You were sitting quietly over there, Darius, all this time, so I had forgotten how—' he searches for the word, and Darius waits for him to insult him again, but he only says, '—how *literal* you are. Look around you, young man, and learn a lesson no one likes spelling out. Everything is stolen. If there is a transaction, you are lucky.

'What do you think happens when I shoot a deer in its heart? Or when those toga-wearing bastards across the sea took over our Nile and the lands with it? You think her king,' he nods at Maderi, 'went over to the tiny kingdom that had those beryl mines and asked for it nicely? He beheaded the local lord for it, as well as the man's cousin who came over three moons later, for good measure. And so those mines became his.'

'So for now,' Madu took his seat, 'we are all thieves here. Except you, I suppose.'

'Enough with the bullying,' Maderi says and Darius realizes with some surprise, that she is angry. 'Put that tongue back in before I cut it out.'

'Ooh,' Madu says, 'the lady has—' but Maderi stops him with a glare.

Instead, they play as the dawn lightens the scene—a fierce, fast game this time, Madu playing for his tattered pride as much as for that beautiful irreplaceable necklace. But this game too, is deeply lopsided, and there is no comeback story waiting here for Madu. Darius thinks that he must be deeply regretting his impulsive bet. But beauty like that necklace is the kind of thing that compels mistakes.

On Madu's hidden throw, Maderi challenges and he loses. On Maderi's, Madu challenges—thinking, might as well, at this point—and loses again. But it's not just that. The sixes fall at the right time for Maderi, allowing her to fly across the board.

When she lands the five she needs on the final throw, Madu breaks the protocol of rising to your feet with hands clasped after a loss. Instead, his hands stay at his sides. He glares at her. 'I don't know how, but you couldn't have won that game.'

The two watchers/attendants/servers stumble over, bleary-eyed. Still effective, Darius hopes in case Madu decides to lunge over the table at them.

'Do you not suddenly know the rules of Ur, Madu? If it's too complicated, you can always try to win the necklace back with a child's game of Two Stones.'

For once, Madu doesn't try to lob an insult back. The last game has eaten through what was left of the night. The sun is blinking through the trees and lights up the bald patches beneath Madu's curls. The lines on his forehead and the bags under his eyes summarize both his immediate sins—a lack of sleep—and older, accumulated ones.

He says, 'You lost the first game on purpose.'

Maderi doesn't deny it.

'I am trying to understand why. Why would someone throw the first game in a best of three?'

The young man interrupts them. 'My dear guests. We value your business but it seems that this game has ended.' He's inserted himself, politely, between Madu and the necklace sitting on the stake stone. 'As always,' he adds, 'the victor settles payment for the space and the game.'

Maderi gives him one of the six gold coins that she's won from Madu. 'For all your lost sleep,' she says.

Madu gazes at them in silence. Nearby, something large—a cat or a langur perhaps—crashes through a bush. The sound breaks the spell between the three of them and Madu turns on his heel and leaves. But Darius felt it. The need for Madu to get even.

The two attendants lean over the gleaming necklace, admiring it wordlessly. Night condensation has gathered on the stone beneath it, and the jasmine creepers and moss frame the polished metal. Maderi gazes at it along with the others. 'I can't believe he gave this up for a stupid game,' she whispers.

'He thought it was his lever to win it all back,' Darius says. But now that the game is over it feels like a weighty thing. Madu has lost too much with this. In letting Maderi agree to this wager, he feels he's made a crucial miscalculation.

Maderi puts the necklace in her scarf bag and they walk out together through the awakening town. They head to a stall that she says is always open early in the morning and has sweet rolls.

'Here,' she hands him the cloth bag.

'Half of this is yours,' he says.

'No,' she says, 'I played it for you. I can always win more. Also, you can't break a necklace in half, especially not that one.'

Darius stops walking. 'I am not going to take it all,' he insists.

'All right,' she agrees, 'I'll take the coins, but not the necklace. It's—too much.'

Darius understands. It *is* too much—too unusual, likely to be badly missed by its original owner, and even trying to trade it would draw attention to her. He, on the other hand, may be able to sell it easily in the port towns he stops at. Merchants in ports outside old Egypt won't hesitate to dissemble the stones and melt down the gold, even if it is worth much more intact.

'All right,' he says. She takes the coins and hands the bag over.

'Madu was an uncorked bottle last night,' he says as they reach the stall, 'all his secrets came spilling out.'

'A game starts before it actually starts,' Maderi says, 'especially games of chance. You take all the opportunities you can to get under the other person's skin.'

They watch the vendor break a brown ball of jaggery with his knife. The chunk of sugar oozes dark brown syrup as he chops. He wastes none of it. After he pours the rice flour on the hot black stone, he drips the syrup over the pancake's pockmarking surface. As it cooks, he mixes the sugar flakes with fresh coconut, packs it into the centre of the pancake before rolling it into a crisp, puffy roll.

Darius takes a bite and feels a deep sense of gratitude, sharpened by sleep deprivation and hunger. Everything is floaty, beautiful. The morning light is very bright, and he sees halos around the trees, the stall, the people walking past. This stall is closer to the river than the others, to take advantage of the morning crowds heading to the boats. Maderi's face goes out of focus and back as he eats, and he can barely hear the jumble of her words, but he listens to the musicality of her voice, her animation even after all these hours wide awake. He can't believe his luck, how he's got here, to this moment in time, in love with the dancing girl, his pouch full of treasure and his heart bursting—the sugar wakes him up a little, and he is able to concentrate better.

'Every dice has a personality,' Maderi says, 'in that way they are like people. Madu's dice is, of course, a trickster. He's using loaded dice.'

'Loaded,' Darius repeats, 'What do you mean?'

'The dice he plays with favours the six, if it's thrown a certain way. My guess? He filled the opposite face with a bit of oil when it was made, so that it falls on that more than usual. But he also weighted the side opposite the two. Someone who doesn't know the dice will get a lot of twos. That's what it looked like when I studied it during the first game.'

'But you didn't get twos.'

The cook gives Maderi an extra-thick roll, one that she can barely get her mouth around. He also offers her a sampling of a brown mixture on a small leaf. 'This is new jaggery from the east, ground with spices. What do you think?'

She dips her finger in it and tastes it. 'It's good,' she nods, 'maybe needs more pepper.'

'More? I thought it was too much.'

'No, it will make the sweet more intense.'

She pays him with a high-value coin, tells her roll-friend that she's just won a game. 'On my own this time. Not for the king.'

'But you didn't get twos,' Darius says again as they walk away.

'The loaded dice is a common problem with the sailors who come here. Getting a reputation as a cheat is not a big deal if you are in port for only two weeks, so they don't care. If you catch a game near the docks, you will see men arguing whose dice to use. Some of the taverns have their own dice. But even with those, there are no guarantees. One of the reasons I played so much in the palace is that I can control the throw.'

'Control the throw, how?'

She curls her small palm into a fist, miming pieces wedged between two fingers. 'You steady the die and throw so that they fall on an axis. It's very difficult to do while looking natural, but I learned it over the years. And the space we played in—I know the tilt of those tables. The one we sat on has a slight downward slope, so his dice from where he sat, did an extra turn.'

Darius stops in the middle of the street so that he can take a look at her full on, and she glances back, amused. 'Every player knows the environment you're playing in has an effect,' Maderi says. 'Nothing is ever pure chance. It's the dice, the player, and yes—the place. I got more sixes because I understood the dice and the table and he didn't.'

'Would he have noticed something was off?'

'He's been playing a long time, so he might have noticed, sure. But he couldn't do much about it because he didn't know where the advantage was.'

'Why would someone throw the first game in a best of three?' Madu had asked.

Because she knew she was going to win. She had known without a doubt.

Sure, with his weighted dice and his box flicks on his hidden throws, Madu was a cheater. A cheater had been cheated out of his winnings. And he knows who Madu will blame. After all, Darius had brought Maderi in to win for him.

Which is, of course, entirely his fault. He should have known that Maderi is not the kind of person that fixes things. She takes them apart.

'He was trying to weasel out of the deal for the necklace, in the end,' Maderi says.

Darius feels like he is seeing her for the first time. There is a sliver of coconut on her cheek from the sweet roll, her hair is wild, her eyes half-lidded and sleepy—she's let her guard down. And the resemblance comes through. It's no wonder she and Madu sparred so easily over the game table. The way they'd crossed swords and amused each other at the same time. She's a hustler too.

Maderi is sweet, charming, and of course, a sight to behold. Even now, the dip of her waist, the arch of her shoulders and neck, that imperious profile—she cuts a lovely figure. He can barely resist her. She also has that gift that young people do, of not seeing herself too clearly.

He looks away from her as he tries to steady himself. It's around the same time in the morning as the day he arrived, so perhaps what happens next is just a coincidence.

A group of girls are walking down the street, baskets in their arms. They don't notice him at all. He sees her among them at once—the same hitched hip, flowers in the basket, the naughty laugh, this time aimed not at him but at a joke someone has just cracked. The girl from his first morning here.

It wasn't Maderi after all. Sure there's a resemblance between the two of them, in the colouring and hair. He'd only seen the first girl for a few moments, even though he'd thought that her face had been burned into his brain. And Maderi had that face paint on from the dance, the first time he'd talked to her. By the time that came off, he'd already been convinced. He sees it now—the eyes are a little different, as is the mouth, the shape of the neck—well, just about everything.

There's a moment of panic, a mind stutter. A feeling that he has travelled down the wrong road.

He watches her go, the woman who'd caught his heart that first day, in her spotless dress and sleek hair. This is clearly a well-cared-for young woman, very different from the orphan temple dancer who stands next to him.

This time, she doesn't notice him at all.

A man he knew and worked alongside at the blighted Berenike port, took every disaster that happened—and Berenike was indeed a place of regular disaster, it was a rare week that went by that a man didn't throw his back, get whipped or lose all his money gambling—with a fatalistic shrug. Caught up in post-drink hangovers, the man, a Greek, cursed not himself but the Moirai.

It was the Moirai, he said—the three sisters Clothos, Lathesis and Atropos—who decided everyone's fate, including the gods, when they were born. Sometimes, you could see your future but could never change it. You owed your miseries and joys to the sisters. You couldn't possibly go down the wrong path—the path was decided for you, long ago.

It doesn't matter, Darius tells himself. He'd been seduced by Maderi's dance, her words. It wouldn't have made any difference if he'd known that she was not the same girl. Right?

His half-eaten roll is wilting in his hand. His fingers are a brown, sticky mess. Their eyes go to it at the same time.

'Tsk,' Maderi says. She takes the roll from him and puts his fingers in her mouth, one by one, licking them clean. While the street is not yet crowded, there are enough locals and seafarers around, and he feels rather than sees the swivelling of heads, the glances.

Even in his current state, his knees turn to water. The sensation of her mouth on his fingers travels all the way down to his toes. But he pulls his hand away. That's a first. Usually, he's as helpless with her as a bird in a net.

Her eyes widen in amusement. She thinks he is embarrassed.

'I need to go to the warehouse, then find a place for this necklace,' he says. 'I'll come see you in the evening. Get some sleep.'

'All right,' she smiles up at him. And he knows he probably won't visit her in the evening.

They are sailing the next day, he remembers as he walks away. And suddenly, he feels fear about being at sea with a man who believes he's been cheated out of priceless treasure.

14

Haroun has returned from his trip with his bags lighter but weighed down with something else. He barely pays attention to Rouhi or Saba, and even the two-headed woman keeps their distance.

His answers are monosyllabic. This time, he works at the dining table, his papers spreading across the surface. The phone, dragged from the living room, sits beside him, and the line creates a tripwire everyone has to step over. Saba loves it, obviously, jumping over and under it, pretending it is electric and something she cannot touch. He makes calls but no one seems to call him back. His pager, which used to ping incessantly, now sits silent, a dead mouse. He growls at Saba when she is louder than he likes, so the three of them retreat upstairs.

He is so busy that he leaves Rouhi alone, coming to bed when it is nearly dawn, startling her out of her sleep.

It's late one evening, four days into his arrival, that he receives a phone call. He huddles around the phone like it's giving him warmth, the handset disappearing into his large hands as he cradles it close while talking. Upstairs, Nita has come out of her room to check Saba's schoolbag for missing books she needs for tomorrow, leftover food from past lunches. There is no telling what it will contain day to day—Nita had once found a web of old chewing gum at the bottom of the bag, with books placed carefully in between.

Rouhi is at the bedroom door, waiting for her. She holds a finger to her lips as she pulls Nita into the room and closes it. She picks up the extension, lifting it by inches. Haroun's voice on the line. Nita's already shaking her head, because, of course, he'll hear the click. But as Rouhi brings the handset to her ear he's still talking intently, angrily and likely hasn't noticed.

Nita watches Rouhi's expressions as she listens—anger, resignation, despair, all of it in a span of a few minutes.

She finally pulls the handset away from her face. The voices are still coming through it, crackly and high-pitched, and she looks at it as if it is a snake that has poured poison into her ear. She grips it like she wants to throw it across the room. Instead, she places it gently back on its cradle. Having to be quiet when she wants to scream.

This bedroom is not safe, Haroun could come up at any moment. But Nita waits. 'Tell me.'

'It is horrible.' It takes a few moments for Rouhi to fight her anger down. She has been listening in on his phone calls for a few days, she tells Nita. To his panicked conversations with his bosses and the other crewmen, and his attempts to cover his tracks. A smuggling scandal is brewing, and Haroun is, if not at the centre of it, one of the principals.

She runs her hands constantly through her hair as she talks, telling her the facts that she's pieced together. Her mouth hangs loose when she pauses, and in a glimpse that takes Nita briefly out of this moment, she sees Rouhi's lower canine, a sharp-edged tooth that usually never shows even when she smiles, but that Nita has felt with her tongue when they kissed. A pointed tooth larger than its neighbours, pointing inward.

The story that Nita gets out of Rouhi explains some of the dinner conversation she'd overheard all those months ago. A port scam came under investigation after an official in Cape Town discovered containers labelled as cookie boxes that turned out to be packed with premium Panamanian hashish. This had happened before with the company's ships, but this time one of the operators ratted out and named names, blowing the scheme (or a corner of it) wide open. Haroun and his captain were both on that list, apparently involved with relabelling containers for exporters who sold banned or sanctioned items.

In Dubai's free trade zone, the checks for container ships coming in are minimal to keep everything moving smoothly. Dubai was tiny at the start, competing with Iran's Hormuz for traffic, and a light hand with the rules has helped draw business away from the far bigger port.

But despite the few checks in place, the laws on the books are clear about the fact that what Haroun had been up to, with a couple of other crew members—relabelling and redirecting containers—is illegal.

Like most long-running scams, it was a simple and elegant one. There are plenty of countries that operate purely on the black market, after having been sanctioned by several nations. The profile of these places tend to be similar—with an unelected head of state who has clawed into power, shirt-sleeves soaked in red, typically after a civil war. The infrastructure is controlled by his people, gang leaders who own the mines, factories, ports. Workers have little bargaining power. Inequality has bloomed and spread, a weed taking over the land. When people riot, they are shot.

Other countries have banned trade from these places, giving the black market a boost.

A container from one of these places—Sudan, Congo, Zimbabwe—would arrive in Dubai with its true origin port and number. The container number was delivered to Haroun's pager after it had been successfully deboarded by one of the two paid-off supervisors on the docks.

Haroun, who was authorized to add and label containers on his ship manifest, would generate a new container and country code, and the container was then loaded for destinations with buyers for its off-label products—Krakow, New York, London. It would travel on the ship under a new innocuous identity. Gold from the Darfur mines became dolls made in Vietnam, Panamanian hashish was rice from India, Iranian components for ballistic missiles became Indonesian rubber. There may have also been some human trafficking in the mix.

As one of the critical links who helped shepherd and coordinate, Haroun was paid handsomely by the black-market exporters for his diligent attention. Perhaps he wouldn't have been pulled up if he'd been smarter or more discreet about what he did with the money, list or no. It was his extravagant taste that caught the attention of his superior officers first. Gold cufflinks with work shirts, beautiful, tailored suits he wore to business events (suits that should have cost a month's salary, easy), the multiplying diamond signet rings on his fingers. Oh, and the Russian escorts he arranged for some of the officers deciding his promotions.

'Now he will lose job,' Rouhi says, 'We lose everything.' Rouhi is scratching at her scalp with both hands. She is, Nita thinks, travelling back in time. Everything catching fire again. Nita begins to say something but Rouhi freezes. Haroun is coming up the stairs, with that unmistakable, heavy gait.

Nita won't be able to get out of the bedroom in time. The rise from the bed, the turn, the dart to the door—it's too much distance. She's thinking up what excuses she could possibly offer of what she's doing here, when Rouhi pushes her down to the floor, indicating that she should go under the bed.

Nita wants to ask her whether she's lost her senses but is now out of time to do anything but scuttle under as Haroun walks into the room. The space underneath is surprisingly clean, free of Rouhi's signature mess—the perfumes, small towels, the used teacups and Egyptian novels. Dust motes rise when she breathes out, but it isn't too bad.

Haroun is opening cupboards and moving hangers about.

'My blue suit,' he says, 'I have a meeting tomorrow. Where is it?'

Rouhi says something. Nita's eyes adjust to the darkness, and she can make out scratches on the bed's wooden underframe. She squints, trying to see, traces it with her fingers. An S with points instead of curves, made with the edge of a compass perhaps, followed by an A. A half-attempted B. Saba's been writing her name here too.

She quietly panics to herself. *When* had Saba been here? When Nita was with Rouhi? But Nita always locked the door (hadn't she?). Has she been here before, while her father beat her mother? Either of these possibilities, impossible to consider. She traces her fingers on the markings. The cuts are deep, as if Saba went over each line over and over with the compass point.

She realizes the room is quiet. Rouhi is on her knees, her hand out. 'He's gone in car,' she says.

'But it's nearly midnight.'

'Well, I hope he become lizard when clock strikes twelve. Reverse Cinderella,' Rouhi says. Another alternate Disney plot. Haroun has gone to talk to his boss, to stop himself from getting fired. A discharge from a government job would mean the loss of many privileges, including this house.

Rouhi has gained her composure back, but Nita can see that something inside her has shifted.

'I will come with you,' she says to Nita. 'Enough. I will leave this.'

The air goes right out of Nita's chest. She wants to say, *are you sure*, but the words don't come out. This feels too fragile, Rouhi's agreement. Out of the blue, and after she's been pushed to a corner.

'We will come,' Rouhi corrects herself. If she goes, Saba goes. And then she smiles at Nita, that smile that looks actually happy.

'Don't tease me,' Nita says.

'No,' Rouhi agrees, taking her hand in hers.

Nita rises to leave, but Rouhi doesn't let go. 'Please, I don't want to sit alone.'

'I feel nervous here,' Nita admits. There's too much Haroun now, in this room. His clothes everywhere, his smell. 'Why don't you come to my room?'

Rouhi opens her mouth to say no, but reconsiders. 'All right'.

Nita closes the door of her room behind Rouhi, locks it just in case—although Rouhi says Haroun's boss lives some distance away and it will take him at least an hour to get back. She pushes a chair below the handle, something that will fall and alert them if the handle moves. She checks that the curtains are fully drawn with no space between their thin drapes. The bunkered-in feeling makes her feel a little safer.

'Tell me the story, Nita,' Rouhi says, 'It will distract me.'

The bed is narrow, and Rouhi fills half of it even when lying on her side. Nita switches on the small lamp on the desk and kneels beside the bed, looking at Rouhi's face, the silhouette of her body.

'I don't want to tell you the story right now.'

'Just a little bit, please?'

Nita finds herself resisting. Instead, she gets into the bed, also on her side—there is so little room. She runs her hand over Rouhi's hips and over her shoulders and neck. Her fingers twist in her hair. The tiniest tug. Rouhi's breathing slows, she lifts her face.

The times they've spent together so far have been lit by the streetlights outside and nothing else, and in this small, yellow light Rouhi's curves are clearer, softer. Nita's heart pounds in her chest as if it is their first time. So much about Rouhi is her physicality—her wonderful body, generous and soft, still voluptuous and in good health. People, when they discuss someone, talk of their life and work, the kind of laugh they had and the things they said. But they rarely talk about the body, not in mixed company anyway. Rouhi's body, with the fullness of her breasts and hips, her generous thighs, was a thing Nita admired even when Rouhi was perched on the edge of a sofa, reading one of her magazines, her legs underneath her, toes curled as if trying to keep warm in a room chilled by the overworked air-conditioning.

A beautiful, complicated, messy, frustrating, dangerous woman. But still, she has no regrets, she realizes, as she examines Rouhi's face. No matter what happens, the sharp joy she has felt in her time with this impatient woman, this woman who never fully understood Nita, is too much for regret.

Nita does not want conversation. Since Haroun arrived, they have barely touched each other. She wants desire to crowd any conversation out. Rouhi unbuttons her dress, and Nita leans in and presses her face into her chest, inhaling the perfume, the lotion underneath that, the shower gel underneath the lotion, and then the scent of her skin, which is what she wants to get at.

There is no place on the bed and Nita has to lie on top of Rouhi, propping herself up on her knees between Rouhi's legs to balance her weight. The position, along with the narrowness of the bed, puts her in charge for the first time, and she discovers that Rouhi likes it. It is power that has been there for the taking from the beginning—to dominate, to kindle the fire, to coax out feeling—and she never really claimed it, letting Rouhi play the lead, just like in the daytime hours. It could have been hers if she'd wanted it.

Perhaps then things would have turned out differently. If she'd taken charge here, been the one moving their bodies, discovering instead of being discovered, maybe that would have changed the way things were outside the room. Maybe Rouhi would have decided in her favour much earlier. Or maybe not.

Their bodies are sweaty—the air-conditioning is off in this room—Rouhi's mouth a pink, nearly soundless O. And then it's over, and the world is coming back in through the window and the walls—muffled traffic sounds outside, the soft ticking of a clock, the misleading quiet of the house.

Nita looks at the door, and the chair is on the floor.

15

The chair is on the floor, and there's someone standing outside the door, their shadow visible through the slit underneath.

Even at their most silent—and they are rarely silent—what they were doing would have been unmistakable to anyone right outside, listening.

The worst way to be discovered, when your back is turned. Nita stares at the door for a moment and looks back at Rouhi, who's lying in bed, eyes closed, hair fanned out on Nita's thin pillow. Nita gives it a few seconds. 'Rouhi.'

'Mmm.'

'Rouhi.'

'I can sleep here, Nita. I am tired.'

'Rouhi.'

She opens her eyes at that. The tightness on Nita's face, and she follows her eyes to the door, sees the chair.

'Maybe it just fell?'

Nita shakes her head.

Rouhi sees it then, the shadow through the gap, as Nita gets up and puts on her dress. Rouhi pulls her knees to her chest. 'Don't open door.'

Nita waits for her terror to subside. The reaction Rouhi is having is fraught with the memory of old bruises. Whoever is outside—and of course it is Haroun, she can smell his perfume even through the door, like a horror movie monster announcing himself from around the corner via a gratuitous stink—waits like they have all the time in the world.

Rouhi finally pulls her clothes on and tries to tame her messed up hair. Nita goes up to her and wipes the mussed eyeliner from under her eyes, straightens her dress, fixing the collar like she does with Saba every morning. In the face of that closed door and the waiting Haroun, Nita feels like the protector, the adult. *I will not let him hurt you again*, she thinks to herself, watching Rouhi's face. From the corner of her eyes, she sees the door handle move. Haroun is getting impatient now and probably angrier with every moment. If they don't go out now, it will only get worse.

Nita looks around and finds the embroidery scissors she uses to mend things. Tiny, but better than nails. She conceals it in her trembling left palm and goes to the door, moves the chair out of the way.

'Ready?' Nita asks her.

Rouhi shakes her head. Her eyes are terrified.

'Ah finally, your majesty,' Haroun says as Nita opens the door. 'I am not used to finding locked doors in my own house. Please come out.'

Cold anger, more dangerous than hot. Haroun smells of Paco Rabanne and whisky. He has a taste for fine things, but expensive whisky smells the same as the cheap stuff when it's leaking out of your pores. To Nita, he smells like the men at the bus stops back home, the ones with shadowed faces who lingered there as buses drove past, watching the schoolgirls. She sensed the same lack of restraint emanating from them as from Haroun now. He's in his blue suit, now crumpled, the tie loose around his neck.

She turns to Rouhi, who's still on her bed. 'Stay here,' she says.

Haroun grabs her neck while her face is turned towards his wife. He pulls her through the door and throws her on the floor, and she has to break her fall with her shoulder to stop her head from hitting the wooden side of the sofa. He's already turning away, still expressionless, as if she's something beneath him, beneath his response. Focused on Rouhi.

'I brought you a gift,' he says to Rouhi in Arabic, his voice sarcastically syrupy, '*Etlaay*'. Come outside.

Nita sits up on her elbows, dizzy with pain. She may have broken her ankle while falling. She moves it gingerly. Not broken—maybe twisted. More concerning is that her head is swimming, the room spins around her. Haroun's voice is a distorted echo.

In the background, Rouhi is screaming. Nita's eyes can't focus. We are mothers, she thinks, as her head still spins. Thoughts come together and splinter. The nausea recedes. The room straightens, putting her back into the nightmare. *Re-entry*. And there is Haroun, coming out of Nita's room, dragging Rouhi out by her arm. Skin white where his fingers dig in. Rouhi in a child's pose, her hand on the door jamb, trying not to be dragged further into the living room as if that will solve something. Haroun reaches behind her, closes the door hard on her hand. Rouhi screams and lets go, and Nita shrieks.

Rouhi falls into the sofa, holding her fingers. The sobs are coming out between closed lips—she's trying to make sure she doesn't wake her daughter.

'Rouhi,' Nita says, her voice low and choked, 'Ma'alesh.' It's what Rouhi says to Saba to comfort her. That's enough for Haroun to cross the room in a couple of steps and slap Nita hard across her face.

It's Rouhi's turn to gasp. 'You know,' Haroun says, 'the bitches in the kitchen told me about the two of you the day I came home. I didn't say anything. I just watched you two disgusting whores sneak around and hide.'

His face twists as he looked down at his wife. It falls into those creases easily, like he's done it a thousand times, for sins big and small.

People, Nita thinks, are made for certain things, like some cut out to be nurses, soft-handed and gentle with low voices, custom-built for the role; or people who command loyalty as soon as they walk into a room, you are somehow drawn to their side; Haroun is made for meanness, his face and his bearing make a certain kind of sense now, a revelation as he towers over his curled up wife, his hands in fists, focused on causing hurt.

But then he turns towards Nita. She is after all, the person who brought his wife to this level.

The first punch lands on her ear, making her head ring, and she immediately loses her bearings again, holding her head, trying to figure out which way is up. He lands the second punch in the soft part of her stomach while she is still disoriented.

She turns on to her stomach and tries to crawl away from underneath him. But he grabs her by her hair, pulling her up to the sitting position, and slaps her hard across her face. She falls backward, but the tearing pain in her scalp has woken her up.

The dizziness is gone. She dives behind the sofa, ignoring the clenching pain.

He is moving after her, and she backs away from the sofa and up against the wall, whittling his possible next moves down to the predictable. As he lunges at her, she feels in the pocket of her housecoat for the sewing scissors. She clenches the small point of it in her fist. She has to wait, however. One opportunity is all she will get.

One of her eyes throbs and turns him blurry. He comes towards her, part man, part blob. She needs him to close the distance between him and her. He has pulled the belt off his suit trousers with a flick of his wrist. Closer now, he whips it at her. She manages to bat the first few strikes away with her palms.

He keeps throwing it, and she pushes it off as it stings at her palms, fingers, wrists. He's growing frustrated. *Come closer,* she thinks.

And he does. He moves quickly for a heavy guy. She blinks, and his hands are inches from her throat, and that's when she brings the scissors up and digs them deep into his flank, guessing at where it will really hurt.

He rears back with a scream, almost a feminine one. Blood springs out between his fingers as he grabs at his waist. He falls on his ass and lies there on the ground, groaning, and Nita, propelled by rage, kicks him hard in the groin. He tries to swat at her, grab her ankles, but the pain is too much—he lies back on the floor, grunting.

She looks up and sees Rouhi looking at them in horror, her hand forgotten. The carpet underneath him is turning to dark brown, the side of his shirt is soaked. He's groaning with clenched teeth, unable for now, to move.

Rouhi disappears into the bedroom, returns with a towel and bends over Haroun. She takes his hand away and presses the towel against his side.

Nita looks at the wound over Rouhi's shoulder. The worst of the bleeding seems to have subsided. But his face is very pale from the pain. The fight seems to have gone out of him.

Rouhi looks exhausted. She kneels beside him for a few minutes, watching his face and then retreats to her bedroom. Nita follows, closing and locking the door behind them in case Haroun gets a second wind. She is still disoriented. Her eye hurts, she is afraid to look into the mirror to see how bad it is. She sits beside Rouhi, lifts up her wounded hand and palpates it gently. Swollen and bruised. One of her fingers may be broken.

Rouhi blinks back tears, looks at her. 'Nita,' she says, but then cannot continue, and instead leans against her shoulder. They sit still, gasping, holding each other.

Nita is worried about Saba. She sleeps like the world is lost to her, and her door had stayed closed throughout that ordeal in the living room. But she might be awake. If she comes out—

But to get to the child, you must cross the monster. They stay in the bedroom, listening, waiting. There are no voices outside. Minutes pass, half an hour. And then the handle of the door moves.

'Rouhi.'

She raises her head from Nita's shoulder.

'Rouhi.' A plea. 'Open the door, please. Talk to me.'

'Don't say anything,' Nita says, squeezing Rouhi's good hand.

Rouhi has stiffened next to her, like she's waiting for something.

'I am sorry. Rouhi, I'll do anything,' the voice on the other side says. 'Please. Just don't leave me.'

Haroun's Arabic turns elaborate and Nita can now understand very little. He's having a private conversation through the door with Rouhi, with Nita sitting right beside her and there's nothing she can do about it. But his tone is unmistakable. Pleading. Begging. Grovelling.

Unable to understand the words, Nita watches Rouhi's face. As he goes on, she seems to sink into his words, swim in them. Nita can almost see her disappear into the dark stream leaking through the door, the empty promises he is making filling up this room.

'Don't listen to him, Rouhi,' she says, 'You know what he's done. How he is.'

Rouhi looks at her, her eyes full of something that wasn't there earlier. Some kind of knowledge, understanding, that right now she is refusing to share with Nita. She pulls her hand away and gets up from the bed.

Nita leaps up with her. 'Rouhi,' she says, 'Don't.'

But Rouhi ignores her, walks to the door and opens it.

Haroun is not standing there, waiting to leap at them, as Nita had feared. He is on the floor, leaning against the doorjamb. His face is worn, all the rage drained out of it, and it's as if that was always the primary emotion on his face. Without it he looks entirely different.

Rouhi looks down at him, waiting for something.

'I have lost everything,' he says, 'I cannot lose you now.'

She sinks down on the ground beside him. Nita watches as she puts her unhurt hand on his collar. She tugs hard and he winces. 'You have hurt me every day of my life.'

'Don't say that. We had good days too, habibti.'

Nita wants to throw up when she hears him using the word.

'You hit me. You hit Nita. You like hitting women.'

'I was jealous. What do you expect?' he winces and sighs as if he wants to remind her of the wound Nita has inflicted on him. The bleeding has stopped, but he has the towel pressed against his side. *Hopefully*, Nita thinks, *I have pierced his kidney, and he will die tomorrow of an internal bleed.* But the colour is back in his face. Monsters are not easy to kill.

'Where is Nita's passport, Haroun?' Rouhi asks, 'You have hidden it somewhere.'

There is a long pause as Haroun considers. For the first time since the door opened, his eyes flicker towards Nita. Quickly, and then back to Rouhi's face.

'If I tell you, will you stay with me?'

What haunts Nita later, what she will remember for a long time, is not the answer. It's how quickly Rouhi says *yes*, without consideration or pause. A possible future for the two of them doesn't merit even a few seconds of thought.

It could have just been courage that Rouhi was showing, a steeling of herself against her fate. But what if it was indifference?

'It's with Reema downstairs.'

There's a thumping in Nita's ears. Rouhi goes downstairs to wake the woman, while Nita watches Haroun, who is still slumped against the door, not getting up. And then for a moment, he opens his hooded eyes and looks right at her. Her head still hurts from where it hit the floor and the wall. Things come out of focus and back. She wants to read the expression on his face but can't.

Out of nowhere, Rouhi is next to her. 'Nita,' she says, 'you must go. Take passport and go to airport. India flight is always there.'

'But I don't have my passport,' Nita says, wonderingly.

Rouhi squeezes her shoulder, and she looks down at the dark blue book Rouhi is pressing into her hand.

'You want me to leave,' Nita says.

'Yes, Nita. You take passport, take bag, you go.'

Haroun is still propped up against the door in his bloody shirt, eyes closed. She wants him to say something that will remind Rouhi of his awfulness, of what it will mean to stay with him here.

She is also waiting for Rouhi to say something else, because it seems impossible that this grubby, painful, miraculous thing that they have, full of the best moments of her life, will end in this hurried and horrible fashion. But the seconds draw out.

Rouhi does not look at her.

Nita goes into her room and packs, putting her things in Saba's cartoon bag. It takes her less than fifteen minutes to pack up everything she has; she's accumulated so little in the past year. Two dresses, three saris, one unnecessary sweater. She washes her face, and Rouhi appears with a band-aid for the cut near her eye. Her throat hurts with unshed tears as Rouhi applies it.

'Can I say goodbye to Saba?' Nita asks.

'No!' Rouhi composes herself and then more calmly, 'I check and she is sleeping. If she wakes up she'll see Haroun –'

'Yes, yes of course.' So Nita will have to leave under the cloak of darkness, under a cloud.

They stand quietly in the room together. Nita can't think of anything to say that would make it work. Not *I love you* or *Come with me* or *If we leave now we will be in another place in six hours with a different life and Saba will be our daughter and she can go to school together with our son and you will get bitten by weird insects. But you will fit right in, you have no idea, everyone will love you. We will fix your hand and everything else.*

But Nita sees in Rouhi's face a negation of anything she wants to say, and it is one outreach too many for her, one that

she can no longer bring herself to do. Maybe Rouhi could have
left a furious, vindictive Haroun. Not a sad, injured one.

'Well then,' Nita says, and Rouhi has her arms around her,
hugging her to herself. Nita inhales the perfume of her skin, her
hair. After a minute, she lets her go and Nita leaves the room,
unconsoled, unkissed. This time, she averts her head from the
bedroom, where Haroun has moved from the floor and is sitting
on the bed, waiting.

She goes downstairs alone, where the house is dark but
unstill. The two-headed woman is awake somewhere. She steps
out and the front door swings closed behind her, and it is only as
the latch clicks that she realizes that this is it—she is outside, and
she will never see Rouhi and Saba again.

No, she whispers to herself. No, no no no no no.

She sits down and hugs her knees on the steps outside
someone else's house that for a while, had felt like hers.

She thinks about how her whole body responded when
Rouhi touched her on her elbow, as she sometimes did, caressing
it ever so slightly with her fingers. How much Saba's hair was
like Rouhi's, and how she'd gone ahead and imagined Saba as a
teenager, as she liked to imagine her son. This too is a child she
has taken care of and come to love. But none of this confers any
rights to her; she would be viewed by anyone looking through the
windows of this house as an interloper, someone intent on theft.

She gets up, eventually. She walks past the pretty houses,
some of which have put tangled party lights out ahead of the new
year. The desert night as always, feels too close to the skin, and
by the time she reaches the traffic roundabout, the back of her
dress is soaked in sweat.

Even at this time of the night—when even the jitteriest
animals are asleep, their mating and hunting and fighting done—

there are the twin lights of moving cars as humans, earth's most sleepless creatures, find reasons to be outside.

Round they go in their vehicles, mostly solitary, hunched over steering wheels, intent on the tunnel view provided by the headlights. When their lights illuminate Nita standing there on the pavement, brown-skinned in her thin, dishevelled dress, holding her plastic suitcase, a bandage near her eye, they slow down for a moment, their foot raising off the accelerator, before they press on, forgetting her, almost as if she'd never been. She watches the cars move around the roundabout like the ticking of a clock—one, two, ten, twelve, fifteen, thirty revolutions pass before an empty taxi stops at her raised hand.

That large ticking clock of the roundabout goes on as she leaves. The neighbours take the tangled lights down, new, even taller buildings dot the skyline, the ruler decrees a giant new aquarium attraction, filled with sharks and sting rays and dolphins, to bring tourists to the desert. The family in the house at the end of the street move on with their lives.

But love ends. It ends and ends and ends, yet the person must go on.

And what about Darius? It's Nita's only withholding, the one thing that she didn't give Rouhi. An ending.

In a way, Darius' story is a funhouse mirror of her own: the immigrant landing in an astonishing place, falling for a girl. She distilled her feelings into him—her longing, her unmatched desire. But Darius had known some things before she did, hadn't he?

It's only when she is in her window seat on the late, late flight to Kochi via Mumbai, that she allows herself tears.

Through the porthole is her final view of Dubai. The exterior of the airport is lit up the way everything here is—aggressively.

The visual brag of an energy rich country. The salt-rich, humid air diffuses the lights, turning them into landlocked stars.

As she watches the city fall away from her, its lights receding, Nita spins the part of the story that she had left out. She had made a plan for Darius. But now in the plane, she changes her mind. So the one who decides Darius' fate, his Moirai, snips the thread of his life in a different place.

16

Darius

Before last night, Darius' greatest worries had been the bad pepper bales and his lover's lack of enthusiasm for him. Simple problems compared to what he has now.

He walks along the beach, holding Maderi's scarf bag with the necklace in it. He is too afraid to return with it to the warehouse. Too worried that he will be seen burying it somewhere.

This unfortunate necklace, he thinks, has landed in the hands of a nervous and pigeon-hearted man.

He remembers that Ebo likes to go out in the mornings and get tender coconuts for himself and whichever girl he's spent the night with. So he walks down to the market he frequents. There's no sign of him, however, and he lingers among the morning carts, waiting. The half-eaten roll roils his stomach. Food doesn't sit well alongside guilt and heartbreak.

He is getting increasingly mopey when he sees a big, curly-headed figure in the distance.

'Whoa,' Ebo says, when he spots Darius, 'you look like one of the washermen grabbed you and whipped you against his stone for a bit.'

'It's been a strange night,' Darius says, and tells him what happened as Ebo buys a tender coconut, then a second, and a third.

Ebo eyes are wide. 'And to think I imagined you as a fellow made of milk and water.'

'What do I do?'

'You can't get on the ship now, obviously.'

'Why?' Despite himself, Darius had been hoping for a different answer.

'Because, you idiot, the most dangerous man that you and I know will be waiting to throw you overboard. The only way you'll see land if you get on the *Tefnut* is when you hit the bottom of the ocean.'

'How can I not go back? A big reason I came here was to get my mother enough coins so that she can stop working at the caravan stop.'

He considers—Ebo is a friend, but he's only known him for a few moons. Still, he's noticed that Ebo is generous, affectionate to his crew, his whores and even strangers, ready with jokes, sympathy and tips.

'I have an idea,' he says, 'if you are willing to help me.'

While they wait for Babu to show up, Darius asks Ebo if he wants to see the necklace. He unfolds it from the cloth and both of them stare at it for a few moments. Ebo stiffens a little, as if he, like Darius, understands the danger of owning something like it. The falcons' eyes glow red with the inlaid gems. Ebo doesn't reach out to touch it.

Babu has been annoyed with the two of them since the messed-up pepper bales. This fresh turn of events doesn't help.

'You are not the first sailor I have lost to the temptations of Muziris,' he tells Darius. 'But you don't know a lick of Tamil and you have nowhere to live. I am not paying for the warehouse space once we lift anchor.'

'I am not asking you to,' Darius says.

'And I am not giving you an advance either,' Babu adds, 'They pay us for the goods once we dock at Berenike and then everybody gets their cut. I am not paying you with money I don't have.'

All three of them know that Babu's chests are full of Ur winnings. But Darius only says, 'I want you to give my cut to Ebo. My mother needs taking care of and he has promised to get the coins to her.'

Babu looks at the two of them, puzzled. 'You are trusting Ebo with a lot of gold.'

'He's a good man. As good as any of us can be, at any rate.'

Babu waves acquiescence at Darius' request that he tell no one that he is not returning to Berenike. They lift anchor at dawn tomorrow, and Darius would like to be still alive when they leave.

That night, he does not visit Maderi. Instead, he goes back to the part of the beach where she took him after the dance. He is the only one here. He sits on the sand and looks out into the deep, roaring darkness. The monsoon wind has arrived on schedule, and it lifts his hair, blows sand across his feet.

He could stay here, he thinks. Learn the tongue, find work, court a different woman. He could find a buyer for this necklace, who might reduce it to gold and stones, and leave him a very rich man. Return home a few summers later than planned, and hopefully find his mother waiting for him.

Someone once said that a happy ending depends on where you stop the story. So that's where Nita leaves Darius, looking out with eyes that are grey-green, a colour that she belatedly bestows on him. The creator and created lock eyes, briefly, before she lets him go.

17

The last connection with Rouhi is one Nita discovers months later, when she picks up Saba's bag from the corner she'd dropped it in after arriving home. She hears a small clink while cleaning it out. In the side zipped pocket is the necklace, wrapped in tissues like some cheap trinket.

She thinks about their final, fraught moments together. Can she ever really know how Rouhi felt about her? The necklace sits in her hand like a message, an apology, an impulsive offering. She can't decipher its meaning.

She had called Rouhi's number from a PCO weeks after landing home, when she couldn't help herself. No one picked up, which was strange considering that everyone usually rushed to the phone to beat Saba from answering it. She tried one more time, days later. The line just rang and rang.

One of Ani's front teeth is coming loose, and he nudges it with his tongue while smiling at her to freak her out. He's started wriggling away from her when she envelops him in hugs. When her sister visits, the three of them sometimes do what she and

Divya used to when they were kids—make up unseemly lyrics to accompany the devotional instrumental music that plays on the radio in the mornings.

But she also wants other things. She wants to be back on the ragged upstairs sofa with Rouhi, watching Channel 33, the *Blockbusters* quiz show, *The Bold and the Beautiful*, shows where she never got to see the endings because Rouhi would interrupt, asking for stories.

She wants to sit there with their hands beside each other, teasing loose threads out of the sofa's old knit. Her emotions can't find a place to settle—she is pulled in different directions at once. A homeless heart is what she's got.

Scan QR code to access the
Penguin Random House India website